The
Last
Great
Hope

By

Wayne Goodman

To Rick and My Mother,

This book would not have
been possible without either

Acknowledgments

The character of Agent Stone is fictional, but much of the information about the Secret Service came from retired Agent Gerald Blaine's book "The Kennedy Detail" (Gallery Books, New York, NY, 2010).

However, this book would not have been possible without the support and faith of the man in my life, Richard May. His insightful suggestions resurrected my unusable first version of this work.

I would also like to thank those who previewed the manuscript: Beryl and Kent.

v 2.21, January 1, 2015

Table of Contents

The Last Great Hope

by Wayne Goodman

Copyright 2001, 2014

YOU PROBABLY HAVE ALREADY HEARD DIFFERENT variations of this story, most cooked-up by the liberal press to make me out to be the bad guy. The law had to pin the deaths on someone, and since they found me holding the smoking gun, I'm the logical suspect. I just wanted the chance to give people the opportunity to hear my version and see it from my point of view. Let me say at the start that I appreciate your interest and your time. Please try to keep an open mind as you read this.

Chapter One

Sunday

AFTER an unusually warm April, with plenty of precipitation, May 2002 appeared to be returning to a more comfortable average, now that rainy season was finally over for Northwestern Indiana. This particular evening reminded me of so many other similar beautiful ones, with trails of clouds in the sky catching the last few ruddy beams of the setting sun.

I had just finished watching my favorite Sunday evening news magazine program, with an in-depth look at that female intern found dead in a Washington park, the one who was dating the California congressman. Having spent years in the nation's capital, I know what a dangerous place it can be.

Last year I finally purchased my own personal computer and had been using it to keep busy during the cold winter months, meeting people online, getting comfortable with word processing, and using email. Once the television went dark, I fired up the computer to check in with the rest of the world.

I just love that little melody the modem plays as it dials in. Kind of reminds me of an old Rolling Stones tune. Especially when the beeping back and forth starts, intermixed with static. Like Mick Jagger and Keith Richards bantering at each other.

Only one new message. From my old boss at the Secret Service, whom I refer to as Top Dog. Haven't heard from him for years. First death in a D.C. park and now this abrupt resurrection. He could have just phoned, but I'm guessing email is probably more secure, with 128-bit encryption. Anyone tapping in on the phone line could intercept a call, but no one would be able to decipher this jumble of hexadecimal numbers. Well, maybe a select few, but it would still take time and I'm guessing time is critical with him, as usual.

The message was quite simple: "Stone, I need you for a special assignment to start immediately. Respond. Confirm."

The specters from all the stray bullets I ever took in the line of duty started moaning simultaneously. Each one had stung individually, but now they vibrated with a coordinated buzz of anticipation. Patience has never been my hobby. I'm more of an under-reactor, hardly ever changing my facial expression. Came in real handy years ago.

"Stone," they called me. Many people still do. Those who know me well use yet another nickname, but I do want to keep a few things private, after all. You might think that a Stone would have infinite patience, but knowing that something is going to happen, and waiting for that thing to happen, is what I don't handle very well. Not that you'd know it to look at me.

I left the Service about 30 years ago, retired from my last post a few years back, and now the old guy wants me to get up out of my comfy recliner to do who-knows-what who-knows-where for who-knows-why. Seems like he should have stopped working long ago. And now that I am retired, I kind of hoped I would never have to deal with him again. Those days are behind me. I don't need to reopen old wounds. But, I will always feel it's my duty to the Country.

He should be grateful I'm a dedicated, loyal American.

My typing could use some improving, and it's even worse when I'm under pressure, whether internal or external, but I managed to tap out a succinct reply: "I'm here. What's up?"

Within seconds another message from him arrived: "Pack for a two-day mission in Boston. Bring 1964 adoption papers. Car will pick you up at 5:45 a.m. tomorrow. See you at the destination. Confirm."

Confirming would be the easy part. Carrying out the order was going to be the bitch.

"Stone hears. Stone obeys."

Washington, Boston, Top Dog. Lots of memories. So many loose ends. What in hell can he want now?

— ♦ —

Top Dog assigned me to the Kennedys mid-1962. In my early 20s, gung-ho, ready to protect my Commander-in-Chief at all costs. Even though he was a loud-mouth, cocky, bush-league liberal from Massachusetts, he was still the President. I was very thankful to get such a prestigious assignment so early in my career.

All the agents who served the President had codenames starting with "D." I'm not sure how I ended up being "Dancer," but I chose to believe it was after one of Santa's reindeer because one of the other guys was Dasher. Our motto was "Worthy of Trust and Confidence," which influenced the duty I had been entrusted to perform.

The President had a family that wouldn't quit. There was a brother, sister-in-law, cousin, mother-in-law, whoever, hanging around all the time. The place was literally crawling with Kennedys. Some of them did crawl around, too. Little Caroline was always trying to get in to see her dad. Mrs. K kept bringing the new baby around to show the Boss.

Kids made me nervous, still do. They're always getting in the way, and the Castle is no place for vulnerable little ones. Especially with all the traffic going through: the tours, the dignitaries, the hundreds of employees. It was a wonder none of the children ever got nabbed. Thank goodness Top Dog didn't assign me to the "Kiddie Detail." I would have had to quit.

With rotating shifts and so much overtime, I don't know how the other agents managed to have a successful home life. Most of the guys spent more time with the Kennedys than they did with their own families. On top of that, we were sworn not to discuss any of the details of our job with others, and all of this made me very happy I remained single.

During August 1963 Mrs. K delivered their third child prematurely. She had a couple of miscarriages already and there was lots of concern.

Born in Boston and dying two days later, little Patrick Bouvier Kennedy never got to take a breath of the stale, muggy Washington air that sustained the rest of us. Given a funeral ceremony worthy of an ambassador or something, he was buried in the family plot in Brookline.

The grieving went on for quite a while around the family. Mr. and Mrs. K wanted lots of kids to carry on the Kennedy name.

November 22, 1963 is a day I will never be able to forget. Many, many hours of therapy and many, many gallons of bitter beer have not done much to dull the throbbing memories of one particular moment in history.

With the shadow of the 1964 election just over the horizon, a publicity trip to two uncertain Southern states, Florida and Texas, seemed like a good idea. A bad polling result must have helped them decide because Mrs. K, who never went on political tours with the President since his election, came along, presumably as the Crown Jewel and crowd favorite.

Tampa and Miami went well, despite the fears that protests by Cuban groups would get rowdy. After that, a two-day, five-stop tour of Texas: San Antonio and Houston the first day; Fort Worth, Dallas and Austin the second.

Having five staging areas thinned the number of available agents, and I was assigned to the Dallas contingent, riding on the front of the old Cadillac convertible nicknamed "Halfback" right behind the President's limousine. We covered every possible precaution for a Presidential motorcade and downtown Dallas flushed with adoring people wanting to see their President.

After a while, the crowd thinned out and the motorcade made a sharp left to get onto the access street toward the freeway to the Trade Mart where Mr. Kennedy was to address a luncheon in a few minutes. I could distinctly hear Governor Connelly's wife when she turned back with a smile to say, "You sure can't say Dallas doesn't love you, Mister President."

When the first shots rang out, we couldn't be sure if it was a gun or just the noise from the crowd. I instinctively turned to the right and behind me to see if I could tell where the noise came from. The next retort was much clearer, and when I turned back to look at the President, I could see that the right side of his head had been blown off. I wanted to puke, cry, laugh, run, scream, kill. The car lurched forward and reminded me I had a duty to perform. Mrs. K had started to crawl back along the trunk of the car yelling, "They've killed my husband! They shot his head off! I have his brain in my hand!"

I ran up with the agent assigned to protect her as fast as I could. He slammed her down pretty hard, commanding, "Get down, Mrs. Kennedy!"

She responded, "Please be careful." I heard that quite clearly, but the next part I wasn't so sure of. "I'm pregnant!" is what I thought I heard, but with all the noises around me, I wasn't so sure. I couldn't really think about it in the moment. Even if Mr.

Zapruder had gotten a clear shot of my face, you would not have seen my stone expression change, shocked as I was.

We all spent the next few eternal hours at the local hospital where idiot surgeons made lengthy and vain attempts to reassemble the shattered pieces of our beloved Boss. All the King's horses and all the King's men…

Top Dog came up to me at one point. He took the remains of a cigarette butt out of his mouth like it was the cork in a wine bottle, dropped it to the floor and ground it into oblivion with the toe of his black oxfords. Tall and lordly, my guess was that he liked to picture himself looking like Gregory Peck or Rock Hudson. To me, it was more like that guy from "The Twilight Zone."

I had taken a seat along a hallway to help get back in my mind. He stared down at me with precision and said, "I saw Mrs. Kennedy say something to you out there. What was it?"

My eyes were still bleary, my heart racing and my hands shaking. Looking up into his armor-piercing glare made me just want to turn away. I was unable. Yes, Mrs. K did say something, but for the life of me I could not remember what it was under that kind of pressure.

I just shook my head and responded, "I couldn't hear what she said, sir. There was too much noise."

Top Dog observed me for any visible signs of prevarication. I gave him none.

"Okay, Stone. If you recall anything later, let me know."

I nodded out of protocol and he just kept staring at me with his inquisitive eyes. It took a few more years of service before I was able to acquire the same reserved, dispassionate attitude that he had. Even though it comes in handy from time to time, it's one of the things about myself that perpetually angers and scares me.

He walked down the fluorescent hallway, staccato steps on the linoleum. His hand rubbed the back of his neck.

Life went on. Slowly at first. We all mourned the passage of a leader and an era.

I got reassigned to a desk job after that, which was okay because I wouldn't have been much good protecting anyone for a while. The images from Dallas kept replaying over and over in my mind. Every time a car backfired I saw the back of John F. Kennedy's head being blown off. Every dark limousine had a woman in a pink, bloody dress crawling on the trunk. Constant reminders of my own inadequacies. Having to write report after report about the details of where I was and everything I did, moment by moment, on November 22, and the night before, didn't help.

Mrs. K disappeared from sight soon after and nobody saw her or the kids for about a year.

In July 1964 Top Dog called me into his office. There was already a nurse in a crisp, white uniform standing by the desk.

"Stone, this is Agent Sarah. She has a nursing license to boot." The brown-haired woman with a low bouffant looked to be about ten years older than me, self-assured and proud, but I still recognized that tiny tremor of nervousness that Top Dog imposes on anyone in his presence. We gave each other the once-over, check-out glance and then shook hands formally, stiffly. She was carrying a standard-issue.

"You will accompany Agent Sarah to Boston," not my favorite place, "where you will put the bundle up for adoption."

Bundle? I'm thinking, *What bundle?*

Top Dog and Sarah glanced down at a basket in the chair near the desk. A blanket in it started to stir.

"Thank you, Sarah. Please prepare the bundle for transport."

She nodded curtly and picked up the baby. The door closed behind her with a distinctive click. I looked back at Top Dog with a question mark. He motioned for me to sit down as he made himself comfortable behind his big desk, lighting a cigarette and brushing the top of his light brown crew cut with the palm of his free hand.

He breathed in and out slowly, placed the lit cigarette in an ashtray and turned to me. "This assignment is top drawer security, understand?"

I nodded. Not to be discussed with anyone, denied when asked.

"Every so often we have to hush up little mistakes, and that's what I'm asking you to do."

Little mistake? That's what he calls the baby? I'm certainly not a candidate for parenthood, but I still consider a living baby a person, not a "mistake."

"There are secrets that need to be maintained." There are so many little secrets around the Service that it's hard to keep up with who knows what and when they knew it. I guess my lack of response clued him in to my bewilderment.

"Sometimes we can't control the people we protect, and they occasionally provide us with new challenges, unexpected turns of events we could not anticipate."

His meandering speech did not make much sense to me, but as long as he enjoyed listening to himself pontificate, I was happy just to nod.

"Good. Then you and I are the only ones who know." About what? I glanced around his spacious yet spartan office for clues, but none were evident immediately.

"What about Agent Sarah?"

"You and Sarah are going to Boston posing as a married couple who can't afford to keep the baby because you've just been laid off and there are no relatives available to help."

This is going to be a tough sell. "Isn't she a little old for me?"

He shoveled a manila envelope across the expanse of his desk. "I couldn't get a younger nurse-agent and you're the only man I can send." Lovely. "We can make her look younger if that'll help you. Hey, it's the '60s, you know, swing a little. Older women are 'where it's at.'" The smug look on his face suggested knowledge by first-hand experience. I had not yet enjoyed such pleasures.

The envelope contained the paperwork and identification I would need to complete this assignment.

"It's a bit risky putting the kid up for adoption, but I figure it's the best way to protect everyone involved. The less they know, the better."

For who?, I thought.

"We'll just have to trust that everything will work out this way. Make sure you get a good contact so you can find the kid later... when we need to."

"Sorry to ask a stupid question, but how will I know that I've got the right child?"

"Good question." I'm glad he thought so. "This one has a birthmark on the bottom of his left foot shaped like a goddamned four-leaf clover!"

I immediately suspected Top Dog of tampering. "Did you have it put there?"

"No. It's the damnedest thing! Check it out yourself. We couldn't have asked for a better identifier."

You know I'd be looking at that foot.

This is not the kind of thing I signed up for. The Secret Service performs many functions, including safeguarding the Nation's financial institutions and protecting its leaders. I guess this is one of the "Secret" operations.

One day I'm protecting the leader of the Free World, a few months later I'm adopting out unwanted babies. This had to be the most uncomfortable mission I ever carried out. Hiding somebody's love child. It had all the smackings of a tawdry dime-store novelette.

And I'm the stinking tin-badge hero.

– ◆ –

The trip to Boston was relatively uneventful. Sarah and I barely spoke to each other; I had no idea how to act like a husband. The baby fussed once or twice, but Sarah responded quickly each time, presumably just like a mother would.

I checked the baby's feet at my first opportunity. Damn! Four purple-red splotches coalesced to form what our human imagination would interpret as a clover leaf. An image I found hard to eradicate from my memory.

The hot and muggy summertime Boston air didn't feel very different from the Washington stuff we just left behind. It's about as tough to breathe but so much easier to swallow.

We found our way to the specified adoption agency with a minimum of difficulties. Boston is a mystery to me, but Sarah grew up in nearby Newton and knew her way around like a native. Top Dog had chosen an inconspicuous, out-of-the-way place in the south part of town, somewhere along Tremont Street. Our assumed name was O'Hara and we were to insist that the baby go to a "good Irish family." I don't think I looked particularly Irish, people told me that I looked like a dark-haired Paul Newman, and my flat Midwestern speech was certainly not native to New England. But that didn't seem to matter to anyone we spoke to.

The staff at the agency was extremely helpful and eager to take our baby from us. Of course, I was suspicious. To my mind, any person that willing to comply with our semi-transparent story had to have a hidden agenda. Sarah did most of the talking, which was probably just as good because I'm not much of a bullshitter.

When the moment came to hand the baby over I could sense Sarah's reluctance to let the child go. She held it out then brought it back to her chest. Perhaps she fought with her own unfulfilled desires to have a child. I had already developed a great deal of respect for this other agent, but that momentary display of emotion raised the level a few notches. It was not in my nature to harbor such attachments to those I protected. Sarah's behavior, whether due to good acting ability or just her natural response to the situation, prompted me to behave in a most uncharacteristic way. I grasped her shoulder and gave it a reassuring squeeze. She eventually handed the baby to the adoption worker, then turned to look at me with an expression I was unable to interpret. The Mona Lisa-like flair of her mouth startled me, and I couldn't tell if she was merely continuing to play the part or whether she was starting to take a liking to me.

Either way it didn't matter. I had no interest in her, except as a fellow agent.

It had been too easy for my money. Two people walk into an agency and put a baby up for adoption with a minimum of effort. I do hope it's more difficult to get "Christopher O'Hara" out than it was to get him in.

Sarah helped put my mind at ease when she asked the very questions I had been wrestling with. We were assured that every adoption is assessed for fitness of parents and that the best possible match would be found for our baby.

I made sure I got a copy of the papers and the names of everyone we spoke to so that I could come back someday to trace this thready trail. Even without such hard evidence, Top Dog would be able to sniff out the clues to the child's whereabouts with only the faintest of scents. This way I wouldn't have to put his talents to the test.

As we walked out of the brownstone building I noticed excess moisture in her eyes. I couldn't tell if this was her acting or a genuine response. After a few blocks we turned and went our separate ways after shaking hands again perfunctorily.

We had done our parts. We did our duty. We followed our orders.

Somebody's baby was going to a good Irish home in Boston.

— ◆ —

It took a few months for the nightmares to stop. Visions of tossing babies and children off cliffs, into gorges and ravines, onto moving trains. Images of walking along beaches and finding bottles, some with threatening messages or ransom notes, some with dead babies, others just with severed body parts. Psychedelic psychodramas about abandonment and shame.

Increasing my nominal beer consumption helped to dull my unintentional thoughts about this, and a few other things. One of my Service drinking buddies suggested I start thinking about getting out from behind the desk. He said it wasn't doing anything for my career, it implied that I couldn't handle the tough stuff, and that the longer I stayed off field work, the more difficult it would be to get back into it again.

I finally requested to return to active duty at the end of September. Hours of stressful testing confirmed my readiness to serve my country's leaders once again.

Working with the Goldwater team left me with some of the happiest memories from my time in the Service. I felt so at home being around other conservatives who were also intellectual. It was like having a family in the workplace. A family I chose to be with, not one that was imposed on me by accident of birth. Or by assignment.

After the election, I got reassigned to the Humphreys. Another liberal. Not as cocky as Kennedy, for sure, but still a bleeding heart if ever there was one.

His wife was real sweet and always treated me like part of the family and not just another piece of furniture. Mrs. H would look at me and smile. Some people thought she had the hots for me. I remember Top Dog's remark about older women and it being the '60s. I still hadn't figured out what the decade had to do with anything. My small-town conservative naivety protected me from all that. To me, she was like a kindly aunt.

Adding to my recurring nightmares was the addition of being called in every so often to assist with training of new agents on the Presidential Detail. Having to watch the Zapruder film over and over and over, discussing what happened, what actions we took and when, brought back ugly memories, not to mention the shame and guilt.

The whole Viet Nam thing started heating up and my job got tougher and tougher. Even though Humphrey was a damned dove, he got just as much blame for the war because he was a part of the government, the Establishment.

I had to endure protesters screaming in my ear as we walked. More aggressive folks would lob bottles and other painful objects at us, and there were occasions when I had to "take one" for the Vice President. This was not my vision of Secret Service work, but it was just as much a part of the assignment as the glamorous stuff. We're not police, and we don't do crowd control. What I wouldn't have given to shoot, stun or bludgeon some of that unruly mob.

The 1968 Democratic Convention in Chicago was the beginning of the end for me. Having to deal with the militant throng of "Peaceniks" was tough enough, but add in the Chicago police force and the National Guard, and you've got all the ingredients for a small war. Just getting H in and out of the convention hall was painstaking and overwhelming. Violence in the name of Peace never made sense to me. Those kids could have found a better way to get their message out without having to resort to protesting and rioting.

I really wanted Nixon to win, not just because I felt he was the right man for the time, which he was. I just didn't want to have to hang around the pinch-nosed, whiny-voiced Humphrey any more. If he had gotten elected in his own right, it would mean moving back to the Castle again, with all its painful memories. I was finally getting used to being back in Washington.

When it was all over, I requested to be assigned to Agnew, but it was declined because he brought his own personal team with him.

It took me a while to figure that it was time to leave the Service. The prospect of yet another desk position wasn't suitable, after my many attempted stints with what I got to calling "paper-losing." Some people are adept at signing forms, stuffing envelopes and arranging meetings. I'm not one of them.

Washington was getting way too hot for me, in many respects. No social ties kept me strung there and I decided to turn tail and head back home to my little town in Northwestern Indiana.

After ten years of Secret Service work, I was immediately welcomed onto the local police force. It didn't take long to move up to officer status, detective, inspector, assistant chief, chief. No scandals, no glaring errors, no embarrassments. I finally mastered the paperwork thing; a computer is the greatest friend you can have. The meeting thing still confounded me; I'm just not a people person.

An exemplary lifetime of distinguished service.

I was hoping to spend my retirement years in peace. I had done my time and I didn't want to do any more. Besides, I had a new interest to focus on.

– ◆ –

My mind made a million flip-flops while I tried to decide whether I should discuss the gay thing at all. I finally figured it would be better if you heard it directly from me, rather than by innuendo, rumors and embellished falsehoods.

You probably already figured out that I don't have much interest in women. It took a long time before I was able to see it, and even longer for me to accept it. Whenever anyone asked why I hadn't married, I always said I didn't have the time for such things. My jobs kept me quite busy, whether by the position's design or my own.

I managed to evade and deflect all inquiries about my personal life, or lack thereof. I'm sure that people had their suspicions, but no one ever said a word to me. At least to my face. There was enough gossip in the rumor mill to keep those wheels well-greased.

It seemed that things have gotten easier over the years for gays. People in general have gotten more accepting or tolerant. I just wish I could get to that level of acceptance for myself.

It's so much easier to tolerate the flaws of other people. It's my own that I have troubles handling.

There are many guys who have these same feelings and can't deal with them. Some guys react with hatred and violence, making gays the target of their lynch mobs or religious crusades. To commit violence against someone you don't even know just because they represent what you hate about yourself seems so twisted.

I just wanted you to know that I have never committed violence against anyone, either physical or verbal, on account of their sexuality. There have been accusations, of course, but every law enforcement officer is perceived as being hateful toward their accuser at some point or other. If you combine all the allegations that have ever been launched against me, it would appear that I hate everyone, including myself.

Okay, it would be difficult to deny that there was some self-hatred in my own make up, but I had become real good at denial over the years. I knew there was something different about me, but I could never quite figure out what it was. It really didn't matter much because I wasn't paying attention to my own stuff anyway. It took another trusted member of my force, and a few big brews, to get me to realize what those strange feelings were.

Henry had been very gentle and supportive with me, having already gone through his own soul-searching around this issue. It was just as difficult for him, if not more, due to a strict Catholic upbringing. He seemed to know just what to say, and what to omit, to keep me engaged in the conversation. Too much, too fast and I would have overreacted. His calculated tone was exactly what I needed to guide me toward my own understanding of the way things are.

The best way I can describe how I felt was that it was like looking in a mirror and seeing myself as I really am, not as the uniform I wore. I wish I could be more accepting of that image, but that's just going to take some time.

The computer has really been my best friend, and I've had a few discussions with other similarly inclined fellows in various parts of the country. Being able to hide behind the anonymity of a screen name has given me the confidence to speak more openly and freely than I could with someone in person. It still makes me nervous that if a guy were really motivated he could somehow trace and find me.

All of us in my little discussion group seem to be grappling with this thing at our own paces. One fellow's divorcing his wife; another is sticking with it and trying to make it work. Kind of makes me glad that I never attempted to play the role of the husband. There would have been a mountain of hurt feelings if I had gotten caught up in that trap.

I have managed to make a few contacts with some guys in the surrounding areas. I try to keep my dates at least some distance away, due to my previous high-profile job. Home is within an hour drive of Chicago, and I've met a few guys who live there. No one set my heart fluttering so far, but my expectations of that happening at this late stage are pretty nil. My best years are behind me. There are times I wished I had come to this realization sooner, while all the parts still worked. I'm sure it would have been much more enjoyable.

I kept vowing to travel to a large urban area where I could get lost in the crowd and not worry about who sees me. It just didn't happen until recently.

Chapter Two

Monday

At 5:45 a.m. a car horn woke me from my nightly quest to retrieve body parts from secluded beaches. I threw on my robe, went to the front door, opened it and waved. As far as I'm concerned, they can wait until I'm good and ready. I'm on no one's clock anymore.

Being the good scout I am, I had packed last evening, retrieving the old dusty suitcase from the cellar and stocking it with a few shirts, pairs of pants, a sweater vest and some undies and socks. I also wondered about taking some more informal togs for, perhaps, making a tour of the Boston night life scene. Then, when I thought about it some more, decided this would be a strictly-business trip. As much as I wanted to explore and experience what the city had to offer fellows of my persuasion, I felt it best not to combine business with pleasure, and I could always go back another time.

The information from the adoption agency had been resting peacefully in a lockbox all these years. Slightly yellowed and looking too fragile to take with me, I wrote out the contact information and made a copy of the agency's certificate. Then the originals rested again in their secure sepulcher. The faked passport held up slightly better but would probably raise suspicion, as it hadn't been renewed since 1964. I'd have to come up with some clever way prove my false identity unless someone from the agency who saw me in '64 still worked there. But I would guess the chances of that are pretty slim.

Ready to face the world, I carried my suitcase out front, locked the door and walked to the waiting sedan. The driver held the door for me and took the suitcase. Oh, the VIP treatment. How nice.

"Agent Stone," he demurred as he took the bag. I haven't been called that in eons, but I'll just go along for the ride, so to speak.

It's about an hour to O'Hare from my place, so I decided to get some more shuteye along the way. I have nothing to discuss with this guy, and I am quite certain he has absolutely nothing to discuss with me.

— ◆ —

On the way to the security gate, the agent introduced himself, not that I can recall his name now. I knew I would never see him again, so I didn't make any effort to remember it.

It almost felt like he was going to board the plane with me. He went through security with me, which is now not allowed unless you have a ticket. At the gate, he waited until I had my boarding pass accepted, then he turned and walked away.

That could have been me, I mused as I walked along the gantry, *if I had stayed on at the Service. Playing chauffeur, nursemaid and personal bullet-proof vest*. Seems like I had made the right decision after all.

Shortly after I sat down, my suspicion gland began to function. It felt like someone was watching and studying me. Not wanting to communicate my suspicions, I waited until the safety demonstration. When instructed to identify the nearest exit, I pretended to look about the cabin for it but was actually scanning the other passengers. A few rows behind me, a dark-suited man quickly averted my eye-contact. Probably yet another agent assigned to look after me. Top Dog likes a seamless trail. I could happily ignore him now that I had identified him.

If it been later in the day, I would have sprung for a beer to help get me through the flight. As it was barely 9:00, a stout didn't seem proper. I don't usually watch movies on planes, and this would be no exception. It was some stupid-sounding comedy about a Greek wedding. The agent pretended to be interested in the movie, but I knew who really had his attention. Still a bit short on sleep, I slept for most of the flight, and Boston arrived mid-afternoon.

The dark suit guy followed me off the plane. When I left the secured area in the terminal, a young man in sunglasses walked up to me, "Stone?" he asked, as if he really needed to. I nodded. "Follow me," he instructed.

We started walking in a direction not toward my luggage. "What about my stuff?" I asked his rapidly-moving backside.

"It will be waiting for you later."

Not very comforting.

We walked out a door, not for the rest of the public, and stood on the asphalt outside the terminal. A dark sedan waited for us. The agent opened the door for me and I got into the back seat. He closed it behind me and got into the driver's seat.

He drove us across runways and taxiways. I could see regular commercial airplanes moving around us. Kind of weird seeing them from this angle. Eventually we passed runways 9 and 4R before turning off onto some old side road, passing a maintenance shed, and headed toward a dirt clearing that looked like a water tank once resided upon it. In the center was a helicopter, blades slowly rotating.

I've been through a lot of action, but never been up in a whirly. Not many things scare me anymore, but the science of helicopters never made sense to me and I could live out the rest of my existence without ever taking a ride in one.

The agent opened the door for me as I looked at the flying contraption skeptically. I guess my usual stone face showed a bit of a crack because I heard, "Never flown in one before?"

I just stared at the young guy, thinking about all the crap I've had to put up with over the many, many years of service, and just said, "I'm okay."

He handed me a headset, opened the door and assisted me in, closing the door behind me. He may have saluted, I'm not really sure because my head started spinning before the thing even took off.

Moments later we popped off the ground and I felt like an ant picked up by a giant-sized human. The view might have been great, but it all melted into a gooey mess until I finally realized I was not going to die in a fiery crash.

We flew along the coast of Massachusetts, south. Sure is a pretty sight. The greyish-blue waves smacking the light brown sand. About an hour later, we crossed the beginning of the Cape and descended into Hyannis Port, the Kennedy Compound.

It hadn't changed too much over the years, and a flood of memories overwhelmed me when the sting of saltwater air blasted my nostrils. I was reminiscing about tackling Bobby on a bright afternoon similar to this when a tap on the shoulder brought me back to the present.

"Stone."

The voice paralyzed me instantly. Top Dog. When I was finally able to re-engage my motor functions, I turned to face my old boss.

"Nice to see you again," he drawled in a folksy kind of way. More wrinkled and paunchier, what hair he had left was silvery bristles, shining in the mid-afternoon sun, trimmed in his signature crew cut. The end of his nose seemed larger and redder. Cigarette in one hand, he reached out to shake with the other. His icy cold eyes had a different kind of fire in them now, still piercing and intense but not so challenging. The smiley expression on his face reminded me vaguely of Muriel Humphrey, and in one blinding moment I realized something I had never grasped during all my years of service: this guy had the hots for me. That explains the plum dandy assignments for such a young agent. Silly as it was, I swept my gaze across the lawn, searching for Mrs. Humphrey, even though I knew she had died a while back.

Now I could sense that he knew that I knew, and the mild awkwardness passed when he continued, "You're looking good." He held out his hand and I instinctively grasped it in a perfunctory shake.

"Thank you, sir."

My palm started to sweat in Top Dog's grip and I pulled away mechanically.

He reached into his jacket pocket and pulled out a small manila envelope. "Here, put this away," he handed it to me, "Don't open it now. It might come in handy later."

With my mind humming about so many other things, I put the envelope in my inside pocket without much thought.

A familiar voice boomed out behind me.

"Good to see you, son."

I wiped my damp hand on my trousers and reached out to take the hand of Ted Kennedy. He stood with the sun at his back and I could barely make out the details of his face due to the glowing aura. I could, however, smell his breath.

"Thank you, sir." Time had not been kind to him. Grizzled and whitened, not even close to the firecracker of his youth.

"We haven't seen much of you lately. Where have you been hiding yourself?"

I had been to Mrs. K's service, and John Jr.'s most recently. It had been a few years.

"Just trying to stay out of trouble. Retired. That kind of thing." I couldn't think of anything to say. He's not much older than me and it gave my pride a pinch every time he used to order me around when his brother was in office. This is one fellow I would not want to have protected.

He gave my shoulder a squeeze with his free hand, "Good job, Stone. I'll, uh, try not to order you around too much today." He chuckled. "You're the man. I'm counting on you," and he turned and walked away.

What did he know about this mission? This is Top Dog's arena and I'll just let him do the talking. Patience, Stone.

I kept my eye on "Uncle" Ted. Even though he's the youngest of his siblings, he still thinks of himself as the family patriarch. No one appeared to challenge him on it either.

Top Dog tapped me on the shoulder, indicating I should follow our host. We walked up to the house and sat at tables on a porch overlooking the ocean.

"Beer?" Teddy asked, holding up what looked like a locally-produced brew.

I looked at the label, saw that it was a lager and held up my hand. "Thank you, but I prefer something a bit darker."

He turned away and back with a different bottle. "Try this," he invited, handing me something that appeared to be more to my liking.

"Thank you, sir."

Teddy giggled and held up his hand, "Stone, there's no need for formality here." This must mean whatever Top Dog is getting me into is pretty important. "Just call me Edward, or Teddy, as you like." He smiled that winning Kennedy smile.

He took the lid off a bucket of soup and I could recognize another familiar aroma.

"Is that from Mildred's? Is she still in business?" One of the perks of having to be in Hyannis was the wonderful clam chowder.

As he doled us each a helping of soup, Top Dog started his briefing.

"Stone, you're probably wondering why we dragged you all the way up here."

This beer is really good. Stout, bitter, tangy. The soup, however, was not as tasty as I remembered it.

"I know you've been out of the loop for a while, but, as it turns out, you're the only man who can perform a particular task for us." He peered at me over his soup bowl.

He's got so many other agents to choose from. *Why me? Why now?* For the life of me I can't figure out where this is going.

"That kid we had you adopt out back in '64. Did you bring the papers?"

Oh now I get it. The baby we took up to Boston was Teddy's. No wonder they wanted to keep it secret. Again I think: *Why me? Why now?*

I nodded so that he would know I remembered.

"You're not going to believe this, Stone. Take a good swig of beer first."

Now my head starting swimming. It could have been the beer, it could have been that statement. Either way, sweat infested my undershirt and I could smell it through the sport coat.

Kennedy looked at me to see if I was understanding what the topic was, and when he realized I had no idea, he indicated I should take another drink and then looked at Top Dog, who nodded gently.

"Stone," the Senator began, "my sister-in-law, Jacqueline, was pregnant with my brother's child."

"That day in Dallas," Top Dog interjected, "Jackie told you she was pregnant." *That Day*, he calls it, like it was just one of a million other days. "You haven't told anyone have you?"

"No, sir." I had actually forgotten about it until he just brought it up. Guess I did hear what I thought I heard. Another beer seems like a good idea. I reached into the cooler for one.

Teddy continued, "I did *not* know about that, no one knew about that until she started showing. We kept her out of sight. As she got closer to delivery, we discussed how to handle the situation."

"They came to me," Top Dog took over. "No one wanted to put the Kennedys at any more risk. I suggested we swap in a stillborn. Jackie had other miscarriages and she probably would have been more relieved than anything not to have to deal with a newborn."

"Bobby and I agreed it would be the best thing at the time."

Top Dog lit another cigarette, took a long puff and swallowed nervously. I don't think I've ever seen him display any fear or worry before. "I took a big risk. With all the talk about a 'Kennedy Curse' and other events of the time, I'm guessing that someone would have wanted to do harm to that little fellow. Jackie didn't need the additional stress."

What the Hell??? He had me put their child up for adoption under an assumed name? *Why me?* Probably because the other guy who knew was too close to Mrs. Kennedy to be detached. Good thing I didn't know who that kid was; I already had enough trauma to deal with. I can't even begin to imagine what kinds of nightmares I would have had if I knew what I had actually done.

"She didn't know…?" The words blundered from my lips without going through my brain first.

"She thought she had a stillborn. The memorial was very hush-hush. They didn't want any more publicity."

Holy mackerel! An unknown, undisclosed Kennedy heir. I probably should have asked a hundred more questions, but my mind must have frozen in shock at the audacity of such an act. Maybe I shouldn't get too bogged down in this quagmire right now. There are more important things to worry about.

Top Dog's stare burned a hole through my left cheek, "So, you and I and Senator Kennedy are the only ones who know about this. Got it?"

Boy, did I get it. This is bonkers! I'm still protecting the guy even after he's gone.

He took one long final drag and then tamped the butt out like he was killing Commies with each stab, his long, pointy nose aimed at the ashtray, his upper lip tight, revealing some teeth. "I had a strange feeling that the family tragedy was not yet over, and that kid may have been our last great hope."

He sure is arrogant and presumptuous, and makes a lot of decisions for people without them knowing about it, supposedly for their own good, but I guess that's what he gets paid for. Stealing a child to protect it from its own fate, lying to its mother to further hide the truth. There's something inherently, instinctively wrong about all of this. And I just followed my orders. The man is deranged or brilliant. Maybe a bit of both. I reached for another dark beer.

One question kept surfacing to the top of my froth-filled head: "Why now?"

Teddy looked at Top Dog, who then spoke, "Remember Agent Sarah?"

Oh yeah, she was the other agent who went to the adoption agency with me. I nodded, or at least I think I nodded. That beer was really, really good.

"She also knew who the baby was."

That would explain her teariness. It wasn't just someone's "mistake" as our boss had told me, but the actual second son of the Kennedys. I would probably have cried as well if I had known.

"She died recently, but before she did, she wrote the Senator a letter explaining what had happened," he continued. "I figure she didn't know that Teddy was already aware of the situation and was trying to let him know before it was too late."

"Honestly, I had about forgotten it had happened until I read her letter," Kennedy volunteered. "I contacted your boss and we discussed what to do."

"We had no idea if Sarah let anyone else know what had happened, so we decided it might be best to find the child ourselves before it's too late. With the upsurge in global terrorism lately, this might just be the right time to, uh…" Top Dog looked right at me. "You were the one who put the kid up for adoption and it's our best bet to have you do the retrieval."

Oh my goodness. That explains the *Why me?* They're saying I'm the only one who can help them with their predicament. Even with my brains stewing in stout beer, I can still figure this situation certainly gives me a great deal of bargaining power. I could probably ask for just about anything I want. Anything. However, being who I am, I asked only one question, "How can I help?"

Top Dog explained the contents of the envelope: a newer set of identification for my O'Hara persona. I was to go into Boston tomorrow, return to the adoption agency and find the missing child. Senator Kennedy stood up, winked at me, said, "Thank you, Stone. You're the man. The right man for the job," and walked into the house.

The secret son of John and Jacqueline Kennedy, possibly lost to obscurity, hidden in the bulrushes, waiting to return triumphantly in the future to reclaim his family's birthright.

— ♦ —

By the onset of evening, I had consumed more dark beer than I usually pack into a lousy weekend. As I staggered back toward the helicopter, Top Dog gave me a knowing wink. Half confidence, half flirtation.

The bastard.

Mixing too much alcohol with the tuck and roll of a small whirlybird flying in turbulence proved to be more than my intestines could handle. Bags for such occasions were handy, I would guess, due to the frequent fliers of the craft, and I had my very first in-flight upchuck. The beer tasted just as bitter coming up as it did going down.

I was never so happy to be at Logan. The same nameless agent waited for me, my luggage in the car. He drove me to an old hotel off of Tremont out near Massachusetts Avenue that was only a few blocks away from where the agency was.

With all the events of today, I felt it best to wait until morning and get a fresh start. Thank goodness for free cable TV.

Chapter Three

Tuesday

MORNING came too soon. The early bright Boston spring sunshine found its way around the edges of the curtains.

When I turned my head to see the clock, the slurpy sludge between my ears started sloshing painfully. Just thinking about the pain made my head hurt. I can't remember the last time I had such a noxious hangover.

Keeping my eyes closed helped a little, but nothing could stop that diesel motor pounding.

A taste in my mouth like unwashed gym socks propelled me up out of bed. Cupping a hand over my eyes to shield out the offending light helped somewhat, but I knew this would be a day I'd live to regret.

After a gentle toothbrushing and a gargle, my mouth felt more human.

The relaxing shower helped even more. Follow that with a cup of fresh instant coffee and I'm almost ready to function.

Strewn around the hotel room were the various pieces of clothing I had worn yesterday. As I foraged around on the floor, I finally got to the suit jacket. Something did not feel right about it; it was too stiff in the chest.

Didn't somebody hand me something yesterday? Wasn't it Top Dog?

I felt around inside the jacket and came across the manila envelope he had given me. This is absolutely amazing! It was an updated passport, current for the O'Hara father character. Thank goodness. I didn't know how I was going to pull this off with the old, out-of-date one. Bless that bastard.

As my head began to clear, I started to put together my plan of attack.

First, call the agency to see if they'd even be able to help me. If not, ascertain the best method of finding out who had the information I required.

The next step would be the more troublesome: finding and contacting the adoptive parents. After that, it's find the kid and try to convince him he's a Kennedy. That should be the easiest part.

I'm hoping that all those years of being an administrator have improved my bullshitting skills. They were near non-existent last time I went to this agency. Plus, I don't have Agent Sarah to cover for me.

Stone can do it. Even Ted Kennedy thinks Stone is the man. Stone gets the job done. Stone is, after all, Stone.

After a while the pounding in my head subsided to a distant thrum, and I was able to proceed. I dug out the contact information and the copy of the original papers.

Calling the phone number on the agency form resulted in a recording with the message that this number has been disconnected and that there was no new number. The address for the place is only a few blocks away and I decided to take a little walk.

I didn't want to go blazing in there like a jack-booted government agent, yet I needed an air of authority to command the information I wanted. My final choice was dress gray slacks with a beige oxford shirt. Over that would go a knitted blue sweater vest. Even though it's almost the start of summer here, the vest seemed to add just the right touch and gave a stately, intentional look.

It took me a bit longer than usual to get dressed this morning. Bending over still made my head hurt a little. Eventually I got into my "Boston casual" outfit and checked in the full-length mirror next to the bathroom. I just hope this is what O'Haras are wearing this season.

Armed with the paperwork, and my "Baby Glock," a small 9mm handgun I carry for my protection, I left the security of my quaint hotel room and descended to the main floor of the hotel. No one seemed to pay me any special attention. Praying that I did not look like a tourist, I strode confidently to the front door. It's a beautiful old building, probably pre-WWI. Lots of rich, dark paneling and scrollwork. Gave the lobby a cave-like ambience, which was just fine for my sensitive eyes.

After putting on my dark lenses, I opened the grand front door and stepped out into the Boston spring. Whew. I had forgotten how oppressive the humidity could be. This sweater vest is going to have to come off some time soon.

The few short blocks felt more like miles, especially since the street slopes uphill. At least I can look forward to an easier trot back.

Again, no one appeared to be looking at me in particular. I guess this outfit is going to be fine.

When I got to the spot where the building should have been, I saw a live-work loft complex that looked only about ten years old. Crap.

At least the walk back is downhill. It'll give me some time to come up with Plan B.

By the time I re-entered the comforting lobby, I had been able to run a few scenarios through my mushy brain. As soon as I got in the room and the door closed and latched, off went the sweater vest.

The big Boston phonebook provided no entries for the agency, which I kind of expected. So, I looked in the yellow pages to find similar places. I called one and asked if they had ever heard of the place I was looking for. The woman's English was hard to grasp, but I'm fairly certain that she had never heard of the place. The next fellow I reached spoke English, but it was that twangy Boston variety that can be hard to understand. He had heard of the agency, that it had closed down about twenty years ago, and he suggested I check with city registrar's office at City Hall. Good idea. I thanked him for his assistance and called for a cab. No more walking for me today.

The vest had to go back on in order to hide my firearm. I was quite sure I would melt in it, especially if City Hall was one those preserved heritage buildings that did not have air conditioning. Otherwise I'd have to leave my protection behind, and I'd feel naked without it in a strange city.

The turban-headed cabbie took me on a small sight-seeing tour. At least that's how it felt. But I do remember Boston being a mess of little streets that disappear and reappear at will. Add to that the haphazard arrangement of one-way signs, continuous construction, and I'm glad that the trip was as short as it was. I gave the guy a twenty anyway. Just in case he's got a big family at home he's supporting on his cab salary.

I balked when I saw the building that was supposed to be City Hall. You figure a city like Boston would have this stately, old, historical building, but instead I was confronted by a modern, megalithic superstructure that looked more like an overblown jail. Molded concrete slabs flanked tall, narrow windows. More blocky chunks stuck out unpredictably at various places. We don't have anything like this back in Indiana. A masterpiece of modern architecture, I'm sure, but I think I would have preferred something that looked like the Old State House or Fanueil Hall across the street. Around it loomed a collaboration of blocky, squarish office buildings, including the requisite JFK Federal Building, and one particularly interesting long, curved brick-covered office.

City Hall gave me the impression of having made a brutal assault into the plaza on which it's situated. Most disconcerting was its look of an upside-down ziggurat, with the floors getting bigger as the building rose, leaving a shadowy overhang around the entrance.

Before going in, I fumbled around for my weapon permit. I would guess the security team would want to keep my gun while I'm in the building. I just want to make sure that I'll be able to get it back on the way out. I flipped open the badge holder, anticipating the questions that would follow.

"Long way from home, Chief?" one of the guys probed when he examined my Indiana license. I didn't suspect people from Boston to be too interested in chit-chat. Guess he's just doing his job.

"Yep. Special research assignment." He nodded, apparently bestowing approval. "Looking for the Registrar."

"Room 213" is what I think he said. It sounded more like "tooth hurting." Luckily I had a few years prior experience of listening to the Massachusetts mangling of the language and could translate with a minimum of effort.

I thanked him and surrendered my gun. He took it, put it in a plastic lock box, locked it and gave me one of the two keys.

Then I walked over to the bank of elevators and pressed the up button. Again, nobody seemed to be taking any special interest in me. The chime chimed and the door slid open. After stepping in I pressed the '2' button, the doors closed after a second or two, and it felt like the elevator started to descend. It was quite disconcerting. I looked up and saw the red 'Down' arrow lit up. I looked

                    Tuesday

at the button panel to see if maybe I had pushed the wrong one. But '2' was the only one glowing.

The cab gently stopped. A brief pause before the doors opened. I stepped out into the hustle-bustle of a municipal office. I could see another security guy standing by a door and I walked over to him, battling the crowd of bodies ambulating through the corridor. The closer I got, the more he looked like his cohort at the front entrance.

With a little hesitation I inquired, "Excuse me, but what floor is this?" I hate having to ask for directions. Maybe it's a man thing.

"What?" he blasted, sounding more like I had just asked him to give me his gun.

"Sorry, but this is my first time in the building. I got in the elevator and pressed the button for the second floor."

"You got it, pally," was his gruff but informative answer.

"But the elevator went down, not up."

As he smiled he revealed nicotine-stained teeth below his scruffy moustache. "Got news for you, Mr. First-timer," he chuckled. "This *is* the second floor. We got two floors below ground. The main floor is the third."

Oh, that explains it. "Thanks, officer, I'm looking for the Registrar's Office."

"Room Tooth Hurting is right over there ('they-ya')."

I thanked him again and walked in the direction he pointed. Who would have suspected that when this inverted missile crashed into the ground it would have buried two whole floors?

At the counter in the Registrar's Office, I faced a Boston public servant, a woman about fifty years old who probably started this job right out of high school. She was in no hurry to help me, and I kept getting the impression that I was keeping her from her next cigarette break.

"Hi," maybe the folksy approach would work with her, "I'm looking to find some adoption records. I gave my child up in 1964 and I'm trying to find him now." I was so nervous playing this part, but I don't think it worked against me.

The woman looked up at me over her half-glasses and smiled absently. She was rubbing the tips of the first two fingers of her right hand with her right thumb obsessively. "That's nice," she boomed with a voice made deep from too many years of too many cigarettes. "Sorry. Can't help you."

"Why not?" I pleaded.

"We only keep current records here. You'll have to go to the Archives over in Hyde Park."

"I see." Studying her face for clues revealed nothing. "How would I get there from here?"

She exhaled a sigh more repulsive than the excessive perfume she wore. This is the kind of person who gives us public servants a bad rap. "Take the Orange T to Forest Hills. Catch the 32 bus to the end…"

"Wait, please, this is getting more complex than I wanted. I'll just take a cab."

"It's a long ride, honey." She handed me a slip of paper with the address: 30 Millstone Road, Hyde Park. "It's the brick building on the corner." With her especially helpful demeanor, it was difficult to tell whether it would be the only brick building around or if the whole neighborhood is nothing but brick. Now that she had completed her Herculean task for the day, she waddled off to get that overdue cigarette break.

I yelled, "Thank you," after her, but there was no response.

Back up in the lobby a news crew was setting up for a location shot. My little, dinky hometown combination city hall and police station had barely enough room to walk through, let alone film in. We used to do our interviews out front on the steps for those rare occasions when we actually warranted news coverage. As uncomfortable as I am talking to strangers, it was a minor miracle each time I made it through an interview. I just kept praying that I wouldn't say something stupid or embarrassing.

The security guard returned my gun without much conversation. As I was on my way he blurted out, "Good luck on your quest, Chief."

I glanced back at him and he had the same brown-tooth smile as his brother downstairs. Who knows? They could possibly be related. Maybe it's working in this weird building that does something to people.

Hailing a cab proved easier than expected. I told the woman driver the address and off we went. She drove us out Tremont

                    Tuesday

Street and I was expecting to see my hotel as we passed by, something familiar, but she turned off before we got that far.

About thirty minutes later I stood in front of the only brick building on Millstone at the corner of Hyde Park Avenue. At least the woman from the Registrar's Office got that part right. You know how it feels when you've started on a "wild goose chase"? I was quite sure that by the end of the day someone would try to sell me some snake oil.

Inside the Archives building I was directed to the Children's Institutions Department. There I discovered that I should have gone to the State Adoption Department, 150 Causeway, near the North Station, under the Fitzgerald Expressway Bridge, back in the northern part of downtown Boston.

I had to call to get a cab in this hamlet. They didn't roam the streets, like in Boston, looking for fares. In the few minutes I had to wait for my ride to arrive, I thought about going back to the wreck of City Hall and demanding the fat bitch pay for my totally unnecessary, and somewhat expensive, cab rides. Then I realized that I'd have to put up with her heavy sighs, heavier perfume, and probably having to fill out a multi-part complaint form which would take weeks to rise through the sifting paper stacks on some civil servant's overcrowded desk. It didn't seem worth the effort.

The cab mercifully arrived before I had totally drowned in my own sweat. It wasn't the newest model, but at least it had air conditioning.

The ride took even longer to get back into town and cost significantly more. This did not look like the swankiest part of Boston, with the ongoing roadwork and the rundown buildings. I was glad to have my ballistic security blanket with me.

Inside the Adoption Department I approached the information desk and explained my situation. The kindly man sadly informed me that the kind of records I was looking for were kept at the State Reunion Registry in downtown Boston: 24 Farnsworth, off Congress. I thanked him as politely as I could muster up and called for yet another cab. I was not about to take my chances standing on Causeway and waiting for a stray cab to happen by. I was really hoping not to have to use my gun this trip. Plus, it was starting to get nearer to 5:00 and I really couldn't imagine staying here an extra day if I really didn't need to.

At least this ride was shorter than most of my other rides. I kept hoping my debit card would hold up for just a few more rides before self-destructing.

Luckily, the Reunion Agency is in a more hospitable part of the city. It took being handed off to a few different clerks, but I finally ended up sitting down with Abigail Adams. No, no relation she says, just a coincidence.

"Well, Mr. O'Hara," lingering on the name long enough to connote some suspicion. Good for old Abby. At least I get the feeling that she's on top of things. "This was quite a long time ago," she muttered while perusing the adoption papers. "I'm sure we'll be able to come up with the information you seek, but I'm curious about your reluctance to come forward earlier." Her nose elevated so that she was looking at me through her quite-powerful reading glasses, which were firmly attached to a beaded necklace.

I'm sure you are, Ms Adams, I thought to myself. The keeper of the key wants to know the reason behind the request. Okay brain, do your thing. Put into use all those wonderful survival skills you've acquired. "Oh, the Mrs. passed a few years back. She never expressed any desire to find Christopher, but I, on the other hand, have always longed to meet the only son I'll ever have. Sorry it took so darn long, but it took me a while to work up the courage before I was able to start this… quest." Good bull, Stone. You have learned wisely.

I couldn't tell if there was a tear in her eye, but her glasses seemed a bit foggier than before. She leaned back in her squeaky wooden chair, looking at me over the glasses.

"Mr. O'Hara, I just want you to know that the Commonwealth of Massachusetts requires the adoptive parents to have signed their consent for the birth parents to have this information. I urge you not to get your hopes up." She stood, again looking at me over the foggy lenses. "Please wait here while I attempt to access this information. There are some vending machines down the hallway if you need some refreshments. I will assume you've had an exhausting day." She turned and walked into a back room.

You know, a little snack right now sounds pretty good. I can't remember what I ate last, and she was certainly right about the exhausting day. A short distance away loomed three old vending machines. I still had a few dollars in my pocket, thank goodness.

                    Tuesday

Oh wow, Snickers. Somehow that magical combination of peanuts, chocolate and caramel has helped me get by on more than one occasion. I can't think of anything I'd rather have right now. It cost me a whole dollar for a rather dinky bar, but how far do you expect one dollar to go these days?

Damn, the soda machine is a Pepsi dispenser and I'm a devoted Coke man. Well, at least there's root beer. Can't go wrong with that. A dollar for one of those tiny half-cans. Two dollars for two nourishing objects. I guess that's fair. I brought my booty back to Abigail's desk and proceeded to enjoy my little banquet.

Halfway through my snack Ms Adams returned carrying a withered folder. My hopes sprung up, despite her previous warning. She settled herself down as she observed me munching and drinking away.

"Oh good, I'm glad you found some refreshments for yourself. You looked like you could use a bit of a pick-me-up." She smiled blandly and placed the folder with measured meticulousness on the desk. "Well, Mr. O'Hara," this time her intonation inflected acknowledgment instead of suspicion. "I have some good news for you." I attempted to swallow the half nut lodged in my throat and ended up having to cough a few times. "Are you okay? Take some of your soda, please." I gulped a bit of the root beer and the naughty nut washed down my gullet with alacrity.

"Better now?" I nodded. "Good. I wouldn't want to have to practice my Heimlich Maneuver just now." I certainly agreed with her there. Now tell me the good news.

"The folks who adopted your child did indeed sign the consent form." It felt like my heart dropped an inch. "I'll take the liberty of jotting down their contact information while you fill out this request form. Please let me also make copies of your ID for our files." She thrust her hand out at me, palm up, eagerly waiting for my verification. I reached inside my vest and retrieved the passport from the shirt pocket and handed it to her. The eyebrows above her half-glasses arched pointedly.

"A passport?" As if I had just placed a wet leech in her hand.

"I travel a lot and it just seems more official, if you know what I mean." Especially if you're pretending to be someone else.

"I see. How… special." She made a photocopy of the passport while I scrawled out the lies I had carefully committed to memory.

Don't you just love committing fraud in the name of the U.S. Government?

I handed her the completed and duly signed form. She handed the passport back to me and I returned it to the shirt pocket without too much fuss.

"Everything seems to be in order," she chimed as she compared my filled-out form to the copy of the passport. Then she handed me the holy grail I had been seeking. "Here you go. I doubt you'll find these people at this address any longer. The file indicates no contact since 1965. They never bothered to inform us of their whereabouts. I'm sorry, Mr. O'Hara, but this is all the information I have."

All the information she had was mountains more than I had. I hoped that my long-day's goose chase might be over. If these names are just what I needed, then, I guess it makes it all worthwhile.

"Thank you, Ms Adams, you've been extremely helpful." More helpful than anyone else I've encountered today.

Outside there was a cab practically waiting for me. Maybe my luck was changing after all. After giving the driver the address for the hotel, I grappled out the valuable piece of paper to look at the names of the 20th Century's Mary and Joseph.

Zachary and Kathleen Walsh. The address didn't ring any bells, but it didn't matter anyway because they probably haven't lived there in over 30 years.

Now, at this point, you might be wondering why I didn't just do all this research on the computer and save myself all the hassle of cabbing around Boston. Makes sense. Most of this information is probably accessible online. However, it has been my experience that over the past few years, as the national economy has cooled from the internet-fueled overheating of the late '90s, less importance is placed on maintaining web sites, and many pages have been left unchanged for years because the entities just don't have the money or the personnel to update them. I guess the bottom line here is that I have lost my faith and trust in information found on the web. Unless, of course, it is mandatory to update daily, like for news sites. I guess most of what I have been using the "information superhighway" for is chat and e-mail. It's helped keep my sanity in a small and somewhat isolated

                    Tuesday

Midwestern town. Being able to discuss things with people from all over this country, and a few others, has helped me oh so much over the past few years. I can't imagine what my personal life would be like if I didn't have the electronic ability to interact anonymously with other folks experiencing the same emotional upheaval.

Back in my hotel room, minus the vest, a phone call verified what had been suspected. The person answering the phone told me she had not known anyone by those names and that she's had this number since 1983.

Zachary and Kathleen Walsh. I will find you. There can't be that many Zachary Walshes, can there? A bit of time spent with my best friend, my computer, will answer that question. But that will have to wait until tomorrow. Right now I'm ravenous and dinner at a local steak house felt like just the thing.

After a brief wipe up to decrease the day's slime on me, I caught a cab and asked the driver to take me to the best Boston steak house he knew. Ten minutes later he dropped me in front of a place called Morton's of Chicago, downtown on Boylston. Guess I can't go wrong with a place named for the Jewel of the Midwest. However, the façade lacked any characteristics of a fancy steak house, and if you didn't know exactly where you were going, you'd never find it.

Once you got inside the street-level door, you had to go down and around a flight of undecorated concrete stairs before getting to the rather understated entry to the best steak house in Boston. The room had a seemingly low ceiling and gave the place a more welcoming atmosphere. The dim lights also helped me to relax a bit; nothing can make me more edgy than bright lights in an eating establishment. The host whisked me to a table for two against a wall, which was just as well; I didn't feel like being on display this evening. After seating me, he cheerfully informed me that my waiter would be Ned, and he would be right out to take my order. I thanked the gentleman politely and wondered if I was supposed to tip him. As he walked away empty-handed, I thought how expensive this trip was turning out to be and figured I'd just be more generous with the dinner tip.

An acrid aroma stung my nose and I scanned the room in an attempt to locate the source. Oh, there it is, on the opposite wall, a middle-aged guy smoking a cigar. In the restaurant! He turned as he noticed me staring at him, making me a bit self-conscious. He then casually doffed the cigar in the air, smiled and winked at me. Okay, now I'm really nervous.

"Good evening, sir. Could I start you off with a beverage?"

There stood Ned, six-foot-something in a Chicago-style waiter's outfit, complete with black vest and spotless, white apron. I hadn't even glanced at the menu yet. "Sure, how about some stout."

"Guinness okay, sir?"

"Yeah, sure. Hey, Ned let me ask you something."

He swallowed nervously, "Yes, sir?"

I pointed to the offensive cigar smoker and inquired, "Are people really allowed to smoke in the dining room?"

He relaxed a little. "Cigars only. Would you like to see our complete listing of Monte Cristo and Davidoff?"

The surprise almost choked me. "No, thanks. I'm just going to figure out what I want."

"Very good. Might I suggest the Filet Mignon? It's our special this evening."

"Thanks. I'll consider that."

He turned away with a bit of a swish and I could not help noticing his bald spot is bigger than mine, and I've got to be at least 30 years older than him.

The menu choices were quite impressive. Unfortunately, the Filet Mignon is served with Béarnaise Sauce. I am in the mood for meat tonight, no fancy Frenchy sauces. It was difficult, but I finally decided on the Porterhouse. It was beef, beef and nothing but beef, just what I had my sights set on.

Ned returned with my beer and a cart of sample dinners and asked if I was ready to order. Oh, yeah!

"Which is the Porterhouse?"

He pointed to a huge slab of beef that would have choked a raging lion.

"I'll have that, please."

"How would you like it cooked?"

I like a little blood, but not too much. "Medium, please."

He jutted his chin to the left as he considered his next statement. "I just want to let you know that the chef tends to undercook, so I'm going to suggest 'medium-plus.'"

"Hey, you know this place better than I do. I'll take your well-given advice gladly." I smiled a little and he grinned back.

"Would you like a salad or some soup to start off? We have the best New England Clam Chowder."

I didn't come here to eat grass or fish. Besides, that recent bowl of Millie's chowder at the Kennedy Compound was enough to keep me for quite a while. Just give me the damn cow already. "No, thanks."

"Then might I suggest a potato on the side?"

That does sound good. I do miss those beefy, big-town taters. "Sure."

He put his pencil to his pad. "Mashed or baked?"

Oh, for crying out loud, get on with the meal! "Baked."

"Butter, sour cream?"

"The works!" Boy, he was starting to get to me.

"Very good. I'll get your order right in." With a cheerful note and a special smile reminiscent of Muriel Humphrey and Top Dog, he waltzed away to the open kitchen.

Once again I was fascinated by the guy with the stogy, puffing away without a care in the world. He didn't seem to mind me staring at him, and I couldn't seem to pull my eyes away. He was about ten years younger than me and had that cocky arrogance I used to find so annoying about the Kennedys. He wasn't bad looking, wavy chestnut hair, chiseled good looks, keeps himself in shape as well. My *petit voyage* ended when Ned returned.

"Here's some bread, sir."

"Thanks." I was ready to start gnawing on the table, I was so hungry. The bread smelled warm and inviting. When it hit my lips and tongue, I could hardly believe it. The subtle taste of onion made it ever so delicious! The place really is a blast out of the Midwest. They sure do know how to take care of hungry customers. I had just started on my second slice of the most wonderful bread I had ever tasted when Ned showed up with the biggest steak I had ever seen. Next to it was a potato the size of a football!

"Hope you're hungry," he smirked. "Take your time. No hurry. Can I get you any condiments: steak sauce? Worcestershire? Ketchup?"

My drool was spilling down onto the table. "No thanks. Just another beer when you get a chance."

"Sure. I'll be back in a few."

Take your time young man, I have a dinner date with two oversized portions. The steak was perfection. I probably could have used the butter knife to cut it, it was so tender. Toppings from the potato melted down onto the plate. I was in hog heaven. Maybe I should have tipped the cabbie more for this marvelous suggestion.

The next thing I remember is Ned bringing the second beer, taking away the glass from the first, and then asking me if I was considering some dessert. Dessert? There was still a half-pound of meat and a half-pound of potato on my plate. "Not really."

"That's fine, but I'll wheel the dessert cart over in a while so you can see what you're passing up."

Ooooh, he's evil in his own smarmy way. I guess if I were a bit younger I'd consider asking him what time he got through working.

A few minutes later I heard the squeaky wheel of a pushcart and knew who was here with what. I turned and saw the most scrumptious-looking mountain of chocolate cake slathered in vanilla ice cream, another chocolate masterpiece which looked like a mousse, and a wedge of cheesecake buried under a farmer's market of fruit.

"See anything you like?" he beamed down at me with a grin. I wasn't exactly sure what he was asking, but after two beers I'm not about to go fishing.

"No, thanks. It all looks delicious." I regretted that last remark after his grin grew even wider.

"All right, then, I'll just tally up your bill." And off he squeaked.

As I was shoveling the last bit of potato into my mouth, he returned and left the check wallet on the table. "I hope everything was satisfactory. We do want our customers to enjoy themselves." Glee, glee, glee.

Tuesday

I wanted to choke, but instead I responded simply, "It was the best steak dinner I've ever had." I reached in for my quickly-waning debit card. "I don't get to Boston that often, but I'll sure be coming back here next time I do."

"Tell your friends about us. On your next visit I'll give you our complimentary after-dinner cognac." He whisked up the wallet with the card in it. I guess he's kind of sweet, after all, in a New Englandy, Bostony kind of way. Ah, if I were younger…

I turned to glance at the cigar man, but I guess he left while I had my face down in the plate. At least the air is cleaner now, but I was getting used to looking at him. Kind of reminded me of a slightly younger version of myself. Once again, Ned broke into my reverie.

"Here you go, sir. Just sign the top copy and keep the bottom one for your records."

How many times have I heard that litany? The steak, the potato and the two beers came to over $50, and I wanted to leave a generous tip. This would be the end of the card, I'm sure. I will have to transfer some money over at my first opportunity. I signed off, after figuring the tip and totaling the whole thing with a sloppy brain. Still not very good at filling out forms, especially when numbers are involved. I handed the wallet back to Ned.

"Come again!"

"Thanks." I managed to make it out the door just as a couple was getting out of a cab. What luck!

I'm pretty sure I dozed off once or twice on the ride back to the hotel. I dragged my butt inside and regretted that Top Dog put me up in a hotel without an elevator. The stairs kept getting longer and longer with each step. At last the top arrived and I wanted to plant a flag.

In my room I threw the clothes wherever they would land, brushed my teeth, used the toilet and fell right into bed and lullaby land.

Chapter Four
Wednesday

My first choice would have been an uneventful trip home, in direct contrast to yesterday's grand tour of Boston. But, of course, I rarely get my first choice.

It started out well enough, with that super-delicious instant coffee provided for my convenience in the room. I certainly wasn't hungry after last night's beef and tater fest. In fact, I couldn't imagine eating anything until I got home this evening, or maybe whatever snacks they might serve us on the plane. Even a bag of toffee peanuts and a Coke would probably hold me over.

The cab ride to Logan went smoothly, and by the time I got my bag checked and had my boarding pass with 15 minutes to spare for the 9:30 a.m. flight, my suspicion gland was active. Too many things went so easily this morning. Some little black cloud is waiting just over the horizon for me, I'm sure of it.

Not that I'm superstitious or anything, but I prefer the aisle seat. Maybe it has to do with being able to get out first in case of an emergency or something. I'm not sure. Windows on an airplane scare me, for some reason. Even when the pilot announces, "If you look out the right side of the plane, you can see the entire Grand Canyon in one view!" I don't make a move; I just concentrate on devouring the in-flight magazine.

When they started boarding, I got in line and handed my boarding pass to a rather handsome young lad in a flight crew uniform. His eyes gave off a certain sparkle when he looked at me. That's nice, but I just want to get on the plane and go home now, thank you very much.

I've never been in an Airbus before. I guess it's kind of nice. Doesn't look too different from American-made planes.

The seat was easy to locate and I looked around one more time to set my bearings. Then, as if planned, once I got settled snugly in my aisle seat with two empty ones to my right, I heard the words I feared, "Excuse me, I've got the window."

Yeah, yeah, yeah.

Wait a second! This guy is gorgeous. I don't easily get worked up like this over other men, but he is definitely a looker. Probably in his late twenties, short brush-cut blonde hair, dazzling blue eyes, a torso sculptured by Michelangelo and tanned under Mother Nature. I momentarily lost my balance as I tried to stand up. Maybe my shoes caught each other or I kicked the seat mounting by accident, but I ended up in his Davidian arms.

"Easy, there, pops," he coos at me.

So, he's standing there, keeping me from melting into the carpeting, and all I can think of is, "Sorry." I'm sure that really impressed him. I struggled to regain my fly-away composure and eventually managed to upright myself. I stepped, cautiously, into the aisle to allow Adonis to pass through. It was difficult to keep my eyes off his backside; however, my consciousness jumped out of my bones when I heard a familiar voice, once again.

"Hello, Stone. I see you've met Agent Hank." The smirk on his pudgy face urged me to punch him in the mouth right then and there, but I figured I'd rather complete my life without any blotches on my escutcheon. Top Dog slid into the middle seat and the whole picture came into view.

Agent Hunk stabbed his right hand in my direction as Top Dog completed the introductions. "Hank, this is Stone. He used to work for me, years ago."

"Hey, Stone."

Oh, now I have to talk to him without drooling all over myself. "How's it going?" We shook the regulation handshake, and then we all sat down.

How did the bastard manage to get seats, and right next to me, on a flight that was sold-out? I'm beginning to think there's nothing he can't get away with. That's kind of scary.

"What a coincidence," I whispered in Top Dog's left ear.

His face screwed up before he responded, "How so?"

I considered a few nasty retorts, but settled on, "It's a nice surprise to see you again so soon, that's all."

"There are no coincidences," he jabbed a finger at me, "Remember that." He then deliberately turned his attention (affection) to the Hunk.

Well, here's that dark cloud I had been anticipating. With its own silver lining, to boot. I wonder if Top Dog just drools over him, similar to the way I would guess he fawned over me, or if they've consummated their relationship. You never can tell with Top Dog.

The plane took off without a hitch and we were on the way home, well, at least I was. I couldn't imagine where agent Hunk lives. Probably West Hollywood or Palm Desert. He looks like that trendy, circuit party, bunny boy type that Henry told me about who can do X and Schnapps shots until dawn. Oh, what I've been missing.

The rather attractive flight attendant wheeled the cart up to our row and asked me, "What can I get you, Gorgeous?"

When I turned my head to face his smiling puss, he then whispered, "I'll give you a premium beverage, comp." Sounds good. I'll have to start learning how to use this power I seem to have acquired. "What'll you have?"

I can't resist a freebie. "Something stout."

"Anchor Steam okay?"

I had never tried that before. I think it's from San Francisco. "Sure."

He uncapped a bottle and placed it on a napkin in front of me on the tray. Then he handed me a few foil packets, "Here, this is in case you get hungry later." He smiled that secret smile and then turned his attention to Top Dog. "And you, sir," all business now, "what can I get you?"

My old boss spat out his commands to the attendant, "Gin and Tonic for me, headphones and a Mountain Dew for my friend, here." He stabbed his right thumb in the direction of his traveling companion.

"Yes, sir," the attendant replied snappily. I'm thinking he's done a few years in the military, or maybe a few men from the military. He expertly popped open the can of tonic, scooped some ice into the cup, filled it almost all the way with the tonic, fished a pre-sliced lime from another cup, squeezed it over the tonic water, dropped it in and then filled the rest of the cup from a miniature bottle of Bombay. Perfect. The fat old queen on the bottle goes to the fat old queen sitting next to me.

The attendant placed the requisite napkin on Top Dog's tray and bent over to place it with military fastidiousness. He seemed to linger there just a moment too long, but it gave me a chance to

                    Wednesday

sample his cologne. Paco Rabanne. It suits him. Then he stood up, resuming his regal bearing once more.

A plastic bag with headphones appeared from a secret drawer, and we passed these over to Hank Hunk. In the meantime, our private bartender poured a toxic-looking, pale green soda over some ice cubes. He then handed the cup, on the required napkin, to Top Dog to pass on. As he unlocked the wheels of his cart, the attendant tossed a pack of Goldfish on each of the other two guys' trays. Top Dog produced a crumpled ten out of his pocket and stuffed it into the vest of our flight attendant, as if he were a Chippendale dancer or something. "Keep the change, son." Oh, brother.

"Thank you, sir!" he responded in obedient fashion.

"Thank you," I murmured with a small smile.

"No, thank you!" and he was off on his merry way to make other passengers happy, but not as happy as he had made me.

Expectedly, Top Dog broke into my momentary tranquility. "Good. Now we can talk."

I shuffled in my seat so that I could face him better. "What about Agent Boy Toy?" By this time Hank had wrestled the packaged headphones out of their cocoon and was shaking rhythmically from side to side, presumably listening to the piped-in sound tracks, but who can tell.

"Nah, he's off in music land," Top Dog waved his hand dismissively.

"Does he know?"

"Know what?" he asked playfully.

"You know what." I was not in a mood to play games.

He turned serious quickly. "No, it's still just you and me, kid."

I guess he's about the only one I know who can get away with calling me "kid."

"Didja get it?" Persistent, inquisitive bastard.

A memory from a few days ago popped into my consciousness. "Let me ask you something first. Did Ted You-Know-Who really know what happened?"

His eyebrows shot up, "What do you mean?"

I searched for a way to describe my niggling thought. "It seemed a bit odd that he knew about the you-know-what and forgot, yet he remembered my name without prompting."

"You're so hard to forget," and he casually placed his left hand on my right arm as though we were intimates. In his wicked wet dreams, maybe.

I shook my arm to get him to let go. He took the hint, after a second too long. "And he said something like, 'You're the man. I'm counting on you.' It really creeped me out. Of course, with all the beer that I had, it's difficult to remember almost anything."

Top Dog chuckled and shook his head in a wig-wag. "Oh, Stone, Stone, Stone," he was really beginning to remind me of Muriel Humphrey now. Talk about being creeped out. "When I was inside with Teddy, he saw you getting out of the helicopter and asked who the supermodel was. Meaning you, of course." I rolled my eyes without anyone seeing it. "I merely reminded him who you were. He remembered instantly. Guess you left a lasting impression, boy," and he gave a little wink in my direction. Barf. How much gin did flyboy put in that tonic? There couldn't have been that much room left after all that ice, tonic and lime. "He started telling me about the pranks he used to play on you back at the Castle. Sounds like you're an easy chump. So suspicious, yet so gullible at times." He laughed a private laugh. "So I told him if he wanted to pull a good one on you, go up and say, 'You're the man. I'm counting on you.'" Oh, cripes. "He asked me what that meant, and I told him not to worry about it because you," indicating me with a pointed finger, "would understand. That's all I told him. I'm surprised he had the guts to pull it off." He laughed to himself again, wiping his eyes with his cuffs.

The bastard.

"So, what'd you bring me?" Back to business.

My diplomacy circuit kicked in. "First, let me thank you for the new passport. I was worried how I was going to pull this off with ID from 1964."

Again, he placed his hand on my arm. "Poppa thinks of everything for his special boys." The sappy grin on his face made the whole thing even more unbearable.

I tried to shake his hand off, but this time he had a tighter grip. "Now, tell Poppa everything he wants to hear." At this point he increased his grip, as though I was an uncooperative informant.

I really hate it when he calls himself "Poppa." It sounds so… incestuous.

After swallowing hard and making one last vain attempt to wrestle my arm free, I relaxed in order to get through the next few minutes. A swig of the beer first. Oooh, this is nasty, bitter putrid stuff. I think I could get comfortable with it pretty fast. An uncontrollable shudder from the bitterness rocks me for a moment. Well, just one more quick pull; it's going to be a long flight and I might as well soften up the bumpy parts.

"Okay," I finally start to answer. His impatient glare tells me I'd better get on with it. "I got the parents' names, but the address and phone number are very out of date."

"To be expected." He eased up a bit on his grip, now that I'm talking.

"But the father's name is fairly unusual and I'm hoping it won't be too difficult to track him down."

He gently squeezed my arm. "How can I help?"

Oh, time for some more diplomacy, "Thanks. I think I can take it from here." This last attempt of snapping my arm from his grasp finally worked. Probably caught him off guard while he was machinating.

"Good work, son. Good work." He dashed off the dregs of his drink. "I want a detailed report, weekly, preferably by e-mail. Understood?"

Okay, that's it. I'm retired. I'm not in anyone's servitude. Especially this overstuffed pederastic megalomaniac. I took a big swig of the Anchor Steam to soften the edge. "Look, you're not my boss anymore."

"But, but…" I wasn't going to allow him to spoil my long overdue soliloquy.

"I am *retired*! I was a goddamned fucking chief of police. I'm doing you a goddamned favor out of the goodness of my tender fucking heart. If you want me to just hand over everything I've got right now and let you finish it up. Fine. You just say the word. Otherwise, get your nasty, bloated red nose out of my tight little ass and leave me the hell alone! I'll tell you what I find when I find it. Because I'm going to be on my time. My schedule. If you want Stone to be your man, then back the hell off and give me the same goddamned respect that you give your twinky little play toys!" Damn, this beer is good!

Luckily Agent Play Toy had drifted off to la-la land and was oblivious to my tirade. Unfortunately, some of the people in the surrounding seats couldn't avoid hearing me, and I swear a few of them actually applauded. With all that beer, it was getting tough to tell fiction from fantasy.

Top Dog slumped back into his chair with a simple smile on his face. He sniffled then cleared his throat. "You got balls, boy. I hoped you would eventually figure that out for yourself." He gently patted the back of my hand and turned toward the window, jostling the sleeping beauty.

There was one more mouthful in the bottle and it went down sour, burning and acid. God. I love this stuff!

Just as I put the empty bottle back on the tray, the friendly flight attendant swooped down to replace it with a fresh, cold one. "You go, girl," he said with a knowing wink which I had no idea what it meant. It was the first time anyone had referred to me in the feminine. I didn't like the sound or the feel of it at all. The remnants of the last beer welled up at the back of my throat and I briefly considered handing the new bottle back to him for making such a rude, insulting remark, but as soon as I lifted it up and felt the cool, sweaty glass in my hand, I changed my mind and took a big gulp instead.

The in-flight movie looked like some stupid romantic comedy with that little gook, Leonardo Di Caprio, and some indistinguishable ingénue. Not what I'm in the mood for right now. As I took another swig of brew, I turned to see Top Dog and his little boy chatting intimately. That was the last image I remember before gently drifting off to la-la land myself.

– ♦ –

When I regained consciousness, two hours had passed and my head hurt a little. Top Dog sat staring at Hank, while Hank stared at Di Caprio's bare chest on the screen.

The flight was scheduled to land at 11:15, Central Time, but the captain announced that we had hit unexpected headwinds and would most likely be landing closer to 11:30. Well, that's not too bad. It just means 15 more minutes of Top Dog.

"Well, look who's joined the land of the living." He still has that punch in the mouth coming his way.

"I shouldn't have had that second beer."

"Your personal flight attendant seems to be taking very good care of you," spoken with a slightly envious note to it.

"Yeah, whatever." Hank was laughing at something happening in the movie. His blue eyes seemed to twinkle whenever he smiled. I could see the movie credits rolling, and Agent Adonis started making silent little applause gestures without actually bringing his hands together. Guess he really enjoyed the show. A few million dollars for Leonardo, ninety minutes of enjoyment for the Hunk.

As the plane landed at O'Hare and we taxied to the gate, Top Dog shared some relevant information with me. "Hank and I won't be getting off the plane with you." I'm certainly glad to hear that. "We're continuing on to Tokyo."

How nice. And good, he won't be around to annoy me. "A little vacation?"

"Top secret. Government business. Need-to-know basis only." Like I care. "Can't discuss it with civilians who no longer have clearance privileges." That indelible smirk is just begging to be smacked.

"I'll let you know when I get something definite."

"Definitely." The cold stare of a man defeated. For now. "Keep in touch."

As I turned and started out of the plane, I looked back over my shoulder and tossed, "Don't hold your breath." I turned my head to see where I was going and didn't look his way again. I secretly hoped he would hold his breath until his beady eyes rolled up into their withered sockets and his icy heart stopped beating.

My favorite flight attendant stood near the door murmuring "Thank you," to each departing passenger. When I got there, he grabbed my hand, shook it warmly and said, "Thanks for flying with us. I hope to see you onboard again soon," and he flashed that certain smile. Yep, I've got to figure out how this thing works.

"Thank you. You've been most accommodating," which made his smile widen. He eventually let go of my hand when I turned to walk onto the exit ramp.

As I walked away I could still hear his cheerful, "Thank you, thank you." He was kind of sweet, if not a bit too effeminate for me. I hope he's got a nice person at home waiting for him.

Finally. Back in Chicago. Only 15 minutes behind schedule. Probably another half hour until I get my bag back. This would be a good time to get rid of some of that beer.

I turned into the first men's room outside the arrival gate. While standing at the urinal, a man in his forties stepped up to the one next to me. Out of the corner of my eye I could see him looking at me out of the corner of his eye. The edge of his mouth turned up ever so slightly.

Okay, now that I know I've got this magic aura, how do I turn it off? There are some things I would rather do without being gawked at. This is one of them. As much as I would like to meet a nice fellow, I don't consider the restroom at O'Hare Airport to be the special place for that to happen.

Unfortunately for me, I had a lot of beer to recycle. That kept me standing there longer than I would have liked. The guy didn't move away until after I was finished. I felt so uncomfortable and icky. No wonder gays get such a bad rap. I took an extra few seconds to wash my hands thoroughly. He stood at the sink next to me and then at the electric hand drier as well. I just hope he doesn't follow me home to Indiana. Maybe he should. That would be just punishment. They don't tolerate his type where I come from.

Back out in the jungle of moving bodies and luggage carts, I aimed myself in the direction of the baggage claim. As I walked, I couldn't help but think about what just happened to me in the men's room. Are there gay men everywhere? Or am I just starting to notice them more now? It seems as though every place I've gone over the last two days, I have encountered some kind of special attention or other from men. I don't know. Maybe I'm getting more paranoid. Maybe I'm just starting to notice what's been there all the time. One thing is for certain, I've got to figure out how to control this whatever it is I've got going. I'll have to ask my buddy Henry when I get back into town.

By the time I got down to the baggage claim area, the carousel for my flight had already begun to move. Slowly at first, one bag, then another appeared up from the mysterious depths below. Of course, with me getting checked in early, my bag will probably be one of the last ones out.

Five minutes and seventy-five pieces of luggage later, my suitcase ascended the conveyor belt. When it reached the top, it obediently fell over and took a short ride until it passed my way. I reached over and snatched it. Okay, now I'm almost home.

Outside, in the warm, humid, smoggy air, I walked over to the area where I usually wait for the shuttle to take me back to Indiana. I wonder how long it will be until one of them is headed in my direction and we can gather enough people going the same way to make it worth the driver's while. Sometimes they wait for a half hour out of protocol, and other times they just give it a few minutes before figuring out I'm the only one headed out to the boonies.

So it's just about noon here in Chicago. I happened to feel around in my pocket and found two foil packages of Goldfish. A little snack would be welcome right now. I chugged down the tiny cheddar crackers and then walked over to the nearest garbage can to throw the wrapper away. After making the deposit, a uniformed driver holding a clipboard approached and asked where I was headed. I told him my destination. He whistled the "Boy, that's far" tune and then said, "Go over to shuttle three. He'll take you,"

And he pointed off to my right.

"Thank you." I nodded. With bag in hand, I walked over to the waiting van. The driver stood at the back with the rear doors open. He reached out to take my suitcase.

"Where you going?"

As I handed him the luggage, I said, "Fort Dyck." The official pronunciation is "Fort Dake," or more like "*Day*-ick," but, of course, we hear everything from the obvious "Fort Dick" to the more disgusting "Fort Dyke."

His eyebrows kicked up a few notches and he tossed my bag into the back of the van with a pile of assorted others. He slammed the doors shut and then opened the side door for me. Inside was a family of five African-Americans. They were headed to Gary. That's almost halfway to my destination.

I snuggled into the only available seat, last row. I thought about pulling out the other bag of crackers, but that would probably be rude to eat in front of strangers.

After the driver got us out of the O'Hare complex, he headed south on I-94. It would probably be twenty or thirty minutes to Gary, if there weren't any unexpected traffic snarls. It was way too early for the evening rush hour, but you never know what kind of idiots are driving out there. Ever since Clinton abolished the 55-mile-an-hour national speed limit, people doing 80 or 90 weave in and out of traffic dangerously. I guess they're in a hurry to get to an accident. Please just let me get back home without too much delay.

As we drove out of Chicago, the scenery gradually shifted from urban to suburban to industrial. Once we headed south from Gary, it would go from industrial to rural. I am so looking forward to seeing open space again. The last few days have been spent in severe civilization without much greenery. I can stand it only for so long, but I need to see trees and open fields to feel recharged, like I'm truly alive. Asphalt and concrete make me feel claustrophobic. I'm not a city boy, and I don't plan to be one any time in the near future. When you're raised in the wide open spaces, you just get used to that sort of thing.

— ♦ —

Once the family I shared the shuttle with departed in Gary, the driver got back on the interstate and then headed south on I-65. Since I was the only passenger at that point, I figured it would be okay to eat the other bag of Goldfish. Guess I was hungry after all. There was no place to throw the wrapper away, so I just tucked it into my pocket for later disposal.

Eventually we arrived at Exit 245 and we headed west on the state route that leads to my home. A few miles later I could see the scattered houses on the outskirts of town. We passed U.S. Route 41 and I asked the driver to turn right on Second Street. The next cross street is Grant, and my house is right around the corner, 209 East Grant Street, just a short, two-block walk to City Hall. A cozy two-bedroom, modest house built in 1880.

I handed the driver my debit card, glad that I had been able to transfer the funds by telephone this morning before leaving for the airport. Instead of including the tip on the card, I handed him the few dollars' worth of coins I had left in my pocket, which would probably have been a nicer gesture if it hadn't included an empty Goldfish wrapper as well. I snatched the bag back with a modicum of embarrassment, and he smiled. We finished the transaction and he opened the back doors, allowing me to retrieve my bag. I waved

Wednesday

goodbye as he drove off, knowing he has at least an hour drive ahead of him, if he's going directly back to O'Hare.

It is kind of amazing that I can live within an hour's drive of such a large urban center and yet you would never know it from the beautiful lawns and trees of our little town.

I opened the front patio door and stepped onto the porch. I had to put my bag down because I couldn't locate the key immediately. It had somehow gotten into the mischievous Goldfish wrapper and it took me a few minutes to figure that out. I felt stupid for a minute, but the lock opened with a healthy clack, and I was home at last.

The clock on the wall read 2:05, but I really wasn't too sure. It felt like it could have just as easily been 6:00 or 7:00 in the evening, with all the activity I've already had today.

The phone machine light indicated I had messages waiting, the suitcase begged to be unpacked, but my tired body said, "Rest!" and I sat down in my easy chair, hit the power button on the TV remote, setting it to CNN. I pushed back in the chair, bringing up the footrest. Within minutes I was snoring away to talking heads on Crossfire.

I woke up in time to hear the wimpy liberal guy whine, "And that's why the presence of the American fleet in the Mediterranean is threatening to the Palestinians. We have to move the ships to a comfortable distance so that they'll return to the bargaining table willingly, and not out of duress!" I switched that shit right off.

There was only one message on the machine. A reminder that the high school is having a rummage sale this weekend, and that we should call the office if we needed to have them pick up any large items we wished to donate.

The luggage still begged me to unpack, and I took most of the contents and threw them in the laundry. The rest of the non-washables I returned to their proper places. I finished at around 3:30 and I dragged the empty suitcase down to the basement where I normally keep it, even though a nagging voice in my head kept telling me I would be needing it again soon.

Even though I had been away a few days, there was relatively little e-mail waiting for me. Mostly unwanted solicitations for home mortgages, credit cards and Viagra.

I entered the URL for our special government people finder. Again, I would not trust the regular websites to have the up-to-the-minute information that I require. After three levels of login codes and passwords, I get to the main input screen.

The search for Zachary and Kathleen Walsh took a few minutes to process; the database is extensive and lists every known person in this country. The screen changed and I found three possible matches: A Zack Walsh in Morgantown, West Virginia, another Zack Walsh in Los Angeles, but the best news is that there is a listing for a Zachary and Kathleen Walsh in San Francisco.

Guessing that the folks in San Francisco are the ones I'm looking for, I figured I better call the other folks, just in case. If it's 4:00 here, it'll be 5:00 in West Virginia. A minute later I was speaking with Zack Walsh number one, a very nice sounding Southern boy who had never been to Boston, and he was too young to match the profile anyway.

In California it would be only 2:00, but I decided to give it a try anyway. The answering machine of Zack Walsh number two picked up, and by the sound of his youthful voice, I could safely rule him out as well.

With nervous fingers, I dialed the number in San Francisco. A woman answered. I asked to speak to Zachary Walsh. She screamed out, "Zack, it's the phone, for you!" I just wish she had moved the receiver away from her mouth or covered it with her hand first.

In a few seconds I heard a click and a man's voice yell, "Okay, Kat, I got it!" Another click. "This is Walsh."

My innards shook as if they were made of jelly. I cleared my throat first, but the frog persisted. "Mr. Walsh," I had to cough to get rid of the lump, "sorry."

"That's okay. What's this about?" The remnants of a Boston twang lurked in his speech.

I swallowed nervously. "Mr. Walsh, my name is O'Hara."

"Yes?" He started sounding impatient.

"I put a baby up for adoption in Boston in 1964."

"Oh my god! Kat, pick up the phone! Pick up the phone!"

A click. "What?" It was the woman who had originally answered.

"It's Chrissy's father!" the man announced.

"No shit!"

"I think so. Is that what you're calling about, Mr. O'Hara?"

I swallowed my uncomfortableness, "Yes, actually."

"Oh my god!" The woman bleated.

"That's what I said," Zack contributed. "How did you ever find us?"

"Well, it wasn't easy," and I wasn't about to launch into the whole episode, "but thank goodness you folks gave permission for the birth parents to contact you."

"Did we do that, Zack?"

"Yeah, but we never told them we moved to San Francisco."

"I guess you could say I was highly motivated to find you."

The woman asked, "What about Mrs. O'Hara?"

"Oh, she's been gone for a few years now."

"I'm so sorry to hear that," and she truly sounded sincere about it.

"Yeah, well, she was part of the reason we hadn't attempted to contact you before. She didn't want to know anything about the baby. It took me a while to work up the courage, but I finally did. I'm so glad I found you two."

"Yes," Zack agreed. "We had always hoped that the birth parents would eventually step forward. We certainly didn't expect that it would have taken so long."

"Well, better late than never, Mr. Walsh."

"Call me Zack, please."

"And I'm Kat."

I had to open the passport to remind me, "Christopher." That sounded stilted.

"Well, Christopher, I'm guessing you want to meet Chrissy."

"That's why I called."

"Yeah, well that's going to be a bit difficult."

"How so?"

Kat answered, "We don't really know where… You're probably going to think we're lousy parents, but Chrissy ran off to a commune years ago and we haven't had any contact since."

"I think it was 1982, Hon," Zack informed us.

Oh boy, a commune. Another damned liberal, just like his parents.

"Well, Zack, Kat, I'm going to be out your way on business later this week. Perhaps I could visit with you."

"Oh, that would be wonderful!" Kat squealed. "You're welcome to stay with us, if you don't already have a place."

"Don't worry about me. I'm all taken care of." Lies, lies, lies. "How about if I call you when I get there."

"Excellent!" piped up Zack. "You seem to have our number. Give us a call when you get into town. We'll be looking forward to meeting you soon, Christopher."

I then realized he was speaking to me, "Oh, yes, me, too. I'll be talking to you later."

"Okay, bye." Click.

"Bye." Click.

I hung up with the biggest lump in my throat. My heart pounded bombastically in my chest. I am still not used to having to keep up such subterfuge. Guess I'm going to get some practice.

— ♦ —

With my hand still shaking, I called Henry, my friend from the force. He wanted to know where I went and I suggested we meet for dinner. He thought it was a great idea. We agreed that he would pick me up at 6:00 and we would go to our favorite Italian restaurant.

I slumped back in the easy chair and fell asleep thinking about having to go to San Francisco.

Henry honking his horn woke me up. I sat upright, stood up, put a few lights on, grabbed my key and wallet, and dashed out the door.

Henry drove a beautiful silver-gray 2001 Honda Accord. Generally you don't see many foreign cars in our parts, but he went up to Gary especially to buy this one. I opened the door and sat down on the soft gray fabric. As he pulled away I fastened the seat belt. His auburn hair reflected bits of late-in-the-day sunlight.

His wide face held a big smile and big teeth. "Long time, no see, stranger. So where did you go?" He turned down Third Street and then made a left onto the state route.

"Well, I can't tell you much."

                                        Wednesday

He turned left into the parking lot of Monica's. "But you still have to tell me everything!"

As we got out of the car and walked toward the door, I thought, *No, I can't tell you anything.*

Inside we sat at our usual table, and our usual server asked us what we wanted to drink. Darlene is a bouncy, blonde Midwestern girl from solid Dutch stock. Someday she'll make one of the local boys a good wife, and mother, but for now she plays the field. And her field is rather large.

I didn't feel like having any more alcohol today, so I just ordered a Coke. Henry had a different sort of day, and he asked for a beer.

The menu looked just the same as last time I saw it, and I decided on a small Thick Crust Healthy Heart pizza. Monica's is famous for their Thin Crust pizza, but I'm Midwestern through and through. Give me the thickest, grainiest crust you can make. The Healthy Heart has less cheese and more leafy veggies. That's for us health-conscious, over-50 (or 60) types.

Henry, a bit younger than me, ordered the Sicilian Sub, a pile of artery-clogging meats (ham, bacon and pepperoni) in a big greasy roll. I guess that would also qualify as very Midwestern.

Once Darlene had brought us our drinks, taken our orders and walked out of earshot, Henry started bugging me about where I had gone. I tried to think of just what I could tell him. I told him that my old Secret Service boss contacted me and requested I help with something ultra-confidential.

Henry is a staunch liberal, and probably the only person in town with a Gore/Lieberman sign still in his window. It helps when you are the Assistant Chief of Police. No one questions your political beliefs. At least not to your face. He would have exploded if I had been able to tell him what had happened and where I had been and with whom I spoke.

Darlene arrived with the food, and not a moment too soon. I had worked up quite an appetite. She set down in front of me a petite pizza with a mound of vegetables on top, and in front of Henry a large roll with vegetables falling out of it.

He looked up with alarm. "Darlene, what is this?"

Her deer-in-the-headlights expression is probably very attractive to the amorous young fellows she meets, but she's at the wrong table for that now. "Didn't you order the Veggie Sub?"

"No," emphatically from the carnivore, "I asked for the Sicilian Sub."

She slapped herself on the forehead and gawked, "What was I thinking? I ordered you what I wanted." She reached down and picked up his plate. "I'll go order you a fresh one. I can eat this one. Can I get you anything while you're waiting?"

"Nah, I'll just nibble on Stone's pizza." He picked up his almost-empty glass and added, "and maybe another beer, when you get a chance."

She shot back over her shoulder as she walked toward the kitchen, "Sure, Henry." She deposited the veggie sandwich on an empty table and then disappeared through the double doors.

While he waited for his replacement, Henry grabbed some of the vegetables falling off my pizza and gnawed unhappily. He also gave me an update about what has been happening in the Police Department. Same old stuff, different names.

Darlene returned with the correct sandwich and a fresh beer.

Henry chided, "Thanks, Darlene, but you're not getting a tip tonight."

"How would that be any different?" she mocked.

"Oh, go away little girl and let me eat." He reached down to grab his steaming sub with a death grip. Our waitress minced off with a bit of a titter. She stood near the table where she had placed the other sandwich and grazed languidly.

I observed Henry demolish the oversized stack of fleshy meats. Sauce trickled down the left side of his mouth. He didn't seem to care.

"I'm thinking about taking a trip to San Francisco." This would be a good time for me to talk, while he fills his face.

"Oh really?" he asked gleefully through a mouthful of sandwich.

"Yeah. There's some things I need to take care of, and I might as well make a fun trip out of it."

"How're you boys doing?" Darlene popped up out of nowhere.

"Fine. Now go away. Police business," mugged Henry.

"I'll get you another Coke, Stone," and off she toodled, big grin and all.

He turned back to me, "Have you made your reservations yet?"

"No, this is just in the thinking, planning stage."

He set the remnant of his sub on the plate to tell me something really important, "Then you have to stay at Beck's Motor Lodge on Market Street."

"Why?" I mumbled through a mouthful of spinach and broccoli.

"That's where I stayed last time, and it had been recommended by a friend."

Henry's "friend" is probably an old trick. He doesn't seem to retain real friends very easily. In fact, he's at the limit of my tolerance. I only maintain this association because of how he helped me gain acceptance of myself. Plus, he's the only other gay man I know in this remote village.

"What's so special about Beck's?"

After sucking in the last bit of fallen meat and a swig of beer, "The place is always full of guys." He busied himself wiping his greasy hands on the tattered napkin. "They leave their doors open and walk around, looking into each other's rooms."

That doesn't sound appealing at all.

"It's only a few blocks from the Castro, kind of in the heart of things." The smile on his face suggested more-than-fond memories.

"I don't know, Henry. I prefer quieter places usually."

"Aww, Stone, c'mon. You've got to start living your life before you're too old to enjoy it!" he clanked the empty pilsner on the wooden tabletop.

One thing I can say about Henry: he sure doesn't hold anything back. That's why he's so popular. Especially because he's usually dead-on right. It's just his confrontational style that makes people uncomfortable.

"You know, you're right. If I'm going to all the trouble to go to San Francisco, I might as well get my money's worth."

"Now you've got it." He reached into his shirt pocket to retrieve his pad and pencil. "Let me write that down for you," and he scribbled out the name of the place. "And a few more suggested stops." He wrote, "Badlands, Does Your Mother Know, Eagle Sunday Beer Bust, Eros" before handing me the piece of paper.

"That looks like a full itinerary."

"Just a few things you have to do before you leave San Francisco."

It felt like a bit of a set-up, but I took the small sheet with his recommendations and studied it some more. "You've been to these places?" I wanted to know.

"Oh yeah," big smile. "I wouldn't steer you wrong, Stone."

"Here's your Coke," Once again our blonde server magically appeared. I quickly shoved the paper into my pocket. She glared at my movement as the replaced the empty glass with a full one.

"Police business," advised Henry.

"Monkey business, if you ask me."

"But nobody has, darling." Henry likes to flirt.

When I looked down, my plate had been mysteriously emptied. Guess I ate the whole pizza without much thought.

"Let me get these things out of your way," and she quickly piled the plates, glasses and used napkins, swooping the collection up off the table in one practiced motion. "I'll be right back with your tab."

"Take your time," Henry teased.

Visions of orgiastic young men slithering around a disco-ball-lit dance floor whirled in my mind. It both excited and frightened me. Henry sat across from me, concentrating on picking his teeth with his pocketknife.

When Darlene returned with the check, he snatched it out of her hand, saying, "This one's on me, Stone. Glad to see you."

"Henry, you still owe me a ride in a squad car, lights flashing, siren going and all."

He handed her a twenty, "Yeah, sure. You commit the crime and I'll supply the ride."

She grimaced at him as she took the payment over to the register. "Will you be wanting any change back?" Even though she knew he had intended her to have the whole thing.

"No, you keep the change. Put it toward your college fund or something."

"Thanks, big spender," and she mocked him with a sneer. "Hey, speaking of college," she's yelling this across the dining room and all the other patrons have to listen, "I'm starting over at Apple Valley next semester."

"Oh, really? They teach underwater basket weaving there?" Oh, Henry, lighten up. We stood and started moving toward the exit.

"For your information, officer," snidely spat out, "I'm going through their two-year beauty-school program. I'll have a beautician's license when I'm finished."

That's a mighty scary thought.

"Maybe I could cut your hair, for free, as practice."

"Maybe you could get the order right next time." He held the door open for me. Darlene stood there with her face scrunched up, glaring at Henry. I think it's about time to go.

We got into the car without conversation. On the way he probed, "You're sure quiet tonight."

I snapped my head in his direction. "Guess I've got a lot on my mind. And you've given me a few things to think about, as well."

He pulled up in front of my house. "Well, Stone, there's a whole world out there you've never seen before. I think it's time for you to take a bite of the apple."

Another frightening, if not biblical, image. I opened the door and got out. "I'm still pretty full from dinner," I offered. He chuckled awkwardly. "Thanks for the food and the company. Oh, and the recommendations."

"You're welcome, Stone. Just have a good time, and then tell me all about it when you come back," he said with a broad grin.

Yeah, like you're the first person I want to tell. I guess my list of confidants is very limited. "We'll see," I responded as I closed the car door.

The taillights moved off into the dusk of Grant Street, and I turned to go into my house. I sure did have a lot to think about.

It has been a rather full day and I'm ready to sleep now. As I finished my nightly routine, I wondered what lay waiting for me in San Francisco.

After turning all the lights out, I climbed into bed and eased off to sleep with visions of courteous waiters, blonde hunks, helpful flight attendants and curious men at urinals dancing through my head.

Chapter Five

Thursday

THIS is the first morning in quite a while that I could actually sleep in. No pressing business at dawn, no Secret Service-imposed rides to O'Hare to catch, no wild geese to chase. So, of course, I wake up with the sun.

After all, I did go to bed rather early last night. As usual, I forgot to set up the coffee pot to have some fresh-brewed ready for me. Oh well, I'll just have to crawl out of bed and do it myself.

The kitchen is bright this morning, glistening Formica and stainless steel. After filling the coffee maker with water and putting in a fresh filter, I got the ground beans out of the freezer, scooped a heap with the plastic measurer and slopped it into the waiting basket.

While the machine dribbled, burped and hissed, I looked out the kitchen window to see who else might be up at this time of day. The only other person in sight is the newspaper boy delivering the *Star*. Slinging papers as he bicycles along, there is a kind of lulling rhythm to his style. I haven't taken a newspaper in years. I get all my news off the web, the radio and the television. I never have to bundle or recycle electronic news.

My yard appears to have accumulated some neglect. I'll have to do something about that. I wonder if the paperboy does yard work.

The machine stops dripping and spitling, and I can smell the rich aroma of morning coffee. I made just enough for one mug. That's all I ever drink. Too much caffeine can be scary.

The exotic perfume of Arabica takes me away to Persian markets and Moroccan cafés. As I poured the coffee from the carafe into my old chief's mug, the smell overwhelms me. The anticipation, the wait, is over. Ahhhhhhh.

Okay, now my brain can function again. I'm not addicted, mind you. I have only the one cup and that's it.

Making arrangements for the flights was its usual simplicity. As fewer and fewer people are flying, getting reservations is much easier than just a few years ago.

I leave tomorrow from O'Hare on the 9:15 a.m. flight. That means I'll have to be out of the house at 6:15 for the shuttle. That's much better than the pre-dawn rising for the flight to Boston. Return from San Francisco one week later on the 10:00 a.m. flight. I'm hoping a week will be enough time to attend to business and have some extracurricular activity as well.

As my suitcase had accurately predicted, it is time to pack again. On the trip down to the basement to retrieve it, the darn thing kept chanting, "I told you so, I told you so." I brought it upstairs, set it on the bed, opened it and stared at its emptiness. I hope I can fit a whole week's worth of clothes in there. Guess I could always buy some new things in San Francisco. It would probably be good to expand my wardrobe a little. Not everything in my closet has to come from the Toggery.

San Francisco is two hours behind us, and I'm guessing that it's a bit too early to be calling out there to make reservations. What was the name of that place? I found the pants I wore last night and pulled out the crumpled piece of paper that Henry had written his suggestions on. "Beck's Motor Lodge," "Badlands" (sounds like a cowboy place), "Does Your Mother Know" (something I don't even want to think about), "Eagle Sunday Beer Bust" (for the birds, but the beer thing sounds good), "Eros" (a place with a name like that can only be trouble).

Beck's is bound to have a website. I just wonder how long it's been since they updated it. If it's as popular a place as Henry says, then they should at least keep it fairly current.

While the computer boots up, I get lost in the fantasy of men being affectionate with other men in an open atmosphere. Enticing but scary. That kind of thing would never fly in Fort Dyck. People still look askance at mixed regular couples (Dutch and anything else).

To my surprise, Beck's did not have a website, but other online businesses, hotel reservation and gay-oriented travel sites, listed it. Most qualified it as "tacky" and "a throwback to the old days of driving your car up to a motel." I don't know–that certainly makes it sound like a guy from Indiana will feel right at home.

Now it was only 8:00 here, and Regis was coming on. There was a guest co-host, some fairly attractive younger blonde fellow. Regis found it easy to joke with him about the local New York happenings. I didn't recognize him nor did I catch his name. I turned off the TV after the opening segment. None of today's guests interested me.

The rest of the morning I went out in the yard and attended to some much-needed gardening. Trimming, pruning, tidying. The lawn could use a good mowing, but I think I'll wait until I get back.

After a quick shower, I ate a snack-like lunch of whatever I could find that had not yet expired. Now that I'm retired, I should really take the time to learn how to cook. Maybe they have a course for beginners over at Apple Valley.

About noon I called to make a reservation at Beck's. Only one room was available: one queen-sized bed, non-smoking, top level, in the back. Perfect for me. I reserved it for the week I would be there. The person who assisted me did not sound gay at all (or at least my concept of what a gay person would sound like), more Middle Eastern or Indian.

Since I was going to be gone a week, I would like someone to take in the mail and check in on the house. Henry is my first choice, so I gave him a call. Not only would he be happy to take care of my house, he also volunteered to drive me up to Chicago to catch the plane. I told him I had to be there by 8:15. He said he would pick me up at 7:00. I tried to tell him he didn't need to do this, but he insisted. I told him I would be just as happy taking the shuttle. He reminded me that you have to give 24-notice to get the shuttle, and that time had already passed.

I acquiesced. There didn't seem to be any stopping him anyway. He seems to be vicariously enjoying my life right now.

We chatted a bit more, mostly about police matters because I caught Henry at his desk. As much as he likes to discuss other people's personal lives with them, when he's at work, he's all business.

— ◆ —

During the early afternoon I went to work out. Part of the reason I still look as good as I do, even though I passed 60 a few years back, is that I go to the gym at least twice a week. Keeping fit has been the biggest boon for me. I feel as healthy now as I did in my thirties or forties. When I look at other guys my age,

Thursday

paunchy and over-padded, I can't help but think they could do something about the way they look, if they were so motivated.

Most of the guys going to our local gym are police or firemen. The ones on the force whom I used to supervise seem to enjoy seeing me there because they are finally able to say things that they never could when I was their chief. I'm big enough to take some good-natured ribbing. It's the towel snapping in the shower room I could do without.

On the walk home I stopped at the CVS to pick up a few travel-sized items: toothpaste, mouthwash, floss. I'm only going to be gone a week, and I'm sure I could just as easily buy these things in San Francisco, but I felt more secure having them with me.

When I got home, I finished packing the suitcase. Now I'm ready for the big adventure tomorrow.

Henry called at one point to see if we could do dinner again tonight. I guess he wants one more shot at me before I disappear into the Bay. He'll be by around six.

After talking to Henry, I realized I had forgotten to ask him about this strange, new power I seem to have over other gay men. I'll get another chance to ask tonight.

I sat down in the easy chair, flipped on the tube and watched CNN with my eyes closed. Promptly at 6:00 a horn from out front woke me. I turned off the TV, stood up, turned on some lights, grabbed my wallet and key. The beautiful Honda awaited.

As I got in I said, "Not Monica's again."

"Oh, come on, Stone," Henry said playfully as he pulled away. "I want to give Darlene another chance to screw up my order." He chuckled and turned up Fourth Street.

"Where are we going, then?" We passed by the Dyck House as we crossed Duncan Street, and it looked like kids from the junior high were dressed up and practicing their parts for Dutch Days.

"I thought we'd do something a little different." He turned right onto Lincoln.

"Are we going to Brittany's?" I asked suspiciously. One of the big news items from last year was the collaboration of the Feds and the Indiana State Police in raiding the former owners of Brittany's Family Restaurant. Apparently, the place had become a front for a drug distribution center. All the marijuana, cocaine and methamphetamines going to northwest Indiana passed through their doors. The local force knew, of course, but they weren't big enough to do anything about it. The owners became complacent, got sloppy, and sold some of their stuff to an undercover DEA agent. Within a week the raid closed the place down. New owners re-opened the restaurant a few months later, but it really hasn't caught on yet.

He turned left into the parking lot, right before the intersection of U.S. 41. There were many parking spaces to choose from. He parked his Japanese chariot near the front door.

As we stepped inside, I could see that most of tables were empty. The rest of the cars in the lot must have belonged to the staff. A slender woman in her early forties with an obviously-dyed, copper-red beehive hairdo told us, "Sit anywhere. I'll be right with you."

I guessed her name was Flo, Agnes or Gertrude. We chose a spot near the door but not too close. Once we sat down, Miss Beehive came over with a tray and two glasses of water. First thing I did was look at her name badge. Winnie. I wonder if that's her real name. It doesn't matter.

"Can I start you gentlemen off with something to drink?" To me, it seemed like her attention was on something not in this room, not in this town or, perhaps, not on this planet. You would think that with the lack of clientele we would get her full attention.

Henry is less aware of this. "What kind of beer do you have?"

She looked at him with a faraway stare and eventually responded, "Beer? I don't know. It's just beer. One kind that's all." Winnie continued to stare at him while she thought about something else.

"Just like at Monica's," Henry chuckled. "Sure, I'll have a beer."

She turned her gaze toward me. I waited for her to ask me, and I guess she waited for me to tell her. "A Coke, please."

The left corner of her mouth scrunched and she whirled away with all the speed of a person in no hurry to go anywhere in particular. We both just stared at her in disbelief.

Henry worked up the nerve to speak first, "I guess that's why they don't get too many customers." I nodded in agreement.

"Henry, you've been to those places you wrote down?"

He smiled smugly. "Not all, but most. You have to go to all of them. It's an initiation rite."

"I'm not as adventurous as you." He giggled. "Would you please tell me what you're getting me into."

"What did you want to know?"

At that moment, Winnie came back with a bar tray and our drinks. She plopped down the beer in front of me and the Coke near Henry.

"Could we have some menus, please?" I thought it was a legitimate question, but from the Oh-God-Why-me? expression on her face, you would think I had asked for her monogrammed kidneys. She slowly walked over to the cash register and returned a minute later with two food-smirched menus, which she tossed on the table without much thought or aim. I seriously considered asking her if we were taking up too much of her time, but during her absence we switched glasses and I took a sip. Not only was it warm, there was no ice in it and it wasn't even Coke. I almost spat it out, but managed to swallow because I had taken only a small sip. "What is this?" I managed to spew.

Winnie looked at me quizzically, "Pepsi. What you ordered."

"No, I ordered a Coke."

"Same thing," she intoned indifferently.

"No. No, it's not. And it's warm and there's no ice in it." I held the glass up for her to take back, but she just stood there looking at it.

"Our cooler's not working and we're out of ice. What do you want me to do about it?"

My frustration level peaked here. "Do you have anything cold to drink?"

Henry piped in, "Not the beer," as he just finished a taste. The look on his face indicated a low-quality product.

"Does it really make a difference, Darling?"

Okay, that's it. I stood up, "Come on. Henry, let's get out of here."

He started to stand as well.

"Hey, who's going to pay for this, fellows?"

I glared at her, "Charge it to the Fort Dyck Police Department. There'll be some boys around tomorrow morning to check out this place. I think the drug lord is back in business."

We were just about at the door when Winnie yelled out, "Oh, you guys are police? Come back, sit down. Your meal is on the house."

By now I wasn't very hungry, and I wasn't about to eat anything coming from this dump. As I stepped through the door I told her, "No, thank you. We'll see you in jail."

— ◆ —

We sat in Henry's car, looking at each other for a minute or so. "Now what?" he queried.

"I guess we make a report." I was still in "cop" mode.

"No. I meant about food. What do you want to do?"

The Donut Hut will not be going out of business as long as Henry is around. Food was the last thing on my mind right now. "Oh, just take me home, I guess. I'm not very hungry."

"Think I'll head out to Burger King. I'll buy you a Coke." He started the engine.

"No, thanks. I think I just want to go home now."

He looked at me with disbelief. "Home? I thought you'd want to hear all about naughty, nasty San Francisco."

"I'm not in the mood right now. How about if we talk about it on the way to the airport tomorrow."

He pulled back onto Lincoln. "Sure. Fine. Whatever you want." It was hard to miss the disappointment and sadness in his voice, but my mind was elsewhere. "I'll send a few boys over to Brittany's in the morning to check out the operation."

As we headed down Fourth Street, I could see the children in their Dutch garb still on the lawn of Dyck House. Soon the sun would be setting and they would have to quit. "Henry, please let me out here."

The car lurched dramatically and came to an abrupt halt. "What's the matter, Stone?"

"Nothing. I just feel like getting a little exercise."

Again he stared in disbelief. "Okay. I'll see you in the morning. About 7. Have a good night."

"Thanks anyway." I got out and stood across the street from the gigantic, historic home. Henry sat in his car, watching me for a few seconds before pulling away. Not only was the Dyck House

                    Thursday

significant to the town, which got its name from it, but to me, personally, as well.

— ♦ —

According to the local legend, a group of Dutch settlers headed west from New York in the early 1800s. The leader of the expedition was Cornelius Dyck (the region in Holland where the family originated pronounced "y" like "*ay*-yuh," hence, "Fort Dake"). Rumor has it he was taking his harem of nine wives and twenty-six children out to the western territories, where he wouldn't be persecuted for polygamy. He had to get out of New York abruptly, leaving his general merchandise store behind, selling the building and all the inventory to a Jewish family for half of its book value. He was in a hurry to leave town, but he didn't have many options.

The party's original destination was Fulton, Illinois, where a growing settlement of other displaced Dutch people had gone, but for some reason, in early 1817, once they got here to Indiana, they stopped west of Fort Wayne. Presumably, old Cornelius realized he did not have enough money to get his troops all the way to Fulton. He called it quits on the hospitable open plain by a small creek. He must have figured that there may not be enough of a customer base to open another dry goods emporium, but at least there's arable land that could be easily farmed and a nearby water supply. After all, he had all his children to help with the farm chores. There was just enough funds in his purse to build a large house for the family and a barn for the animals and grain storage. And the farm equipment and the seeds for their initial crop of maize and wheat.

As no one else lived in the vicinity at the time, they homesteaded the land and the government eventually deeded it to them.

Indiana had been granted statehood in 1816 and it wouldn't be until 1818 that nearby Illinois would officially join the Union. After the first harvest of 1817, uncivilized displaced Native Americans of the Miami Tribe appeared out of the West, raided the farm, killing two of the younger children and making off with half the livestock and much of the harvested grain. What they couldn't carry with them, they tossed out into the fields to fallow.

Devastated by the loss of his two children and most of his assets, Dyck appealed to Governor Jennings for assistance. Moved

by the touching story about all the casualties and damage caused
by the attack, the Governor ordered the state militia into the area to
protect the family while a defensive perimeter could be
constructed.

Of course, Dyck withheld the part about him having nine wives,
possibly due in part to that being the reason they were originally
ejected from New York. The family presented themselves as
relatives, aunts, sisters, cousins and such. The construction troops
were duly suspicious, but what were they to do? They had their
orders to follow, and they concentrated their efforts on building a
stronghold for these attractive new settlers.

Eventually the fort was completed and the construction crew
returned to Corydon, over near Louisville, Kentucky. It was the
original state capital; Indianapolis didn't exist until the 1820s.
Some of the militia men stayed behind, some because they wanted
to help protect the Dyck family, some because they grew to like
the area and began to think of it as home, some because they had
taken a fancy to Cornelius's older daughters, and some for a
combination of these three reasons.

The site was named in honor of the town's founder and it has
been called Fort Dyck ever since. The wooden defensive walls are
long gone, having had seen a bit more damage from the local
tribes. But after Illinois became a state, the attacks decreased in
frequency and the walls were eventually dug up and transformed
into houses for the growing community.

Across the street from where Henry left me off stands the
original Dyck House, with some restorative assistance from the
local preservation society. It's open to the public on weekends,
with tours given by docents in period garb three times a day.

— ♦ —

My paternal grandfather was a traveling John Deere farm
equipment salesman at the turn of the 20th Century, based out of
the company headquarters in Moline, Illinois. He got the plum
assignment of the agriculturally prominent Northwestern corner of
Indiana. He arrived in this town in 1902, sold a fleet of plows and
other accessories. He had the grand notion to attempt to make a
sale at the Dyck House. It was the largest building in as far as you
could see.

Old Cornelius had died long before the Civil War, but his grandsons fought for the Union, rising up to officer's ranks, serving with Generals Meade, Burnsides and Hooker. They all returned decorated military heroes. By the end of the 19th Century, their grandchildren occupied the grand old family home and when my dapper old granddad happened by, one of their daughters (the great-great-granddaughter of old Cornelius himself) took a liking to him.

He ended up settling down here, making Fort Dyck the base of his operation. As it was a burgeoning farm community at that time, he maintained a brisk business until he retired in 1932, mostly due to The Great Depression. Between what he had put aside from his profitable endeavor, and the Dyck family fortunes, they lived a very comfortable life during a time when most of the rest of the country had difficulties making ends meet.

Our family never knew poverty or want. My father chose a life as a fireman, and I continued the tradition of public service. I was not brought up in the lap of luxury, but there was always food on the table, a roof over our heads and clothes on our backs, even during the leaner years. Using my inheritance enabled me to purchase the home I live in now. I might not have ordinarily been able to afford it solely on a policeman's salary.

Well, if you look at our family tree, which we can trace back over 200 years now, I am, through marriage, the great-great-great-great-grandson of old Cornelius Dyck. It was an honor, and it filled me with civic pride to serve as my home town's chief of police until my retirement a few years ago.

I just stood there watching the children reenact scenes from my family history. Something intrigued me in the way these kids attempted to recreate my ancestors' lives. Of course, they were all too young and too short, but something powerful came from their juvenile portrayal of the Dyck family. The boy playing Old Cornelius couldn't have been more than twelve, and he probably weighed almost 200 pounds. For some reason the role of my great-great-great-great grandfather is always given to the fattest boy.

"Evening, Chief." One of the younger patrol officers saw me standing there. "Enjoying the show?"

I had only met him briefly before I left. His name escaped me, but I remember he had just moved down from the Chicago area.

"Yeah. Out for a little walk. How's the patrol going?"

"It's a beautiful night for a stroll." Static buzzed through his two-way. A female voice cut through, "407 in progress at Third and Duncan. Who can respond?"

The young officer grabbed at his mike and called out, "This is Petroni. I'm a block away. I'll cover." He looked at me. "Sorry, Chief. Gotta go. Want to join in the fun?"

I'm too old for this. "No, thanks. You go have all the fun."

"All right. You take care." He turned and trotted down Duncan. Petroni. Definitely not a Dutch name.

The sun touched the horizon, and the children started wandering off. I headed down Fourth wondering what fat Old Cornelius would think of his gay offspring who also served as the town's chief of police.

I reached my house just as dusk arrived. The automatic street lamps began lighting up as I stepped into the porch. There was one beer left in the fridge, and I brought it over to my chair as dinner. Guess I was hungry after all.

The TV fare wasn't holding my interest, and after a few swigs of the beer, I dozed off to "Will & Grace."

When I woke again, it was after 10:30 and Jay Leno amused himself with a joke about former President Clinton. The guy's been out of office for years and Leno still manages to poke fun at him. He is married to a senator, after all. Off went Jay and off I went to bed.

Chapter Six

Friday

IT was difficult to sleep with the adrenaline anticipation of flying to San Francisco. I got out of bed before dawn, made the coffee I forgot to set up last night, and prepared the house for my absence.

After a warm shower and my one cup of java, I was ready. All packed, dressed and battened down. Henry would only have to bring the mail in a few times.

Promptly at 7:00 the doorbell rang. I glanced around one more time to make sure that I took care of everything. I opened the door and Henry stood at the rear of his car with the trunk open. The suitcase is a bit heavier than I had intended, but I managed to haul it over to the car and lift it into the trunk without assistance.

He pushed the lid closed and got into the car. I opened the passenger door and got in. He smiled a knowing smirk and asked salaciously, "Ready for your big adventure?"

I may be ready for the trip, but I don't think I'm ready for Henry at 7:00 in the morning. He took a gulp of his Donut Hut coffee and started the car.

"You're awfully quiet this morning." He turned down Third.

Sure, I thought, I'd be more chipper if I had as much caffeine as he had. However, I don't think the world is ready for that. "Still have a lot on my mind."

He chuckled, "You never stop thinking, do you? This trip is going to do you a world of good. I can tell." At this time of day there was little traffic and he had no trouble turning left onto the state route.

I'm glad he's optimistic about this. I'm terrified.

He's probably right. This trip will do me a world of good. I will finally be in an atmosphere where I can feel comfortable with myself. I might actually learn something.

And now that I think about it, I never do stop thinking.

As we head out of town, he looked at me judiciously, "Are you ready to hear all about Sin Francisco now?"

No, not really, but I think he's ready to tell me. "Sure. It'll give me some more things to think about."

A smile spread his lips. Plus, the caffeine was kicking in. "What would you like to know?"

We were close to the interstate now, and I almost wanted to wait until we got on the freeway so that nobody from town could know what we were talking about, as if anyone could hear us anyway. "Mostly about the places you wrote down. Can you tell me about Beck's?"

"Did you get a room?"

"Yep."

"What's the number?"

"How in hell am I supposed to know that?"

He smiled, "Because I want to know approximately where your room is."

"Is it that important?" The turn-off for the interstate is right ahead. Henry let the car coast as we approached the on-ramp.

"It kind of makes a difference." He guided the car up the curving slope. At this time of day the traffic is pretty light and we were up to 80 miles an hour fairly fast.

"It's on the top floor, in the back."

"Must have been the last one available."

"As a matter of fact, it was." How did he know that?

"Most people want the front because it's right on Market Street and they can… observe people better."

"It sounds like this is more than just your average motel."

"You could say that," and a grin appeared.

"Is that where you stayed?"

"Not the first time I went. I just happened to be lucky enough to be an invited guest. As we walked up the stairs and toward his room, there were doors open and men laying naked on their beds."

"Henry, I don't think I'm ready for that kind of experience." It sounded scary.

"Don't worry, Stone. It's not usually the attractive ones who leave their doors open."

"Oh, gee, that really makes me feel better."

"I liked it so much, that's where I made my reservations for the next trip. You're going to have a great time. Don't worry so much. What else do you want to know?"

                    Friday

"Tell me about the other places." I already had them memorized and did not need to look at the paper for prompting. "What's Badlands?"

"Oh, that's a dance bar in the Castro."

"For cowboys?"

He giggled. "I hear it used to be quite rustic years ago, wooden-plank floors with sawdust, rough-hewn wooden paneling with old license plates all over the place."

"Sounds charming."

"It got remodeled. It's all tech with polished aluminum, plastic and video screens."

"What kind of crowd goes there?"

"It's pretty mixed, but predominantly younger guys looking for sex or drugs."

"Lovely." This is beginning to sound like a nightmare. "Does Your Mother Know?"

"I haven't told her yet, but I'm considering having that discussion next Thanksgiving."

"Very funny. And how many times do you get to use that joke?"

"Not often enough." The closer we got to Gary, the more traffic we encountered. Henry had to actually slow down to the speed limit. "It's a card shop a block down from Badlands. Gay-oriented stuff. Naked men and guys in bad drag. Not the kind of thing you'd find at our local CVS."

"I'll try to get you something nice."

"My favorites are the ones that fold out, like a Z, and they show full frontal nudity and big old whangs."

I couldn't picture myself being able to purchase anything like that, even in San Francisco.

"I'll see what I can do. Next, Eagle Sunday Beer Bust?"

"Yeah. You'll enjoy that. It's an old biker bar in the Folsom with an open-air patio in the back. On Sundays they charge admission and give you a cup. It's usually a fundraiser, and volunteers from the sponsoring agency walk around with pitchers to keep everyone happy. The beer isn't particularly good, but after the first glass it all tastes the same anyway." He smiled to himself. "It gets kind of crowded, and there's usually entertainment of some sort. After a while they start the barbecue and serve a meal."

"And I'm going to enjoy this because…?"

"You'll be hanging out with a bunch of gay men and having fun. Some of them don't wear any pants under their chaps."

"Oh, yeah?"

"Unfortunately, they're usually the out-of-shape, saggy-ass ones that you'd rather not look at. But after a while, especially on warm days, guys start taking off their shirts."

"That sounds better."

"I would guess that you'd get quite a bit of attention if you took your shirt off."

"I'll be keeping my clothes on, thank you."

He smiled disbelievingly, "Sure, let me know if that happens."

"And, lastly, Eros."

Henry did not answer right away. No self-clever quips, no nasty innuendos. At last, he turned to look at me, "It's a sex club, Stone."

"What's that mean?" Although I'm sure I could guess, I just wanted to hear him explain it in his own special way.

"Guys walk around in towels looking at each other. If the mood strikes, they play around. Usually a crowd forms and people stand around and watch."

"And you've been to this place?"

He hesitated again, "No, I just heard about it." His stare focused on the road ahead. Traffic slowed, and we were getting close to the interchange.

"And you want me to go to this sleazy place for your edification?"

He appeared to be concentrating on the traffic and the off ramp. Silence from Henry is so refreshing.

Now we headed west on I-94, toward O'Hare. Silence rode with us for a few minutes while I chewed over things in my mind. Some of my questions remained unanswered. "What else have you heard about this place?"

Without looking at me, he continued his verbal tour, "I hear they put out bowls of snacks and you can buy soft drinks. There's a steam room that sees a lot of action, but I hear most of the goings-on happen on raised platforms in the play area." His stare was steady forward.

"Sounds interesting." His head sprung in my direction. "For someone else, perhaps." He looked forward again. "Henry, how could you recommend a place like that for me?" His expression turned regretful. "I'm just getting used to this. I'd like to wiggle my toes a little before jumping into the pool."

"I figured you'd find out before walking into the place."

"It just feels like such a set-up, Henry." I stared forward as well.

Neither of us said another word until he pulled into the O'Hare labyrinth. I didn't want him waiting with me. "Just drop me off at the departing flight curb. I'm going to give my bag to the Red Cap."

"Okay," sounded a bit dejected.

He pulled up in front of the door. The clock on the dash read "8:10." Plenty of time. I got out and walked to the trunk. The taillights started flashing, the lid lifted slightly and Henry popped out of the car. He opened the trunk for me. I said a silent prayer against hernias and lifted, with a single snatch, the heavy bag from the car.

"Thanks, Henry. I appreciate your help."

"Yeah, well, have fun. Give a call when you get back. I've got a date with Brittany." He closed the trunk gently and walked toward the driver door.

"Thanks again for watching my house. I'll try to call you next week."

"Okay. Sure." He climbed in and drove off. I'll bet he has a quiet ride back to town.

I shuffled the suitcase over to the Sky Cap desk. One fellow stepped forward to assist me. He lifted the bag with one hand like it was a docile cat. After setting it on a cart with other luggage, he tagged it and stapled the receipt to my ticket envelope. I handed him a dollar and he accepted it blandly.

Inside the terminal I checked the display to determine my flight's departure gate. As I started the long walk down the pavilion I started thinking about the trip ahead. Dance bars, card shops, nostalgic motels, sex clubs. Not to mention the missing child of John and Jackie Kennedy.

Once I got to the gate, the check-in line consisted of six people. I waited patiently; there was no rush. Finally at the desk, I gave the agent my ticket and she processed it, handing me back the boarding pass. An empty seat near the departure door appealed to me, and I sat there in meditation until boarding started. The people flying first-class rambled by, attempting to look bored. Some day I'll get to fly first-class. At the rate I've been accumulating flyer miles lately, it shouldn't take very long.

Eventually the agent called my row and I got in line to board. Most of the other people on the flight looked Asian, which I guess made sense because its final destination is Shanghai.

This time I decided to wait for the people with the window and middle seat to sit down before I made myself comfortable. After a few minutes, a middle-aged Asian couple, juggling more carry-on than is permitted, stuffed the overhead compartments with gift boxes and small pieces of luggage. The man pointed to the two seats and I stood up to let them by. The wife smiled and placed a tote under each seat in front of them. As they sat down she handed her husband a magazine, presumably printed in Chinese. We all smiled at each other.

Once I got comfortable, the nagging thought that Top Dog would mystically appear in the seat behind me kept me from relaxing completely. Just to make sure, I peeked over the top of my seat. Another Asian family sat in hushed conversation. Maybe now I can relax.

"Well, hello again!" The voice sounded familiar, but at least it wasn't Top Dog. When I swung back into position, the flight attendant from the other day stood looking at me. I smiled and shook my head. "You sure get around, don't you?" he teased me.

"Business," I stated.

"In San Francisco," his voice went even higher, indicating innuendo. "How lucky for you." He was laying it on thick. At least the other passengers probably did not have a clue what he was saying. "By the way, this time I'm cutting you off after one beer. Last time was a teensy bit embarrassing." He smiled playfully.

I guess I'm getting more comfortable with this style of conversation. It didn't make me upset, like last time. Of course, I hadn't had the beer yet.

He started moving off, "I'll be back in a while with beverages. Behave yourself." Again, that secret smile. He turned to the other passengers, saying something like, "Knee how Ma."

Friday

The issue of the in-flight magazine had not changed since last time. Having already gone through it twice, its appeal diminished greatly. Without anyone to talk to, I tilted my seat back after we were on our way and closed my eyes. The tap on my shoulder made me jump a bit, and when I looked up, my favorite flight attendant held a sweaty bottle of Anchor Steam. He placed a napkin on the tray and set the bottle down, "Go easy with this, Tiger, it's the only one you get." He winked.

The Chinese couple looked askance at my beverage. They both said, "Cha" almost at once, making it sound like, "Cha cha." I couldn't tell if they were chiding me or telling the guy what they wanted. He repeated, "Cha," and produced two cups of hot water and two tea bags. Then he gave them each a packet of Goldfish. Before he wheeled off, he slipped me a handful of bags, "Here you go, Gorgeous." I inhaled the familiar scent of Paco Rabanne. He maintained his contact with my hands a little longer than was comfortable for me. I flinched and pulled back. He half-smiled. "I'll check in on you later," and off he went.

As this flight is headed in the same general direction as the last one, the movie offering is the same. I toyed with the idea of watching it, especially because this is a longer flight. However, the memory of Agent Hank Hunk going giddy over young Master Di Caprio clouded my mind, and I decided to pass. The Chinese couple eagerly paid the ransom for headphones.

With not much else to do, I took a few swigs of that nasty-tasting, powerfully potent Anchor Steam. It had the same effect as last time and made me shudder uncontrollably again. Maybe I can get a tour of the brewery while I'm in San Francisco.

The small amount of alcohol from the small bit of beer helped me relax enough to transport me to a dreamy bliss for most of the rest of the flight. At one point the pilot's voice jostled me into consciousness when he made some announcement about the Grand Canyon. I fell right back into my reveries and did not wake again until a familiar tapping on my shoulder jarred me.

"We're just about there, sir," the flight attendant informed me with a very business-like air. He then smiled broadly, "Is this your first time going to San Francisco?"

I couldn't decide how to answer. If I told the truth, he might start giving me yet another list of things I must do. But I hate lying. "It's a business trip," I decided on. It wasn't a lie, but it wasn't exactly the truth either.

He rolled his eyes and said, "Yeah, whatever," with intentional nonchalance and a flap of his hand. Then he walked off. Guess I need to work on my being flirted with.

The plane landed about 11:45 Pacific Time. Only a dozen or so of us departed. Most of the passengers were headed for China. My friendly attendant sent me off with, "Have a nice stay. See you again soon."

"Thanks again," I smiled my best smile for him.

Within a minute I stepped into San Francisco International Airport. Another modern salute to concrete, sheet metal and tinted glass, but this time a bit classier and refined.

Again, I needed to respond to the call of nature due to my beer intake. After the experience at O'Hare, I had heightened anxiety about using public restrooms. And this was San Francisco.

Carefully following the directional arrows, I rounded the entry-way to the nearest men's room and found I was the only one in there. Just in case, I went to the last urinal in the back. One older gentleman came in, but he stood far away and didn't even look at me. Mission accomplished.

Back out in the pavilion, clumps of people walked to and from flights. No huge crowds bombarded you, like at O'Hare. I could sense a few younger men looking in my direction, but nothing threatening.

The art exhibit displayed a collection of pins and brooches worn by former Secretary of State Madeleine Albright. Apparently, people accused her of communicating, openly or secretively, by her choice of accessory. My favorite was the snake she wore, in lieu of a nametag, when meeting with Saddam Hussein, who had publicly called her "a snake." I guess that's one way to get back at people.

The terminal is tall and lofty, almost big enough to fit a plane into. Following the signs, I got to the Baggage Claim, one flight down. The carousels seemed more old-fashioned than the avant-garde design of the pavilion above. The lights indicated which one would have my flight's luggage. This shouldn't take very long, given that so few of us deplaned.

Within minutes the mechanical shuffler started moving and a minute or so after, the parade of suitcases began. Despite having arrived so early, my bag came up sixth. Maybe taking the suitcase to a Sky Cap ensures later placement in the luggage compartment. I'll have to keep that in mind. However, it hadn't gotten any lighter, and it almost defied my attempt to retrieve it.

If I didn't know better, I would have thought someone put something in there to make it heavier while I wasn't looking. I did manage to haul it over to the elevator, up and onto the shuttle train platform and waited to go the car rental agency.

In just about a minute, a train came by. I struggled a little but managed to get the suitcase on board. We stopped right at the pick-up desk, and I was assigned my car, a late-model, white Dodge Intrepid sedan.

Once I got outside, I immediately noticed the change in climate. No humidity. No heat. Except for the sooty contribution of internal combustion engines, the air felt lighter and fresher.

I hated doing it, but I asked for directions to the motel.

After studying the marked-up maps, I navigated out of the parking area and onto the access road. Getting onto the freeway seemed fairly easy, and traffic flowed smoothly.

I'm driving to San Francisco! The airport is about 15 miles south, on the Peninsula, as they call it. Heading north on U.S. 101, the scenery did not merit mentioning until I got to the interchange with I-280. All of a sudden you could see the downtown buildings glistening in the cold sunlight, and I instantly fell in love with the city.

The roadway curved quite a bit for a freeway, making it difficult at times to drive and gawk simultaneously. At one point, two rather tight curves back-to-back caused the traffic to slow down to about 40 miles per hour. I would guess this section was designed long before the current speed limits.

When I reached the Mission-Duboce exit, I stayed in the left lane, as instructed, stopping midway down the ramp behind a string of cars waiting for a traffic signal. The scene looked like something out of The French Connection or Dirty Harry. The area under the elevated freeway had not been cleaned in quite a while. Black-smudged girders supported the freeway above. Severe shad-ows created an eerie, mid-day darkness. Panhandlers stood by the side of the road with crudely lettered cardboard signs requesting handouts for assorted reasons. A couple of the drivers ahead of me rolled down their windows and gave alms. I don't think I'll be doing that.

Once the light changed we moved on and I headed up a slight incline. Eventually the road gently curved off to the left and we were on Market Street. I passed a large Safeway on my right, one of the landmarks on my navigational aid. Palm trees lined the center strip, giving the place a quasi-tropical air.

Two blocks later I saw the sign for Beck's. The eye-catching yellow and pink paint made it difficult not to look. The parking lot had but a few spaces left and I managed to aim the rental car into one of them. I later discovered that this little lot is a godsend in a city that disdains easy parking.

The desk person confirmed my reservation and handed me the key to room 340. He pointed in the general direction of the room, and told me in broken English about the ice machine and the no-open-doors policy. I nodded my assent and walked back to the car to wrestle with the big bag. Somehow I maneuvered it to the little elevator and we were on our way to the third floor. The stench in the elevator seemed odiferously familiar but not overpowering.

The door opened and I lugged my luggage along the walkway to the room. Inside, the place looked like any other room you might get in Indianapolis or Cincinnati. I don't see what all the fuss is about.

Once I got my personal effects arranged for my stay, I went to the telephone to call the Walshes. It was almost 2:00, but I sensed that they are retired or work at home.

"This is Walsh."

"Hello, Mr. Walsh, I mean Zack," remembering a little too late that he preferred the more casual address.

"Christopher? You're here in San Francisco?"

"Yes. How did you know that?"

"Oh, the Caller ID shows a local number, not like the last time when you called from… Indiana, wasn't it."

This guy definitely has too much time on his hands. "Yeah, that's right. I hope I didn't catch you at an inconvenient time."

"Not at all. We were just planning our menu for dinner. Would you please join us?"

                    Friday

"Well, I'd hate to impose."

"No bother! We generally make more food than we can eat anyway. Our usual habit is to give the leftovers to the homeless in the neighborhood."

"Oh, okay." I can't even begin to imagine what these guys would be cooking for dinner. "What time would you like me to arrive?"

"Anytime is good. We'll be here."

"Is there anything I can bring?" Indiana state law requires the guest to ask this question.

"No, don't worry about it. We've got all we need here."

"All right," I acquiesced, "Where am I going?"

"Where are you now?"

I guess his Caller ID can't tell him everything. "Beck's on Market Street."

It sounded like Walsh covered the phone with his hand, "Hey, Kat, the guy's staying at Beck's!" A woman's laughter could barely be heard in the background. His hand came away. "We're at 717 Ashbury. Do you need directions?"

"Yes, please."

Zack gave me a list of streets and landmarks guiding me to his home.

"Okay. See you in a while. I have a few errands to run first. Maybe around 5."

"Perfect! See you then." He hung up.

What was I getting myself into?

— ◆ —

One of my "errands" consisted of finding a place to eat some meat. My sense is that this dinner is going to be strictly vegetarian, and I still have not yet met my daily requirement of flesh consumption.

I changed into some jeans and a T-shirt. The weather felt warm enough for that. I have heard how cold San Francisco can get in the midst of summer, but today is not one of those days.

As I left the room, I noticed a rather large balcony overlooking Market Street. Several men stood gazing down at the passers-by. They appeared to be my age or a little bit younger. Not one looked at me as I went by.

Down on the street people walked in small groups. Some stood casually in conversation. Hardly anyone by themselves.

I started in the direction of Castro Street. At the end of the block sat a café unlike any I had ever seen. A coffee house surrounded by an outdoor patio nestled into the odd angle of acutely intersecting streets. The name on the glass wind screen read "Café Flore." The people inhabiting it constituted an eclectic collection of personalities and styles. Pretty young men brandishing cigarettes, chattering away as if everyone in the neighborhood wanted to hear their conversations. Serious, bookish writers with laptop computers creating the next wave of poetry and fiction. Garish drag queens hoping that someone, anyone, would engage them in dialogue. Students studying against all odds in this disquieting atmosphere. Not my kind of place at all.

As I stood grazing over the crowd, my you-are-being-watched alarm went off. In two seconds I spotted the person looking at me. Sitting at a table by himself with a mug and a long-handled sundae spoon, a young man with spiky brown hair and a slightly off-center nose burned holes through me with his eyes while he licked the spoon slowly and unabashedly. The intensity of this interaction overwhelmed me and I had to get away from there as quickly as possible.

As I crossed the intersection I noticed that the street branching off to the right and up a hill was 16th. That's my first turn on the way to the Walshes. The next block included Italian and Mexican restaurants, but that's not what I was in the mood for. Across the street I spotted a Subway. Not exactly what I would call local fare, but I pretty much knew what I would be getting.

No other customers around, I gave the order to the counter person, barely out of high school, I imagined–a meatball sub.

"A what?"

I pointed at the picture of it on the menu above his head, "Meatball sub."

"Oh," and he set to work creating a meatball sub exactly like every other one I've ever had at a Subway.

I sat on the small bench out front and chewed the sandwich with gusto. Again, people passed by in groups, practically no one alone. Bits of conversation stuck with me as clots of young folks went by: "…not in that movie…"; "…a year!? It's already

                    Friday

been…"; "No, where do *you* want to eat?"; "…he's so over me…"
That last one left me pondering its meaning.

It still amazes me that same-sex couples can be so open about their orientation in public. Many of the couples, both man-man and woman-woman, held hands or had their arms around each other as they walked. It repulsed and excited me. Our society at-large disdains this behavior, but I wanted to experience it myself to see what it was like. However, without a partner, temporary or permanent, there was no one for me to walk with.

After polishing off the sub, I thought it was time to see what all the hubbub was about. I stood up and walked around the corner onto Castro Street proper. Right on the corner is a bar named Twin Peaks with large plate glass windows. You could easily see who was in there. Nothing like this would ever fly in the Midwest. The guys were mostly my age, and I felt an urge to go in, but to stand in a gay bar with the possibility of someone I know walking by and seeing me through the window terrified me.

The grand old Castro Theater loomed a few doors down. In the midst of a John Waters festival, "Polyester in Odor-A-Rama" proclaimed the marquee.

Across the way was a bar named Daddy's. I'm not sure I want to know what that's about. Cliff's Hardware looked rather inviting. The display in the over-sized front windows depicted a day at the beach, except all the people, equipment and scenery were made from hardware, tools and knick-knacks, presumably sold within.

When I got to the corner of 18th and Castro, I saw Does Your Mother Know on the other side of the street. People seemed to be crossing despite the flashing red hand of the signal. Some even continued to go even after the light changed to red. Very daring.

The petite shop held thousands of cards, as well as little gay gift items. I browsed for a few minutes, embarrassed by some of the frankness and nudity. I chose a card for Henry, the Z-fold type that he specified. The front portion showed a young hunk with a pretend sad expression and the caption, "I miss you." Upon opening the card fully, his naked butt is right in your face with, "Wish you were here." I think he'll like that. Plus no blatant penis to make me feel squeamish.

After the card shop I happened by a place called The Midnight Sun. Inside the soft lighting contrasted the bright sunshine outside.

On two large screens music videos played at either end of the room. The few people there looked at me and then went back to staring at their drinks or the video. This does not seem like a very happy place, but at least there are no windows.

Back outside in the light, I realized the time had come for me to get back to my motel and get ready to visit with the Walshes. The return trip passed uneventfully. Just more groups of young people walking nonchalantly, apparently unaware of how lucky they are to be in a place where their behavior is not questioned or persecuted.

— ◆ —

A brief splash and wipe up was all I needed to get ready. I figured I could keep the same clothes. They sounded pretty casual.

On the drive over I passed through the neighborhood known as "The Haight," which used to be "Haight-Ashbury." How unusual that a place so identified with the radical politics of the 1960s has a Gap and a Ben & Jerry's.

Parking a car in San Francisco differs greatly from parking in Indiana. At home, all you have to do is drive to where you want to go and there's always a parking spot waiting for you. Not so in the City by the Bay. It took circling and searching five minutes before I could find a place to park the Dodge. Someone else was just pulling out of a spot on Waller, right around the corner. The handling of the car impressed me greatly as I maneuvered into the tight space. I hadn't parallel parked in years, and it took me a few times back and forth before I got it right.

Across the street from the Walshes stood a stately, old house with a low, wrought-iron gate. People gathered in the street taking pictures of it. I guess it has some significance that I don't know about.

I climbed a flight of rickety wooden stairs and stood at the door of 717 Ashbury Street. As there was a hole where the doorbell probably used to be, I knocked loudly. Within seconds I heard footsteps approaching. "It's open!" someone yelled. Through the lace hanging behind the oval window in the upper part of the door, I could see a shadow getting closer. The door opened and behind it stood a fellow about five-foot-five, bald round head surrounded by curly gray fluff, round-lens spectacles, looking very much like a professor emeritus.

"Christopher!" It took a beat before I realized he was talking to me. "How nice to see you. Come on in!" He opened the door fully and bade me enter. He shook my hand vigorously, holding mine with both of his. The long entryway carpet had seen better days, but I would guess it's a valuable antique, similar to one I saw on that Roadshow program.

"Kat's in the kitchen finishing up. Dinner should be ready in about 15. Can I get you anything to drink?"

A beer would certainly decrease my anxiety. "Thanks. Sure. Do you have any Anchor Steam?"

"Oh, a hard-core kind of guy," he chuckled. "I think we have one left over from last week. Have a seat," he indicated a richly decorated lounge overlooking the street, "I'll be right back. Please make yourself comfortable."

He scooted down the long hallway to the back of the house. I cautiously peered into the lounge. A dark purple, crushed-velvet, overstuffed sofa and loveseat dominated the decor. It had the feel of a Victorian drawing room, complete with fringed curtains and tall, dark, dusty bookcases. Newspapers and magazines covered the low coffee table in the center of the room. Most of them looked like local underground organs: *The Bay Guardian, The Independent, The Western Edition.*

"Christopher!" Mother Earth herself screamed as she strolled down the hall. Beads in her graying hair, a multicolored tent dress with fringe, plastic jewelry up each arm. Without asking, she threw her arms around me and gave me the biggest bear hug I had ever known, leaving slight indentations with her bracelets. She took a step back, "We're so glad you could make it."

When my ribcage returned to its normal girth, I replied, "Thank you for having me into your home."

Zack returned with an open Anchor Steam for me and two clear, fancy bottles of slightly green fluid. He handed one to Kat. "Let's all sit, shall we." He indicated the loveseat for me and the sofa for them. It was just as uncomfortable to sit on as it was to look at.

Through the bay window I could see another group of people taking pictures of the house across the way. "Excuse me, but is there something special about the house over there? I keep seeing people taking photos of it."

"Oh, that's the Dead House," Kat tossed out as if everyone knew what that meant. But I did not, and I just stared at her. "In the old days a few of the Grateful Dead lived there. Jerry… Garcia visited a few times. Tourists get a big thrill out of it. It's nothing special," she waved her hand downward. "Now, this place," she indicated her home, "this place saw far more action than that dump!"

"Kat, I doubt our guest wants a history lesson." He raised his eyebrows in a Groucho Marx kind of way. Then he turned to me, "What brings you to our fair city, Christopher?"

Again, I didn't respond to the name immediately. A swig of beer would go well before answering. The first swallow produced the same uncontrollable shudder. "Business. Pleasure. You know." I didn't know what to say. I certainly did not want to talk about me. Or Christopher. "I really want to hear about Chris."

"Chrissy," Kat corrected. It sounds awfully girly, but this is San Francisco after all.

"Yes. I want to hear all about Chrissy."

"I wish we could tell you more," Zack started off, "But it's been nearly 20 years. We've spoken on the phone from time to time, holidays mostly, but that's about it."

I had no clue what to say.

"We don't see eye-to-eye on a lot of things, Christopher. Especially when it comes to politics," Kat winked at me, incorrectly assuming I understood her innuendo.

"Maybe we could start with some *hors d'oeuvres*," Zack switched gears. "We have olives, pickled veggies and feta."

"I'll get it," and Kat shuffled toward the kitchen.

"Tonight is Mediterranean night. I hope you like Middle-Eastern food."

I have never eaten it, nor had I heard of anything he mentioned, except olives, and they just go on pizza or in drinks. "I'm not familiar with it, but I'll give it a go."

Kat returned with a tray full of stuff: olives I recognized, pink-tinged wedges, and crumbled cheese. She held the tray out to me but did not offer a plate or napkin. There was no serving fork and I stared at the food blindly.

                    Friday

"I'm sorry, Christopher," Kat blurted, "We're kind of casual here. Just use your fingers. It's okay," she smiled to increase the permission level.

Not knowing what to expect, I tried to take one of everything. She then offered it to Zack, who made a pile of goodies in his left hand.

"Just put the pits in the tray on the table." Kat indicated an ornate silver-plate ashtray worn from years of use. Pits?

Zack extricated a small stone from his mouth and deposited it in the container. I guess the olives have pits. They didn't look like the type I am used to seeing on my food. The first one I tried tasted nutty, felt slightly chewy and reeked of vinegar. After gnawing the meat off the large seed, I didn't know how to get the thing out of my mouth. I observed Kat as she daintily pursed her lips, allowing the pit to slip out into her waiting fingers. I attempted to duplicate her action and ended up losing the thing on the floor as it slipped past my hand.

"Oops!" shouted Zack as he reached down and swooped it up deftly. He dropped the pit diligently into the tray. "I'm sorry we don't have a great deal of information for you. What can you tell us about Chrissy's mother?"

Nothing, I thought to myself. "I really don't want to talk about her, please. I'm sorry."

Kat reached over and patted my hand, "That's okay. We understand."

"I would really like to hear more about… Chrissy."

They looked at each other before either spoke. Zack started, "It's just as difficult for us to talk about someone we feel we lost, too." He looked at Kat.

She continued, "We wanted to raise a child to value our values, believe our beliefs and continue our work." She shook her head. "That's not what happened." She glanced at Zack.

"Chrissy totally rebelled and has adopted an extremely conservative way of life. We told you about the commune." I nodded and popped another olive into my mouth. "It's a community of skinheads, Christopher. Nothing could be farther from our philosophical principles."

"Running away and joining this cult devastated us." I nodded in agreement as I nibbled away. "We wanted her to believe in all the right things."

I nearly choked. Maybe it was the pit, maybe it was, "'Her'?"

"Chrissy," Kat cooed. "What's wrong, Christopher?"

I simply spat the seed into my hand, "Our baby was a boy!" The pit clinked in the metallic ashtray. "I must have made a mistake."

Again they looked at each other. "No, you haven't, Christopher," Zack demurred. "It's just been so long, sometimes we forget ourselves."

"Maybe we should continue this discussion over dinner," Kat suggested and then stood up, heading toward the rear of the house.

This is getting even weirder. We followed her to the dining room, an alcove off the main hall with a beaded curtain. A very solid, dark wooden table hid beneath a feast of food, most of which I could not identify.

"I'm very confused. Please explain."

"Let's sit," Kat invited. "Just help yourself," and she indicated various plates of strange-looking foods.

Zack took a big breath and exhaled audibly. "It's a long story, Christopher," and he glanced at Kat. She glanced down at the food, avoiding his gaze. "We found out early on that we could not have children of our own. Of course, we both wanted a child to raise. Adoption was our only choice at that time."

"There was always child piracy," Kat teased, "But court costs. You know."

They chortled together, then Zack went on, "The agency's waiting list was long, and we had to go through lots of hoops to prove our ability to be fit parents."

Kat continued, "One day we got a call saying that they had a baby for us. We rushed over and were shown your son. I fell in love immediately." She looked over at Zack, "Maybe you should tell this next part."

He had started to collect various lumps of things on his plate. After clearing his throat, he went on, "Yeah, well, Kat wanted him circumcised."

"They told me it would be cleaner and healthier for the baby. What did I know back then?"

Zack reached over and grasped her hand. "I was adamantly opposed to it, having suffered my own genital mutilation at the hands of the medical establishment." That made me wince and squirm.

"One day, while Zack was out," Kat narrated now, "I took little Christopher–we decided to keep the name you had given him–to Mass General for, you know," and she made snipping motions with her fingers. Now I was really uncomfortable. "First, they strapped him onto a board. Then a medical student applied a clamp–if I had known they'd be using such painful-looking hardware I would never have agreed to this–a big metal clamp when the instructor wasn't looking. Apparently he put it on wrong, applied too much pressure and little Christopher's little penis ended up on the floor." She began getting teary.

Zack patted her hand. "The doctors presented a few options, and we discussed it thoroughly with the medical team, some psychiatrists and our families. After much deliberation, we decided it would be best to surgically alter the child and raise a girl."

"I'm sorry, I'm sorry," Kat openly wept now.

This poor kid. Everyone else trying to decide what's best. No wonder he, she, ran away.

"It took a few years of surgery, but they finally managed to get the appearance right. We stayed with the name, changing it to Christina. Of course she can't function in the same way as a woman, but at least she looks the part. Luckily, she was young enough and doesn't remember all the operations."

They both had started eating, scooping bits of things with pieces of flat, round bread.

Zack continued, "The settlement with the hospital was more money than we thought we'd ever see."

"It was 1967. We were flower children and decided to move here to San Francisco to become part of the movement. It was a wonderful time."

"With the money from the settlement, we bought this house and kept the doors open. People knew they could always get a meal or crash here."

"Janis Joplin once slept right where you were sitting." She pointed out toward the front lounge. "Tim Leary stayed with us whenever he was in town. Eldredge Cleaver, Angela, Bobby. Even Dr. King himself visited with us once."

Zack let out with a huge sigh, "But Chrissy hated all of it."

"She was always an angry child. Wanting what she couldn't have. Never happy with what we gave her," Kat drifted off into memories.

"The difficult part came at puberty when we had to explain the facts of life, and a few other things."

"All her friends were getting breasts and curves. She wasn't developing the same."

"One night we had a family discussion about the issue. She screamed about how we made her into a freak. We tried to explain as best as possible, but she wasn't interested in our compassion. She just wanted to be angry."

"When the screaming was done, she agreed to more surgery–for breast implants–and hormone treatments. She still has to get those treatments, and I think the last I heard, she still goes to the Haight-Ashbury Free Clinic, but they won't tell us anything," and she trailed off, tearing up again.

I didn't know what to say, or whether I should even say anything. In those instances, it's probably best to keep quiet, and I just stared at the food.

"We're sorry, Christopher," Zack offered. "I know you came here looking to make contact with your son. We feel terrible about it."

I just needed to make absolutely sure, "There's an identifying mark."

"The clover leaf!" Kat piped up.

"Left foot?" I asked.

They both nodded.

"Have some babaganoush," Kat prompted. I hadn't touched anything. "Or maybe some taboulleh."

I did not feel like eating. "I'm not hungry right now."

"We understand," Zack comforted.

— ◆ —

The bitter taste of the beer comforted me more than anything else that evening. I made vain attempts at sampling the food, but it might as well have been chopped octopus, mashed stinkweed and boiled shoe remnants.

Zack and Kat described their charitable work and how they invested the settlement money to continue serving their community. Clairvoyant timing in the late '90s allowed them to ride the crest of the dot-com phenomenon and walk away before the tumble. They presided over a treasure chest that would last them the rest of their lives and still allow for generous doling out of charity.

I could stand only so much liberal crap. And they were Liberal, with a capital 'L.' After a while I excused myself, claiming a headache. More and more lies.

At the door, Zack called, "Feel free to drop in anytime. You're always welcome here." They waved vigorously and I walked around the corner to the car.

Somehow I managed to get out of there without talking about myself, or Christopher. A couple of radical, liberal hippies making a ton of money off business and financial investments. There's something very unnatural about all that. And, speaking of unnatural, there's Chrissy to deal with. Nothing is going to come easy here.

As I approached the rental, I could see a piece of paper under the wiper. Oh no, a ticket. When I got to the car, it turned out to be an advertisement for a band called The Dead Kennedys playing this weekend at the Fillmore.

Ignoring the obvious irony, I crumpled the paper but discovered no trash receptacles in the immediate vicinity. Instead, I pushed it into my pocket for later disposal.

As I drove past the corner of 16th and Market, I could see the denizens of Café Flore on the patio, in their loud outfits and amazing hairdos. One parking spot awaited me back at the motel, and I thanked the goddess of parking for that little miracle.

I climbed the stairs and noticed the big balcony was empty. It seemed very inviting. I walked over to the rail and peered down. People passed by, to and fro. One face I did recognize: the guy with the spiky brown hair and off-center nose. He looked up at me as he went by.

I ignored the sight of a beautiful setting sun blending into the cloud layer over the hills of San Francisco, and in a minute my mind wandered off to the real purpose of this trip. The missing Kennedy son, emasculated, rejected a radical liberal upbringing, ran off to join a secretive, ultra-conservative commune. Top Dog is just going to love it. I'm not sure I want to continue chasing this wild goose. Something inside tells me it's time to hand his baby back to him. I'm 2,000 miles from home and have no idea where to go next. At least I'm here in San Francisco where I can let go and relax.

"Hi!" The word shot out behind me and my muscles tensed reflexively. I turned to face the spiky-haired guy. "Hi!" he erupted again, thrusting his right hand at me, "I'm Jeremy."

At least a second of time passed while I sized him up. About 30 years old, slender, a bit shorter than me, not ugly, but no model either.

I responded by grasping his offered hand firmly, and maybe a bit too firmly on purpose, "Stone."

He pulled his hand back as soon as I let it go. "Hi, Stone."

Not knowing what to say, I just stared at him, looking for cues or clues. I found it difficult not to focus on his nose. Bright, emerald green eyes gazed up at me.

He went on, "I saw you earlier. What a pleasant surprise to find you again." His smile was part wicked, part delight. This boy-man is quite bold.

"Aren't I a bit old for you, Jeremy?" The name melted soothingly in my mouth.

Staring into my eyes he replied, "I've been looking for a daddy just like you."

I'm packing my bag and leaving tonight. This town is way too weird for me.

When I turned to walk away, he shouted, "Wait! Where are you visiting from?"

I took one more step and then stopped. Why should I respond to his invasive question? He's socially aggressive and seems to have no regard or respect for privacy.

The gnawing bit of mystery he just created propelled me back to the railing. I stared at him again, trying to infer motivation from his appearance.

"You're from the Midwest, aren't you?" he accused. I guess I'm fairly obvious. "Me, too. Ohio."

"Indiana," slipped out before my mouth had gotten the signal from the brain not to give this guy any information.

"I'm so glad to be away from all that bullshit," he prattled, "This is the only place I feel I can totally be myself. Ohio is so limiting, and everyone has expectations of your behavior and goals. Not to mention your sexuality." He stared up at me now.

The growing lump in my throat went down painfully with a slow swallow. The intense gaze of this young man started blood flowing to a region of my body I wouldn't have expected. How many times does a guy over 60 get propositioned by someone half his age? My biggest fear is that this might be the very last time. He's not a visual heartthrob, but he seems to want me very badly.

Henry is screaming in one ear, "Do it! Do it!" while my Midwestern sensibility is purring, "You just met. Wait. Give it time."

As I turned again to walk back to the room, Jeremy grabbed my hand in an obsessive, yet gentle, way, "Can I come with you?" his dew-filled eyes pled with anguish.

Henry whooped and hollered with joy. My innards felt wet, but I was determined not to show any interest.

"You are the hottest man I have ever seen, and I just want to be with you and make you happy." The intensity mounted.

I shook my hand free and started walking again.

He stood at the railing, finally getting the hint. "I'll be at the Eagle on Sunday. It's a fundraiser for The Godfather Fund. I'm singing." The look on his face mimicked a little boy whose favorite toy lay at the bottom of an inaccessible well. The pout got bigger as I moved farther away.

By the time I got to the room, my heart pounded so loudly in my chest it was all I could hear. Maintaining my calm took every ounce of inner strength. I can't remember ever being so sexually aroused. The door slammed from my being distracted, and it brought me back to partial reality.

About an hour of television went by, but I could not possibly tell you what was on. The image of a brash, young, asymmetrical face kept usurping my thoughts. The rerun of Jay Leno prompted me to start getting ready for bed.

Even though it was late and I had already had a long day, I did not feel tired. My arousal had turned physical, and while I enjoyed the long-missed sensation of engorgement, it kept me from sleeping.

The thoughts in my head kept floating back to Jeremy and his intense, green eyes. It wasn't until I relieved the tension, while reliving the subdued intensity and imagining his offbeat face, that I finally felt spent enough to sleep.

As I drifted off, I wondered and worried if I had, one time more, let a never-again opportunity pass.

Chapter Seven

Saturday

Such vivid dreams but much restful sleep. I replayed the Kennedy Assassination over and over, except this time they kept taking him to hospitals where quacko doctors hacked various parts off of babies.

Not the kinds of themes you wish for. However, when I awoke to a gloomy San Francisco morning, I did not feel tired at all. Getting out of bed was not difficult and I looked though the slightly-milky window at the precipitation hovering in the air.

An image of something green lingered in my foggy mind. Round, bright and emerald green. Misplaced memories suddenly dislodged, and I sat down in the chair to keep from falling over.

Back in the early '70s, a handsome, young police officer named William transferred up from Indy. He moved to Fort Dyck to care for an elderly aunt. Chief van der Hook assigned him to me for mentoring. At the time I was a sergeant awaiting my imminent promotion to lieutenant.

At first, his I'm-from-the-big-city attitude got in the way. William thought he knew it all. Nothing I told him stuck or sunk in. That really frustrated me. I had even considered appealing to the chief to move him to somebody else.

About the time I had reached the end of my patience with him, his whole attitude changed. Instead of strutting with superiority, he shuffled and looked down. Rather than chattering at me endlessly, he slumped quietly in reflection. I figured his aunt must have died or something.

While we stood in the backroom of the station together, he told me that he received his draft notice and he had to report back to Indianapolis the next day. We looked into each other's eyes, and for the first time, I realized his were beautiful emerald green.

I didn't know what to say or do, and we both just stood staring at each other for a while. After a few minutes, William stepped forward and hugged me. Everything in my body went stiff.

He sensed the erection and moved a hand to my crotch, then quickly pulled it away. The closest I ever came to intimate contact with another human being.

"Geez, Sarge, I didn't know I meant so much to you," he teased and then kissed me politely on the left cheek.

William ended up being sent to Viet Nam. We kept writing letters to each other, and I anticipated his return so that we could continue where we left off.

When I got the promotion, I wrote a long letter to him, telling how much he meant to me and that I looked forward to him coming home soon. Every day after that I checked my mailbox at least twice, looking for his reply. None ever came.

At first I thought he might have been embarrassed by my finally expressing the feelings we had both been avoiding. As time went on, I started to hate myself for having those feelings and even more for writing them down and sending them to William.

A few months later, an elegantly-dressed, elderly woman with a cane came to see me at the station. She introduced herself as William's aunt. I invited her into my office so that she could sit down. Turns out she wanted to let me know she had received official notice from the U.S. Army that William had died in combat. The old woman felt she needed to tell me about it personally because her nephew spoke so highly of me. Said he thought of me as a big brother.

Okay, now I need some coffee.

One thing this city does not lack is places to get coffee. That and Thai restaurants.

Across the street is a place called Peets. As soon as you walk in, the aroma of fresh-roasted beans rouses you like a playful slap on the cheek. I requested the darkest, most bitter brew and got the best cup of coffee I ever tasted.

Once I started sipping the French Roast, my mind began to wander. For some odd reason I mulled over the trip to Boston in 1964, the time I placed the baby up for adoption. Sarah, the other agent, connected somewhat with the child, perhaps because of who it was or maybe due to her own motherhood, but I had no such bonding experience. In fact, I felt so relieved when it was all over. I was just Top Dog's minion carrying out his perverse plans. Who the hell does he think he is?

With my thoughts buzzing from the introduction of caffeine, I made my mind up to pack it all in and head back home, to the security of Indiana, where people don't just walk up to you and ask to go to your motel room.

"Excuse me," a young mother said as she bumped a stroller into my leg.

"Oh, that's okay," I responded. "No harm done."

She fetched the child up into her arms, "Come on, Christopher, let's get mommy her morning coffee so we can go for a stroll in the park." She waddled up to the counter, babe in arms.

When she said the baby's name, "Christopher," the muscles at the back of my neck pinched. I cringed.

"Are you okay?" Mommy had turned around just in time to see my pained expression.

"Fine. I'm fine." Little Christopher looked so peaceful in his mother's arms. She turned back to ordering.

Coincidence? Who knows? I just stood there with my coffee cup and my soul, both half empty.

What else in my life is so important right now? A sense of duty prickled my conscience, and I realized that I at least owed it to Chrissy to tell her who her real parents were.

As I gulped down the rest, I remembered what Kat had said about a free clinic, and the planning part of my brain took over. I'll go back to the motel and look in the phone book. Then I'll go for a drive.

— ◆ —

The Haight-Ashbury Free Clinic is at 558 Clayton Street, a block off of Haight. I ended up taking the same route as my first trek to the Walshes. Parking proved to be even more difficult on a weekend, but I eventually found a spot a few blocks away.

Walking along Haight Street I passed quite a few young people mumbling something about "kind bud." At first I didn't know if they were talking to me or what, but eventually I realized they were trying bum marijuana off of people. What a strange city.

At the clinic I attempted to explain to the volunteer at the desk that I needed to speak to someone about records. She told me to try the used record store on Haight. I explained I was interested in medical records and she instructed me to sit and wait.

While I sat, I watched a cross-section of the underclass accessing a working model of socialized medicine. People getting their daily methadone, people without shoes who hadn't eaten recently, people with disfigured bodies, people with nowhere else to go.

A prim young woman eventually prompted me to follow her to a small office down the hall. She introduced herself as Marla and asked how she could help.

"I need some information about a particular patient of yours."

"I'm sorry, but we can't give out confidential information without a signed consent."

I knew that. "Well, maybe you can assist me without breaching confidentiality." She turned her head away from me. "A long time ago I put a baby up for adoption. Zack and Kat Walsh adopted that boy," she swung her head back to look at me directly, "and I have come here to San Francisco to find out what happened to the child with the cloverleaf birthmark on his, now her, left foot."

She exhaled audibly and pouted slightly. That encouraged me. "I know Chrissy comes here to get her hormones, and I was just wondering if there was any way you could inadvertently let me know when she'll be in again."

The young woman bit her lip pensively. "I can't tell you when actual appointments are, but she was just here last week and doesn't come back for another month."

That's not going to work. "I'll be gone by then. Is there any way to contact her?"

She shook her head slowly, "No, I'm afraid not. No one knows where she lives. We don't even have an address for her. I'm sorry."

Another dead end. I started to stand up, "Thanks anyway. They said she lives on a commune. I guess some communes don't have phones or addresses."

As I reached the doorway she blurted, "Wait!" I stopped and looked back. "She talks about 'living in Paradise' on Pale Face Ranch."

"Paradise?"

"I think it's a small town out past Sacramento. She said she liked the idea of being 'in Paradise' while living in a town called Paradise."

"Thank you." It's a slim lead, but so much more than what I walked in with.

"Wait!" Marla stopped me again, "have you ever met or dealt with a person like Chrissy before? I mean someone who has had gender reassignment."

Gender reassignment? Political correctness has gone too far. "No. No, I haven't."

"I suggest you get acquainted with some of the issues before making contact with your child," and she smiled at me with a hint of experience. "And remember, I never gave you any information about any of our clients."

I winked at her and said, "Thanks for at least giving it a go."

– ◆ –

From there I drove to the Main Branch of the Public Library. I figured I could get some basic research done there. Parking on a Saturday in the area known as Civic Center was much easier, especially because of the parking meters.

The striking building facade looked new but seemed old, as if they had just steam cleaned it. Inside, it's a lofty place with a tall central open space. In the lobby, when you look up, you can see one of the upper floors jutting out into the central shaft. In fact, that view is the basis of their logo, which is imprinted all over the place.

Behind the information desk is a wall a few stories tall with plastic ovals bearing people's names. At first I thought it was a list of contributors because I didn't recognize any of them. Then I saw "William Saroyan" and realized they are authors' names.

Across the way I could see people working at computers. I asked the woman at the desk about scheduling computer time.

"You can schedule computer time on the third floor, but you need a valid library card."

"Any library card?"

"Any library card from within the state of California."

"Indiana won't work?"

She smiled. "No, sir. California only."

"Thanks anyway. Where can I find the main card catalog?"

Her smile grew. "There is no card catalog, sir. You can use the terminals on the third floor to access the collection."

"No cards?" I squeaked.

"Well, the old ones got used as an art project. They're along the walls up there."

"Thanks again." This place gets even stranger as time goes on. A library with no card catalog. I hope they still have books.

A graceful staircase led up to the third floor, past a colorful children's collection. A bank of computer terminals stood waiting to serve patrons. The interface seemed old-fashioned, menu-driven. I guess that way there's no need for a mouse. The search engine is fairly similar to doing a web search.

I tried various subjects: gender, castration, circumcision–which led me to sexual law. Lots of titles appeared, but most pertained to the legal treatment of transgendered or homosexual people. Finally I found "As nature made him: the boy who was raised as a girl" and that sounded more on target.

I looked around for the stacks of books; there weren't any. I went to the information kiosk at the center of the floor and asked where to find the books. The obviously-gay man in his late 40s looked up over his reading glasses, adjusted his paisley vest and told me that you have to write down the call numbers and take the request to the library page. He pointed to a window along the wall.

Hmmm. Just as I suspected. No books. Back at the terminal I had to recreate my search, as I had cleared it before I left. It took a minute but I found it again. Scratch paper and golf-scoring pencils are provided for this purpose. I scribbled out 305.9066, the name of the book and author, and walked over to the paging window.

I handed my slip of paper to the distracted boy with a matted goatee. He handed me a form to fill out without even looking at what I held. At first I felt disrespected, but then I had to think: who is dehumanizing whom?

Even though paperwork is still not my favorite pastime, I filled in as much information as I could. On the second try he grudgingly glanced at the form and mumbled, "Be right back."

While I waited, I happened to notice the wall covering is made from old catalog cards which had been written and drawn all over. Some of them were quite intricate and ornate. What a fascinating idea.

The distinctive sound of a book being slammed on a counter brought my attention back to the window. The book I had requested sat waiting. My plaid-shirted friend continued to ignore me. I didn't know whether I should thank him or spank him.

I brought the book over to a cozy chair overlooking the central shaft, and started to browse.

The story concerned twin boys born in Winnipeg, Manitoba, during the 1960s. As the first received circumcision, the doctor used too high of a current on the cauterizer and fried the little guy's penis. After hours and hours of consulting and counseling, the parents made the same decision as the Walshes: raise the child as a girl. Around age 18, the child decided he wanted to be a man. More surgery, more hormones. He eventually married. I seem to remember seeing this news story a few years ago on TV.

Of greatest interest to me was the emotional turmoil of the boy raised as a girl. Having to play with dolls when she really wanted guns. Not being able to date. Looking in the mirror and not being able to accept the image.

After dropping the book off at the paging desk, I went back to the central kiosk and asked where the maps are. The vested man told me I could find them on the first floor.

There I consulted a map of Northern California and located Paradise up in the foothills of the Sierra Nevada Mountains. I sketched out the route on another piece of scratch paper. From what I could tell, it would be an all-day trip, about two hours to Sacramento and then another two hours to Paradise. A backroads drive might be just the thing to help relieve the tension of being in a city again.

I left the library with more questions than when I had entered. Why am I doing this? What do I hope to get out of meeting JFK's long-lost offspring? Is this just another attempt to appease my guilt about things I cannot go back and change? Has rekindling William's memory turned me romantic and sentimental? Am I hoping to make up for lost opportunities?

When I got back to the car my mind flashed on Jeremy again. Henry wanted me to go to the Eagle Sunday Beer Bust. Jeremy mentioned he will be singing there tomorrow. What a coincidence.

Just to make sure I would be able to find the bar, I drove past 12th and Harrison. I had expected an old biker bar to look like something out of the 1950s, with lots of chrome or shiny metal. This place is mostly old wood. Lots of empty spaces on the street promised good parking.

Heading back to the motel, I considered my options for the evening ahead. Badlands was on the list. Maybe another walk to the Castro. Maybe an evening in front of the TV. No, I did that last night. Henry's right. I do need to get out more.

— ◆ —

Pasta Pomodoro, an Italian restaurant at the next corner, provided my evening meal. I got to walk past Café Flore again, just as bustling as usual. Pomodoro has some good food and attractive serving staff. Along the way I noticed a very black place named Detour. Maybe later, if Badlands doesn't work out.

I liked the sliding-glass windows at the front of Badlands because they were open. Some younger men sat at the table there and held conversations with various other young men standing outside.

The back part of the bar had a dance floor with strobe lights and video screens. People moved in rhythm to over-the-hill singers attempting to make yet another come back. The accompanying videos had to be filmed in soft focus or long shots.

A few of the younger guys smiled shyly at me. I wasn't about to make any moves, dance or otherwise.

One particular fellow kept trying to catch my eye, but I had no interest in him. His hair needed washing, and he didn't seem to be able to stop moving. After a while he walked up and announced, "I'm Ted. Me and my buddies are going out to my BMW for a snort. Want a little bump with us?"

I couldn't decide if it was his nasal twang, his obnoxious cocksure attitude, his oversized floppy polyester shirt collar, his bad teeth, his ugly collection of friends or his invitation to go do drugs that repulsed me most. I decided not to start any trouble and politely declined with, "No, thanks."

He walked away with an expression similar to when you put what you thought was steak in your mouth and then someone tells you it's liver. "Get her!" is what I think I heard him whine to his cronies.

Thirty minutes had passed and I saw no reason to stay any longer. I will be able to tell Henry that I have been to Badlands

Saturday

without lying. The fresh air felt good on my face when I got outside.

On the walk back I noticed a Pottery Barn store at the corner of Castro and Market. It seemed very much out of place with all the independently-owned businesses here. Kind of like the Gap in the Haight.

When I passed by Detour again I considered going in. Loud music boom-boomed through the walls. The door opened, the music got louder, two people walked out, but I could not see in because a leather curtain blocked the view. Intriguing. Figuring I may never be here again, I decided to give it a go. Inhaling to brace myself, I pulled the door open and stepped inside. The leather smelled strong as I pushed it aside.

Although the main room of the bar is fairly dim, lights from pinball and video games glowed eerily in the gloom. In the midst of it all, a cyclone chain-link fence looms over the patrons. Some people leaned against it, others hung from it. One fellow hand-cuffed himself to it.

The line for the bar was only a few men thick. Directly in front of me stood a tall, lanky, gray-haired fellow about ten years younger than me. He wore a black leather vest and pants with boots to match. Something about him attracted me. Maybe it was the musky scent of the leather or the commanding stance of his pose. I considered starting a conversation with him after we both had our drinks.

When he got to the front of the line, the young and scruffy bartender asked, "What do you want, Butch?"

"Oh, girlfriend," the leatherman squealed, "I need a big, tall cocktail! I've been hiking the hills in these heels all day!"

I'm really beginning to hate this city.

Once I got my Anchor Steam, I found a spot by the fence to occupy. The first sip provided the anticipated shudder.

"Good stuff, eh?" inquired the brown-haired young man standing next to me. "I like it, too." He showed me his matching bottle, took a swig and wiped his mouth on the sleeve of his flannel shirt. He held out a brawny hand, "I'm Bruce." His accompanying smile included bedroom eyes.

We shook. "Stone."

"We don't have anything like this back home," he indicated the beer.

Which begged, "Where are you from?"

"Winnipeg."

"Really?! I was just reading about Winnipeg today." On second glance he seemed quite nice.

"Oh, yeh? What about?" which he pronounced somewhere between "a boat" and "a boot."

This didn't seem the time or place to go into details. "A pair of identical twins, one raised as a girl, one as a boy."

"Oh, the Reimers!"

"You know them?"

"We went to school together. Sad lot."

I wanted to ask him all about the one raised as a girl. Just as I started my question, he shouted out.

"Hey, look!" and he pointed above the entry door.

In the small space between the top of the door and the ceiling stood a dancing cage with bars like a jail cell. Within it gyrated a person in a trench coat and fedora. In an odd way, it reminded me of the outfits we used to wear at the Secret Service. As the music bumped and ground, he undulated his body, somewhat in rhythm to the song. Off came the coat, followed by a dress shirt and pants. The crowd mostly ignored the performance, but the few who watched gave a big hoot. The striptease continued until he only had a spangly G-string and the hat. At one point a light caught his face. It looked quite severe, pock-marked and war-worn. I understood why he kept the hat on for so long.

He teased the few of us who watched by suggesting he would take off the G-string. Over and over he pulled on the straps, put his hand through the pouch and pretended to take it all off. One man hooted and whooped. At the end the dancer yanked on the little strap and it sprang off his body, revealing an even smaller G-string beneath.

The lights dimmed on the cage and the dancer disappeared. I turned to continue the conversation with Bruce, but no Bruce. As I continued slurping the beer, I waded through the crowded bar looking for the Canadian I had just met. Couldn't find him.

My bladder asked to be emptied and I found my way to the restroom. A line had formed and I waited patiently while I looked at men and they looked at me.

Too bad about Bruce. I really wanted to hear what he knew about the twins.

As I got closer to the bathroom, I noticed no doors, no stalls. The urinal had a low mirror above it, perfectly positioned for indiscreet observation. I had to close my eyes and think about waterfalls in order to complete the task at hand. It still took a long time and I realized I should have just gone back to the motel.

After one more sweep of the bar in hopes of finding Bruce, I gave up and made my exit. I almost knocked into a fellow with short, curly gray hair leaving at the same time. Through his round, wire-frame glasses I saw pale blue-green eyes. His stare focused far away. Across the street a line of people stretched down the sidewalk, waiting to get into a dance bar.

Without thinking about it, I said, "What's so special about that place?"

He responded, "Yeah, who wants to go there anymore?"

We looked at each other for a few beats. I kind of hoped he would ask me another question, any question. Having a decent conversation with a man in San Francisco is proving harder than I thought.

He smiled an alcohol-induced smile and walked off. I headed back to the motel wondering when I lost the whatever-it-is I had wanted to get rid of, and pondering how to get it back.

Chapter Eight
Sunday

As it was Sunday morning and I didn't have to be anywhere in particular, I allowed myself the luxury of staying in bed with the cable TV on.

After a brief shower I left my cozy room to forage for food. Near the pasta place where I ate last night I found Squat & Gobble, a crêperie. While the name conjures up indecent and lewd acts, the food served is rather good and plentiful. I had a meaty sausage omelet and some dark, strong coffee.

Again the warm day defied the prediction of a cold San Francisco summer. After eating, I took the time to browse along Market Street and peer into various shops. Crystals, antiques, stylish sunglasses, glitzy watches and gay-oriented books all had their chance to lure me, but none succeeded in finding their way into my luggage. Examining the other casual shoppers fascinated me more than any of the merchandise.

Eventually I got bored with that. Most folks were from out of town as well. Some even spoke English.

There doesn't seem to be too much to do in this area other than shop or eat. Or go to bars.

Back in the room I went over my choices of wardrobe for the afternoon ahead. Knowing the Eagle is a biker/leather bar certainly helps, but I really didn't bring anything very appropriate with me. I guess my old patrolman's outfit would have been popular. Of course, I haven't worn that in umpteen years.

I settled on a black T-shirt and blue jeans. I hope that fits in.

Parking at the place proved harder than promised yesterday. It took a few minutes, but I did manage to find a spot a few blocks away on 12th Street. Again, just as someone else was pulling out. I guess that's the secret to successful parking in San Francisco: look for people getting into parked cars.

On the walk back to the bar I passed buildings with businesses that looked defunct. Many had leasing signs. I suppose the economic downturn hit this area fairly hard.

At the Eagle, leather-clad men took money for the Beer Bust. Eight dollars bought an all-you-can-eat dinner and a plastic cup for beer. One of the guys stamped my hand to show I had made the required donation.

Inside the fence, an outdoor patio contained an eclectic assortment of men, many with leather clothes or accessories. The ages ranged from somewhat young to older than me. Most, however, looked to be in the 30-50 range. I did not feel so out of place, like I did at Badlands.

Within a minute a tall, slender fellow sporting an open leather vest cheerfully splashed beer into my empty cup and moved on to the next thirsty soul. The first taste of their watery-weak barley pop was my last. Ever since I've tasted Anchor Steam, nothing can compete with its nasty, stout taste. I realized that I had better not dump out the cup because someone would just refill it with more piss-water beer.

Guys began to set up a public address system on the stage area above the barbecue pit. Cooks had already started grilling good-looking hunks of meat and I waited expectantly for my share.

Through the crowd I could see a bar in the back under an awning. As I pushed my way through the jungle of cigar and pipe smokers, I noticed another faint smell of a different type of burning leaves. Probably for medicinal purposes.

At the back bar I ordered an Anchor Steam under the gaze of a way-past-his-prime biker, even older than me. Perched on a chrome-legged barstool, this denizen of the shadows watched everything with a glazed-over expression.

I set the plastic cup on the bar as I picked up the bottle. As expected, the first sip made me shudder uncontrollably. The old biker watched and then went right back to staring off somewhere.

Loud pops and crackles announced the power-up of the amplifier. Standard tapping of the mike and, "Testing... One, two, three" followed. "Welcome to the Eagle everybody. This afternoon we're having a fundraiser for the Godfather Service Fund, an organization whose charity knows no bounds. We're glad to have you. Hell, at my age I'm glad to have anyone." No one laughed. Most weren't listening. "We have some wonderful entertainment for you, including the internationally-famous Kinsey Sicks!" That drew some intermittent applause. "Stick around and have some beer. The barbecue should be ready soon. Our show will start in just a few minutes."

I had walked back to the stage area during the announcements. Leaning against a wooden pillar posed a gorgeous young man without a shirt. His light-brown hair and dreamy green eyes suggested steamy sensuality. The bottle almost fell from my hand as I transfixed on him.

"I see you like my boyfriend. Me, too." A middle-aged fellow with a large bald spot hiding under a comb-over inquired through a graying Van Dyke, "What's your name?"

"Stone." I extended my hand to shake. He used his to indicate the pretty boy.

"That's James. I'm David."

"Hmmmm." I returned my hand to my side.

"So, where are you visiting from?" His inquisitive eyes examined me with curiosity.

I swallowed. "Is it that obvious?"

"Well, I haven't seen you here before. We're here every Sunday."

I didn't know if he was bragging or complaining.

"On vacation?" He wouldn't give up. At least I'm finally having a conversation with someone.

"Not really. It's a business trip."

"Oh, I see. And what sort of business are you in, Stone?"

Okay, he wants something from me, but I can't figure out what it is "Actually, I'm retired."

"Ah! A retired business trip," he mocked. "I get it." He rolled his eyes and raised his eyebrows.

At that moment the announcer returned to the mike and saved me from further persecution. "The barbecue is just about ready, so if you want to line yourselves up, we'll start dishing it out. Dishing... Get it? Good. And speaking of dishing it out, it's time to wring out, I mean, bring out the Kinsey Sicks. So here they are, the ever-popular superstars, the Kinsey Sicks!"

Those who paid attention applauded generously. Disembodied voices sang *a capella*. The tune sounded like "Route 66," but the words were different.

Soon four men in drag appeared from different directions and walked onto the stage as they continued to sing in beautiful four-part harmony. The song described their group and introduced each member. One looked like the librarian went mad, one aspired to be a society matron, one imitated 1960s chic, and the last one had an overblown version of That Girl's hair and a flared-out baby-doll skirt.

The quality of the performance rivaled professional groups. Especially having to do it here, in the open, walking among the groping hands of the crowd. Impressive, indeed.

By the time the number ended, the four of them stood on the stage. We applauded. The matron grabbed the onstage mike.

"Thank you. Thank you, everybody. Welcome to the Eagle. This motley crew is the Kinsey Sicks. We just flew back from our fabulous tour of New York... and Newark."

The guy with the That Girl hair interrupted, "And boy are my arms tired." He raised his muscle-bound arms, flapping slowly, revealing two mounds of bushy, black armpit hair.

"Thank you, Rachel," the matron hammed it up by waving a white-gloved hand in front of his nose. "That's our precious Rachel. The others are Winnie, Trampolina, and myself. I'm Trixie! Next we have a very special treat for you on this special day of fundraising for the Godfather Service Fund. Our next performer is just breaking onto the local Country-Western scene here. This is his very first debut right here at the Eagle. Gentlemen and gentlemen—are there even any gentlemen here?—please give this little cutie a big, warm welcome, not like the paltry one you gave us. Here he is, direct from open-mike night at The Edge—Destiny!" They walked off as twangy music started.

Jeremy stepped out onto the stage wearing a lavender gingham cowboy shirt, a Stetson and chaps. He scanned the crowd and stopped when he saw me. The music played on as he continued to stare. A moment later he shook it off and asked to have the track started over.

Again, the twang of guitars hit the smoky, afternoon air. He pranced around the stage, swishing his smallish butt in time with the beat.

"I'm looking for a brand new Daddy, a spanking brand new Daddy," he sang. "Won't you help me?"

The crowd whooped and hollered. As he turned his head from side to side, you couldn't see the off-centeredness of his nose. He continued singing as he stared at me.

"The old one treats me very rough, but never nearly rough enough." Jeremy writhed in rhythm. Very seductive. "I need a man from the wrong side of town to tie me up and tie me right down."

I'm guessing he writes his own material. The more he sang, the more he stared, and the more uncomfortable I grew. People started looking at me to see who was the object of his affection. That made me even more uncomfortable.

"I think he likes you," taunted David, clapping a hand on my shoulder.

As he finished up with, "I'm looking for an ever-loving, never-stopping, always-topping, even-handed spanking brand new Daddy. Won't you help me find my man?" I set the bottle down and tried to manage my way through the crowd toward the exit. Applause and whistles erupted.

By the time I reached the gate I originally entered through, Jeremy had jumped down and pursued me through the throng.

"Stone, wait!"

I had started back toward the car. "What?" I barked.

"Where are you going?"

"Anywhere away from here." My mood did not exactly match his. I just kept walking.

He kept after me. "Is something wrong?"

I stopped and turned to face him. "What?"

"You came to see me and now you're leaving." He looked at me expectantly. The kid doesn't get it. I don't want to be singled out in a crowd.

"So?"

"Do you want to go get something to eat together?" His please-please-please eyes looked up at me. Bright emerald green.

My stomach rumbled on cue. It had wanted some of that meat from the barbecue, and now it wasn't getting any.

"If you wait here I'll run back and get my stuff. It won't take two minutes."

My heart fluttered. My mind zoomed. The Stone expression held steady.

"Hurry up."

His face exploded into a joyful smile unlike any smile I've ever seen. Off he ran, his cute little butt framed by the chaps.

What is going on here? The more I try to push him away, the more aggressive his advances. I will never be able to figure out the men in this city. I just hope they're not indicative of all gay men in general. Again, I considered heading back home, where people are just people.

However, something I cannot figure out about this pup revs up my juices. He intrigues me in a way no man has so far. Maybe it's the cultural differences, the age thing, the vastly different styles or some quality I can't even put into words. Perhaps it's the emerald green eyes. Why him? Why now?

"Where are we going?" he asked, jerking me out of my mental soliloquy.

"I was headed back to my car."

"Where are you parked?"

"A few blocks away. On 12th Street."

"Oh good. We can go to Harvey's." He still wore the purple and leather outfit. What will people think when they see me with him in those clothes?

His pace exceeded mine and I had to speed up to maintain a comfortable speaking distance. "What's Harvey's?"

"Oh, a restaurant."

Nonchalant, self-confident, cocky. I just want to hug him. Or at least hold his hand. But not in public. Not just yet.

We crossed Folsom Street and he held a door open for me. I might have passed the place by because it really does not draw much attention to itself.

The inside looked like a garage sale exploded. Pieces of old furniture hung off the walls at odd angles, strange antique photos and ads hung amongst kitschy knick-knacks. The host ushered us to a rickety table painted in some unusual colors, at least purple and orange.

Mismatched flatware smirked up at me. A small baby bottle filled with milk anticipated being overturned to empty its contents through the chopped-down nipple. I had a difficult time deciding the intent of the decor and ambience. Part of me wanted to laugh and other parts wanted to examine some of the curious items.

"This is some place," I said neutrally. "Looks like it's been here a long time."

"This place has been around forever, at least from the '60s. It's only been Harvey's a few years. Before that it was Hamburger Mary's. Thank goodness they had the sense to retain the original decorations."

"Thank goodness," I replied, mostly to myself.

He picked up the menu and placed it at the edge of the table without looking at it.

"Aren't you going to read the menu first?"

"Nope. I already know what I want. Same thing I always get."

Nothing jumped off the page to demand ordering. "What would you suggest for a tourist from the Midwest?"

When I looked up from the menu, Jeremy sat staring at me. Part creepy, part interesting. It's nice to be admired, but I'm a bit shy.

"What would you like?" the server asked us.

"Him," Jeremy responded, pointing at me. He laughed: ha, ha. "Castro Turkey Club Sandwich. Extra mayo, please. And a Coke."

The server then turned to me. The very last item appealed more than anything else. "A burger and a Coke."

After the server moved off, Jeremy grilled me, "What did you think of my singing?"

I like Country music, but I'm no critic. "I liked your moves. Very, umm, sensual."

"But did you like the song? I wrote it myself."

"I had a feeling."

The server placed two large fountain glasses of Coke on the table and walked off.

"I'm trying to build a bridge between Country music and being gay. There aren't many choices for songs, so I write my own."

Not knowing how to respond, I merely smiled and took a sip of soda. The asymmetry of his face continued to fascinate me.

"Destiny?" I asked quizzically.

"Oh, that," he dismissed. "I wanted a stage name with impact and a slightly spiritual feeling. I had also considered Jericho."

"Stick with Destiny," I advised him. "It suits you somehow."

He smiled again. "I see you met David."

"David?" I had no clue what he was talking about.

"The guy talking to you at the Eagle."

"That one," I recalled with dismay.

"Don't worry. He goes up to just about everyone. He's some bigwig attorney with a continuing series of cute, young boyfriends."

"Were you one?"

"Me?" he exclaimed. "No way! Not that guy. He's not my type."

"I thought you're looking for a daddy."

"Daddy, yes. Grandpa, no."

The server placed the plates on the table as I chuckled. It was the first happy laugh I could remember in a very long time. Jeremy dug into his sandwich like he hadn't eaten in a few days. I couldn't take my eyes off him.

He looked up and asked through the food in his mouth, "Aren't you hungry?"

"Not as hungry as you, apparently."

"Sorry. Performing makes me ravenous." He continued devouring and devastating the large sandwich.

My burger tasted like a regular burger, except the whole-wheat bun's dense chewiness diminished the experience for me. I like my pizza crust doughy, but give me air-filled bread for my burgers.

As he inhaled his food, Jeremy frequently stopped to lick his fingers. One-by-one he started at the palm and stroked his tongue to the end of each long, bony digit. This behavior transfixed me, but he seemed unaware of my amazement. He is so unabashed, doesn't seem to care what people think, and is very up front with his feelings. We don't have people like this at home.

By the time he emptied his plate, I had gotten through about half of mine. He gave his fingers one more licking.

"So what brings you to San Francisco, Stone?"

I'm getting tired of answering that question, but I guess it's standard fare. "Some business." I'm getting tired of giving that answer, too.

"Ummm," he offered. "What are you up to later?"

"I really hadn't thought about it."

He looked directly at me and asked, "Could I come visit with you at your hotel room?" His puppy eyes glinted in the soft lighting.

I felt scared, annoyed, exhilarated, aroused. He just kept pushing and pushing and pushing. Even though I ached for such carnal interactions and wanted to fully experience him, I just could not allow myself to express it, especially directly to him. I did not know how. Perhaps it was time to open a new door.

Atlas shifted the globe to the other shoulder. "Sure," I mumbled down at my food.

I didn't need to look up to know that a smile consumed his face. I took one more bite of the burger and pushed the plate away. For some reason my hunger abated.

The server returned, cleared the table and left the tab. I picked it up, pulled enough cash out of my wallet and left it on the table.

"Thanks," Jeremy said. "I'm a little short right now. I'll make it up to you later." His smirk made me wonder about the meaning of "later."

We stood up and walked out. I couldn't think of anything to say, and he didn't speak either.

I put the key in the door and unlocked the car.

"Nice," he admired. "So butch." He got in.

"I have to go out of town tomorrow on an errand and I'm leaving fairly early. It's a long drive." I hoped maybe he would take a hint.

"Where you going?"

"Some place up north called Paradise."

He turned to look at me, "I'll take you to Paradise tonight."

"It's a long drive." I had been concentrating on where we were going and didn't pick up on the double entendre in time. "Oh, I get it."

He giggled a childish laugh. Normally I would find that annoying. At that moment it was merely charming.

"What's up in Paradise?" He sure is inquisitive.

I didn't know how much I could tell him. He hasn't given me any reason to be suspicious so far, but earning trust with me is a long-term venture. Of course, I don't have to tell him everything.

"I'm looking for someone."

"You've got someone right here. You don't need to look any farther."

The smug expression on his face defied response. I pulled into the motel parking lot and had some choices for spots. The one closest to the back stairs looked best and I aimed the car there.

We got out and I locked the doors. He leapt up on the stairs while asking, "Which room?"

It almost surprised me that he didn't already know. "To the top," I told him, and up he scampered.

As I got to the room door, I looked nervously left then right to see if anyone observed us. Old habits, fear, embarrassment.

Jeremy chided, "No one cares, Stone. This is San Francisco."

Once inside I locked the door and switched the deadbolt to prevent the maid from accidentally wandering in. This is San Francisco, they keep telling me.

"I need to go pee," Jeremy announced and then jaunted off to the bathroom.

The sweat from my palms began to drip on the carpeting. Pounding from my chest blocked out all sounds. I can't believe this is happening. I'm in a motel room with a man I barely know. It's so scary, exciting, nerve-wracking, tension-filled.

"I would have invited you to my place," Jeremy said as he stepped out of the bathroom wearing only the chaps over a jock strap. "But I have a roommate, and she doesn't like it when I bring men home." He tossed the shirt, pants and boots by the chair across from the bed.

His flat, hairless chest gleamed in the light from the table lamp. I could not stop staring.

"You can touch, if you like," and he stepped closer to me.

Instinctively I backed up. He stopped.

"I make you nervous, don't I?" he asked, looking up with his bright green eyes.

"My turn to pee," I excused myself and trotted to the bathroom. Again, I had to think about waterfalls before anything would happen.

Back in the room, Jeremy lay face up on the bed, legs spread apart casually. So tempting, so foreboding.

"Can we talk a little?" I stalled.

He sat up. "Sure. What do you want to know?"

My mind did not offer any immediate suggestions. "You said you were from Ohio."

"Maple Heights, just outside of Cleveland. Moved here five years ago. And you're from where?"

From where I stood I could see his crotch, and he knew it. "Indiana. Fort Dyck. South of Gary."

"I know where that is." He shifted his position to sitting on his haunches. "We went to Dutch Days once a long time ago. Kinda boring. Not a big, exciting thrill for a six-year-old. What do you do there?"

"I'm retired."

"What did you do there?" He's relentless.

"I was the chief of police." I don't know why I'm telling him this.

"Oh, really?" His eyes opened wide. "May I call you 'Chief Stone'?"

That sounds so crass the way he says it for some reason. "'Stone' will be sufficient."

"Yes, sir," he retorted. "Would you please sit here with me on the bed?" He patted an empty spot.

The pounding increased in volume and blocked my thoughts.

"Come on," he prompted. "I won't bite. Unless you really want me to."

The ex-chief of police, afraid of one young man. Or what the young man represented. Ridiculous. What is there to be afraid of?

I re-examined him through squinting eyes and realized it was time to take control. Choosing to sit on the bed, I picked the place, not where he indicated. He smiled at me. I did not smile back.

He cocked his head, shaking it slightly from side to side. His gaze floated to the ceiling. Once again he looked at me and smiled. This time he reached over and started to lift my shirt up. I tried to protest, but he shushed me with a finger to his lips.

The shirt slipped over my head. He tossed it to the ground and I sat half-naked on the bed with him.

"Hmmmmm. Nice." He examined my chest. "Somebody still works out."

As he placed a hand on my chest, he brought his face closer and smothered his lips into mine. Up until that point I had never really kissed a man. Or at least more than just socially.

When he tried to invade my mouth with his tongue, I reacted and pulled back.

"Relax," he cooed. "It feels like your heart is beating a million times a minute."

It was. If I wasn't careful, it might burst right out of my chest.

He used both hands to caress my torso. His touch communicated calming energy. The stiffness of my posture gave way to a feeling of trust I had never known before. I allowed him to connect with both the outside and the inside. My overloaded sensibility shriveled up and blew away. Here is the passion I had been seeking.

When my eyes met his again, he whispered, "You're a man of many secrets. I respect that."

For the first time in my life I felt like I had met someone who wanted me for me, and not the image, the name or the family lineage. I wanted to trust him, but I couldn't. Not right now.

"How did you know?" I inquired.

"That you have secrets? We all have secrets, but you hold yours deep in your heart, where no one else can get to them."

"I meant, how did you know, just by looking at me, that we would be compatible?"

"Mmmmm. I'm not sure." He glanced around the room. "Some things you just feel are going to be right."

"Sometimes," I mumbled, "Sometimes it takes me a while to realize that for myself."

He grasped my hand tenderly, "I know. I know." I caught his gaze. "I'm in no hurry either. I've been hurt many, many times before, and I'm in no rush to repeat those particular experiences."

My curiosity aroused. "You've had relationships?"

"Oh yes. More than I care to remember."

"You're so young." His eyes widened. "Well, compared to me. Have you always been attracted to older men?"

"Mostly." He began caressing my chest again. "I find guys your age easier to talk to. They're usually more settled and way more understanding."

"I'll try to take that as a compliment. Have you ever been involved with someone your own age or younger?"

His cheeks flushed, "There was one under-aged guy a few years ago. He was always high on speed and couldn't get an erection if his life depended on it. I used to call him my 'Boneless Chicken.'"

"That doesn't seem like a very workable relationship."

"There was more to him than that. I tend to see deeper into others than most people." He stared at me so intensely it hurt. "What about you? Any previous broken hearts?"

"No. None that I know of."

"I kind of figured that this would be your first relationship."

I sat straight upright. "What are you talking about? We just met."

He gently tagged my shoulder. "Just you wait."

So insistent and sure of himself. Yet I still wanted to lose myself in him. Just not yet. Not yet.

He reconnected with my chest and slid his hands down to my waist. I tensed.

"Relax, relax," he comforted, "I'm not going to take advantage of you."

Against somebody else's better judgment I released control of my muscles and let him position my body across the bed. I figured now would be as good a time as any to give him a chance to demonstrate his trustability.

Jeremy slowly removed my shoes and socks. Off came the pants. I wanted to protest but did not. As I lay vulnerable before him, he merely touched and stroked me with his fingers. This helped to relax me. Soon he was licking all over in a playful fashion. At first it repulsed me, but then I discovered the pleasurable sensations that accompanied his affection.

He focused most of his attention on my chest. The first time he lapped one of the nipples I practically sprang off the bed. I guess that's what happens when you quickly release pent-up tautness. His hands gently caressed me back down.

When he put his nose in my armpit I wanted to get up and walk away. The nipple thing was bad enough. This felt really dirty and I couldn't imagine anyone wanting to do it, or me doing it to anyone else. His downward pressure on my ribcage kept me from moving anywhere and I had to lie there and endure it. Thank goodness I'm not very ticklish. Otherwise, I might have gushed into spurts of laughter.

Jeremy used his tongue like a massager and applied pressure with it on some of the more knotted places. He forced me to relax. Eventually I gave up and gave in.

For the next hour or so he worshipped my body without it being sexual at all. He sensed my apprehensions before I had a chance to verbalize them, and my trust in him grew. Not once did I feel violated or taken advantage of. I only felt adored and respected.

He had busted through the guarded ramparts and touched my soul. It surprised me; it angered me; it thrilled me.

My original plan included driving him home early enough to get a good night's sleep for tomorrow's journey. With the usual tension drained and my always-tight muscles relaxed, I gently drifted off to sleep in his protective arms instead.

Chapter Nine
Monday

Waking up with another body in the bed is something I had not yet experienced in adulthood. At first it startled me. I'm used to being the only one there.

I had hoped that waking up with someone would have included some sex, but that's not the way things went. Of course, if I weren't such an uptight, old-fashioned, fuddy-duddy there would have been sex. I'm just not ready for that yet.

I stared at Jeremy's back, studying the slight imperfections: acne scars, freckles, scabs. I wanted to caress his skin, but felt I shouldn't wake him.

"You can touch, if you like." Somehow he sensed my being awake. He continues to surprise and amaze me. "I can be ready to go in two minutes." He rolled over to face me, smiling.

"What?"

"You said you had to leave early. I don't want to keep you."

Now I remembered. Last evening I had told him I had an early obligation in order to get him out sooner. Guess that plan didn't work.

"Don't you have to go to work today, young man?"

"Nope." His smile brightened. He leaned over and kissed my nose.

I sat up. "I'm sorry about last night."

He shifted as well. "There's nothing to apologize for. I thoroughly enjoyed myself." He hugged me.

"I thought all guys your age just wanted sex."

He studied my mouth briefly before answering, "There's more to life than sex, Stone." He jumped out of bed and flounced into the bathroom.

Now I was in unfamiliar territory. I wanted him to leave. I wanted him to stay forever.

At last reason won out, as it always does. I have a mission to complete first. There will be time for personal pleasure later.

"It's a long drive." He stood naked by the bed. His hairless body radiated vibrant youth. "Paradise is at least four hours away."

"You've been there?" I found it difficult to concentrate on conversation.

He started some sort of stretching routine. "Once. A few years ago. I have friends in Chico. That's nearby."

Sounds like he wants to play tour guide. He's already taken me places I've never been before. But do I want to spend all day with someone I hardly know?

It would be a very boring drive by myself. However, this is a Top Secret mission. But it certainly would give us time to get to know each other. I shouldn't.

"If you want me to go with you, I'd have to stop by my place first to change clothes."

So confident. Was I ever like that?

"Ummm. I'm not sure I can take somebody with me today."

"Top secret mission?" he teased with a touch of sarcasm.

I decided to respond flatly, "Yes, as a matter of fact."

"Oh, I see." He glanced at the floor.

"Jeremy," I really didn't know where to go from there, but when he looked up with please-oh-please in his eyes it made it so much easier to say, "If only I could, I would."

The side of his mouth wrinkled up. "I would really like to go with you," he admitted while he gathered his few belongings. Then he sat in the chair and dropped his gaze. "I'm ready to go whenever you are."

"I need to shower first. Maybe you could go across the street and get us some coffee." He perked up. "I should be ready when you get back."

"Cool!" He stood up and placed his stuff back on the chair. "What do you want?"

I walked over to my pants from last night and fumbled out a ten. As I handed it to him, I requested, "French Roast, black."

He grabbed the bill and headed out. "Be right back."

During the brief shower I had the chance to revisit last evening. He certainly has been sweet and has not given me any reason to suspect or doubt his motives. It was so hard for me to accept that someone like him would have been looking for someone like me.

"Better enjoy it while you can." Henry's voice seemed to be coming directly out of the spray of water above me. I hate it when talking showerheads are right.

But there are so many issues to consider. Top Dog wants this kept confidential. And what is the point of that? As soon as this man-girl finds out where he-she came from, the well-kept secret will be no more. Since when have I really cared what Top Dog wants? And I *am* retired, I remind myself. My main allegiance should be to me, and me alone.

When I looked at the showerhead again, it was smiling. The smug kind of smile you just want to punch in the…

Okay, okay. He can come with me. But he's going to get some background first so he knows what he's getting himself into.

Knocking at the door made me leave the bathroom with just a towel. When I opened the door Jeremy stood there with two cups of coffee and a big grin. "Yummy!" he drooled as he walked in, staring at me. He handed me one of the cups. The acrid scent of beans perfumed the air.

I took a quick sip. "Jeremy, I've been thinking."

He handed me the change. "Yeah, me, too." After taking a tentative taste from his cup, his face screwed up.

"Something wrong with your coffee?"

"Probably not." He wiped his long tongue around his mouth. "I've never had this before. I decided to give it a try."

"What did you get?" I started putting on some casual clothes.

"Same as you." He attempted another taste but with the same result. "What is it were you thinking about?"

"Oh, yeah," I recalled my thoughts. "It might be nice if you could come along with me."

He interjected, "That's what I was thinking."

"However," another sip, "I need to fill you in on a few things so you know what you're getting yourself into."

"Okay. Do you think you can trust me?" He sat wide-eyed, anticipating my words.

We locked glances for a few seconds. Nothing helps build my trust in someone more than being able to stare into their eyes and them not flinching. He held steady, staring back.

Before I went out last night I had locked my gun in the suitcase. I retrieved it in front of Jeremy and told him, "I have a license to carry this. I don't anticipate using it, but I feel safer with it. Especially when going into unfamiliar territory."

His eyes bulged. "Are you a private detective or something?"

I rolled my eyes to the ceiling. "It's a long story. Let's save it for the drive. Are you ready?"

He stood up, grabbed his things and said, "Let's go!"

We left and walked down the stairs to the car. I unlocked the doors and we got in. "Where to?" I felt like a taxi driver. Maybe I'll get a nice tip.

He directed me to his place about a mile away, in an area he called Noe (pronounced '*No*-ee') Valley. For some unknown reason he had me wait in the car. A quaint little neighborhood, not as bustling as the Castro. I continued to sip on the French Roast as I waited.

It's a little thing, but I feel a bit better about Jeremy now. Having sent him for coffee, him coming back, and with change. The few moments of serious eye contact. Silly, I know, but those are the kinds of episodes that help build trust for me.

He returned in a few minutes, smelling of Lifeguard, hair spiky again.

In jeans and a sleeveless T-shirt he looked very casual–and distracting. He smiled when he caught me looking at him.

Once again he guided me. I followed his directions to the freeway onramp, and we were off on our adventure.

"So why wouldn't you let me see your place?"

He grimaced and launched into his story while we traversed the Bay Bridge. "My roommate is kind of weird. Her name is Alice Latrell, but I call her Alice La Tourette's because she's got that freaky syndrome. All the time she's home she's talking to herself–blah, blah, blah, blah, blah–it's so hard to put up with. Sometimes she suddenly screams stuff like, 'No, no, no, it shouldn't be like this!' Freaks me out." He pointed toward the left. "You want to be in the left lane toward Sacramento. She works at some store called–I forgot the name, but I call it Linens For Days. She's the evening shift manager, so I knew she'd be home."

For a while we drove without talking. He seemed to be content just to watch me drive. Eventually we passed some industrial-looking places that turned out to be oil refineries.

"If you don't like it, why don't you move?"

"Yeah, well, she gives me a good break on the rent and I can't afford to be on my own right now. I'm only working part-time while I'm trying to get into the country music biz. You're going to need two dollars for bridge toll up here."

We drove across a rather short span. Certainly not worthy of the two dollars, but I guess there's no other way around.

"I can't imagine what it would be like to work with her," he continued. "She's so weird! They probably play tricks on her all the time. I mean, I certainly would if she were my boss." He looked directly at me. "So, who's your boss?"

I guess this is the time for the long story. After clearing my throat, I started, "Actually, I'm retired, so I don't really have a boss, *per se*." I turned to look at him looking at me. I felt a shudder similar to the one I get with my first sip of Anchor Steam. "But a long time ago I worked for the Secret Service."

"Cool!" he blurted out. "Did you have to protect the President?"

"As a matter of fact, yes."

His eyes smiled. "Which one? Reagan? Bush?"

I laughed to myself. "A long, long time ago. Kennedy."

"Wow! Were you at Dallas?"

A stinger pierced my chest and I swerved slightly. "Yes, and I was with the agent that slapped Jackie back down into the limo."

"Oh, cool! That was you."

"That was me."

Jeremy seemed quite curious. "And what happened to the other guy?"

"Clint Hill? Oh, he stayed on and retired a few years after I did. We see each other from time to time at reunions." My mind replayed a short version of the day in Dallas for me. The driver in the next lane honked when my car started to cross over the line.

"You're, like, history!" he grinned.

Oddly, that did not make me feel old. Rather admired, actually. And appreciated. A feeling I had been looking for without much success lately.

"My older cousin was obsessed with the whole Kennedy thing," Jeremy rattled on. "He used to tell me all about it and then quiz me on the facts. He would have loved to meet you."

"Where does he live?"

"Oh, he's dead now. Killed in the Gulf War. Got that strange brain fever. Never made it back to say goodbye."

"Sorry. He sounded important to you."

"Yeah," he shrugged. "We spent a lot of time together. I used to hide out at his place when I didn't want to go home. The guy loved guns. He had a small collection of pistols and rifles. Loved to disassemble them, clean them, reassemble them, shoot them and then clean them again. We used to go to the local practice range together. It pissed him off because I was a better shot than he was. Afterwards we would just drive around and talk. With so much crap going on, I needed somebody to talk to. Nobody at home ever listened. He was like a substitute father to me." After a brief pause he mumbled, "More than my real father."

Not wanting to delve into the boy's family history just yet, I picked up the previous thread, "My boss was a particularly con-niving fellow I call Top Dog. As it turned out, Mrs. Kennedy was expecting again when the President was shot." He did not react to this news. "Top Dog took it upon himself to protect this innocent baby boy from possible foul play by having me adopt the kid out under an assumed name." Again, no reaction. "Only a few people knew about this. And now you. One of the others recently disclosed this information and Top Dog thinks it's time to make contact."

Then he turned to me. "Does Clint Hill know about this?"

I'm not sure he does. "I don't think so. I mean, he knew that Mrs. Kennedy delivered a child, but he probably thinks it was a stillborn like everyone else."

"And so it's up to you to go to Paradise to tell this long-lost guy he's really a Kennedy."

I flinched. "Not exactly." Unfortunately, the scenery on this part of the trip is fairly bland: outlet malls and barren hills. Nothing to help distract me. "It seems that 'he' is now a 'she.'"

Jeremy cocked his head. "You mean like a transgendered person? With a sex-change operation?"

"Yes, but not what you're expecting. This change happened when he was a baby, not because he wanted to be a girl."

He scrunched up his nose. "How did the baby know it wanted a sex-change operation?"

A large sigh fell out of my mouth without consent. "His adoptive parents had to make this decision after some doctor botched the guy's circumcision."

A few moments passed in silence. Jeremy squinted tightly and said, "Ewwwww."

"That's what I thought when I heard about it." We exchanged an uncomfortable glance. "Top Dog doesn't know it yet. I'll bet he's not going to be the happiest camper when he finds out. He thought he was creating the savior of the nation, or perhaps the whole human race. He even referred to this kid as 'our last great hope.'"

"You don't think a transgendered person is capable of such greatness?" I could sense his arms akimbo as he defended the entire transgendered population.

"That's not what I mean," I corrected. "I think Top Dog had grand political plans centering around this kid. Unfortunately for him, his last great hope has turned out to be a raging ultra-conservative with a sex change."

"Ooooh. How did that happen?"

"Rebelled against his ultraliberal parents, I guess. They're a couple of new-age hippies."

"You've met them?"

"Yeah. They live in the Haight. Right across from the Dead House."

"Cool."

"Yeah, cool."

"And we're driving all this way because Victor/Victoria Kennedy lives in Paradise with the skinhead Nazis?"

I turned to look at his astuteness. "Yes. How did you know?"

He shrugged slightly. "I don't know. It all fits in, I guess. That area is very popular with white supremacists."

"I see."

"There's a large group centered around Oroville called Aryan Nation, neo-Nazis. Over the last few years some of them have splintered off into different factions." He glanced at me with a raised eyebrow.

"Pardon my inquisitiveness, but how do you know so much about all of this?"

"I told you," sounding rather smug, "I have friends in the area. They've mentioned some of the goings-on. I hear the group in Paradise is the most extreme separatist movement. They call themselves Kinder von Hitler and live at some place called Pale Face Ranch."

"Yes! That's the place they told me I could find her. Do you know where it is?"

"Not a clue." He shook his head. Without asking, he switched on the radio. Static hissed from all around until he started pressing buttons. After a few tries he found a country station. "That's what I want to be doing someday. Singing on the radio like that."

I scowled unintentionally. "Not with the kind of stuff I heard you sing. I don't think the country music scene is ready for someone like you."

"Someone like me?" he emphasized the last word with a flourish. "What do you mean?"

"You know," I floundered.

"No, I don't. You mean young and cute?"

"Not exactly. You are young, and you certainly are cute," and I quickly glanced over at him smirking, "but I don't think the good-ole-boy circuit could handle someone who is so up front about being, well, you know."

"No, I don't know, Stone. What are you talking about?"

"You know. The fact that you… like guys."

He turned to me suddenly, "Can't you even say the word 'gay'? Is that so hard?" His eyes bulged a little. Mine focused tightly on the road ahead. "You're still uncomfortable with your own sexuality, Secret Service man. Well, I'm not. I don't care if the whole world knows I'm a fairy, queer, swishy, poofy, queeny, faggot, gay homosexual." His hands flayed about with each word. "From San Francisco." He dropped his hands onto his lap and faced front.

I didn't know how to respond, so I just waited for him to pick up the conversation again.

A few minutes passed while we listened to Lee Ann Womack wail her woe. The lack of conversation felt refreshing.

"I'm sorry," he spoke finally, "I keep forgetting we live in very different worlds. I've been in San Francisco long enough to have had the chance to experience my sexuality and become comfortable with it. You're from a repressed little town where there is no opportunity to explore and learn what being gay is about. Please accept my apology for blowing up on you like that." He looked up at me with his head hung down.

Not knowing what to say exactly, I just reached over and held his hand. We drove like that until we got to Sacramento and I needed both hands to navigate the Route 99 interchange. After we got off the main road we stopped for some drive-thru food to take with us.

As we headed north to Paradise, our route led us through a variety of fruit orchards and some open grassland. We chatted about the various country singers we admired, which ones Jeremy thought were gay, and how he planned to make his big splash on the country scene. From time to time we also exchanged glances. Eyes sparkled, smiles twitched.

— ◆ —

By mid-afternoon we pulled into Paradise, California, a snapshot town of well-off retirees. I pulled into the first convenience store we came to, the Fast-N-Easy Mart. Inside I asked the clerk about Pale Face Ranch. He stiffened noticeably and told me to stay on Skyway and turn left at the Antique Mall. That would be Honey Run Road. Follow it for a few miles, past the fire station and the covered bridge. The ranch would be on the right and we couldn't miss it. I thanked him and bought a couple of Cokes for the trip. He looked at me suspiciously but still took my money just the same.

Within a minute of driving farther into the town, I had found Honey Run Road and headed out. The scenery changed from small town to rural to a downright deserted one-lane road. The tall, brown grass needed water and the few trees appeared long-dead.

After a few miles of twists and tight curves, we saw the fire station. Around the next bend an old covered bridge spanned the creek on the left. A couple of seconds later I looked off to the right and saw a large wrought-iron gate topped by a huge wreathed swastika. This looked like the place. I pulled into the driveway and stopped the car at the gate. Next to it was a call box. I got out of the car and pressed the button. A few seconds went by, then a gravelly voice asked, "Yeah?"

I spoke into the box, "I'm here to see Chrissy Walsh."

"And who shall I say is calling, sir?" sounded a bit sarcastic.

After a moment I replied, "Friend of the family."

I heard a few clicks and then the curt response, "Chrissy has no family."

Three, two, one. "She does now."

More clicking. "Wait there, please."

"Thank you," I shouted to no one in particular. Back at the car, I requested Jeremy to stay inside, just in case there was any trouble. He nodded his understanding.

A few minutes later a rusty old jeep in a whorl of dust pulled up to the other side of the fence. Out stepped a camouflage suit covering a medium-height, slightly-muscular person with a shaved head and a swastika tattoo above where the hairline used to be. One hand held a cigar, the other an Uzi. Mirrored glasses hid the eyes, but the nose and lips looked vaguely familiar.

"Who the hell are you, old man?" The voice rasped of tobacco, and the low pitch was not exactly feminine.

I wanted to smile; I wanted to slap her. I did neither. "My name is Stone. I put you up for adoption in 1964 in Boston, where the Walshes found you."

"The hell you did," she spat back.

"You have a birthmark on the bottom of your left foot that looks like a clover."

She tilted her head back and looked down her nose at me. Then she took a puff off the cigar and lifted her glasses. It felt like I was looking at John Fitzgerald Kennedy in 1963. My throat filled with razor blades.

She let the glasses drop back into position. "Are you my father?" she asked, more softly, but still raspy. The gun still pointed at me.

"I would like to talk to you, but could you please lower your weapon first?" I pointed to the gun.

"I said, 'Are you my father?'" Louder and gruffer, waving the gun at me. "Answer the fucking question." She glared at me.

"No. No, I'm not. Your father's dead, but I used to work with him."

"Yeah? Well, who the hell are you, then?"

"Is there somewhere we can go and talk? This is going to get pretty complicated." I held my hands out, sweat-drenched palms up.

"We can talk right here, old man." She continued to brandish the gun nervously. "Whatever it is you have to say to me, you say it right here." She inhaled another drag from the cigar.

"Okay, that's your choice." I swallowed and stalled so that I could formulate a plan of action. Eventually my brain kicked out the words, "Your parents were President John F. Kennedy and his wife, Jackie." There, I had said it. My duty is complete.

"The fuck they were!" She aimed the Uzi right at my mouth. "You lying sack of shit! What kind of trick is this? Who the hell are you?"

"It's hard to talk with a gun pointed at my head."

"I don't give a fuck! Answer my goddamned question!"

After swallowing a few sharp-edged lumps, I responded, "Secret Service. Retired. Assigned to the Kennedys. Jackie was pregnant in Dallas. You are that child. My boss had you adopted out for your protection."

"Bull—shit!" she hollered.

At that instant, I looked at my reflection in the lenses of the sunglasses and some of the stuff I had read in the book at the library flashed across my mind. I said gently, "Chrissy, I know what it's like to look in the mirror and feel disconnected from the image I see."

She glanced askew at me, "What's that supposed to mean, asshole?"

I just kept staring at the unexpected image of this rather unhappy child. "I think you know."

She spat at me.

I went to reach for my contact info and then thought better of it. "I want to get a card out of my pocket with my name and number so you can contact me when you are ready to talk more about this."

A moment of intense staring passed between us. She exhaled breathily.

"That's all you better pull out of your pocket, mister. Or my little friend here will remove your hand from your arm." She shuffled the gun around. "Move slowly. No surprises."

In slow-motion I retrieved the card I had prepared to give her so that she could reach me. I passed it through the iron rail and she snatched it quickly.

"All right now. You're done here! Go away! Get the fuck out of my face!" She turned and strutted back to the jeep and drove off.

"You're fucking welcome," I mumbled to myself.

Mission accomplished. I strolled back to the car, one ton lighter.

— ♦ —

"Wow, she sure is a brick," Jeremy commented.

"Built like one," I concurred.

"How did it go?"

Good question. I'm still breathing, so it couldn't have been too bad. "As well as could be expected, I guess. I certainly gave her something to think about." I started up the car and backed out of the driveway. Now we all had something to think about.

"It's a shame we drove all this way for such a quick chat."

"Yeah. A shame," I contemplated.

"We can actually get back faster if we go this way." He indicated continuing the direction we had come in on. "This road takes us back to Skyway just outside of Chico and we can get to I-5 from there. It'll cut out a lot of that small-town traffic we had to drive through earlier."

"Okay." It's nice to have your own private guide. Especially when you're in unfamiliar territory.

"That was so cool. I always wondered what the entrance to that place would look like. Now I know." He smiled at me, but I don't think it was about me.

Chico reminded me a bit of Fort Dyck, but with newer houses and an abundance of college kids. Jeremy told me the state university used to be the premier party school, but the administration has tried to play that down over the last few years and those honors now lie elsewhere.

After a short while we reached the interstate. It actually felt good to be heading back to San Francisco, which surprised me. The wide-open spaces seemed nice at first, but I realized that I felt more secure back in the city. Mostly because San Francisco did not make me as claustrophobic as Boston or Chicago. It's more spread out and comfortable. Plus, the human scenery is nicer to look at.

We stopped at a roadside diner in a town called Vacaville. The food didn't kill us and we hit a good conversational stride. He talked more about the family he ran away from and his dreams of being a county music star. I didn't have to reveal much. Jeremy seemed content to be the focus of the conversation. Just as well; my mind kept going over the events from earlier in the day.

Driving back into San Francisco at night is fantastic. As we crossed the Bay Bridge, we were treated to a sparkly view of the lit-up downtown buildings. My heart revved up a bit. It amazed me that I had that strong of a reaction.

"Pretty, isn't it?" Jeremy asked.

"Sure is."

"Bet you don't have anything like this back in Indiana." He smiled maliciously.

"There are quite a few things I found here I can't get back home." I glanced at him slyly.

He grasped my hand. I started to pull away out of habit, but he maintained his grip. His hopeful smile comforted me.

"Where do you want me to drop you?" I asked.

He stared in my direction for a few seconds. "Your hotel. If you don't mind." He smiled that secret smile, and my heart melted. Honking from the next lane snapped me back to reality and driving.

— ◆ —

Only one parking spot left at Beck's, but that's all we needed. Walking up the stairs felt more like gliding. Up, up, up.

Inside the room we hugged briefly. Jeremy broke away and held out a closed fist. He turned the palm up and revealed a blue, diamond-shaped pill. "Here, take this," he prompted.

I stiffened. "I don't take drugs."

"It's not what you think. It's Viagra."

"Viagra? What do you...? Oh." I guess he's prepared for everything.

"I like older guys, but sometimes there are drawbacks." He held the tablet closer to me.

Henry's voice rang up from Jeremy's hand, "Take me, take me!" My Midwestern conscience would not allow for such frivolity. The little blue pill tempted me, taunted me, terrified me. I applied my ultimate test of sane thinking: "What possible good could come from this?"

I filled one of the drinking glasses on the bathroom counter with water, snatched the thing away from Jeremy and swallowed it hungrily. In a little while we will discover what possible good can come from one little blue pill.

He flopped onto the bed, toed off his shoes and turned on the TV from the remote. After flipping through most of the channels, he stopped on the Country Music Channel. With a come-hither smile, Jeremy patted the bed and requested, "Sit. Relax."

I undid the gun holster and gently placed it on the dresser. You would think after 60 years of tying my own shoes I would be able to accomplish removing them with some ease. I fumbled with the laces, attempting to tweeze them with my fingernails, growing more impatient with each failed attempt.

After reaching an impasse, I grabbed each shoe by the heel and yanked it off my foot forcibly. Jeremy commented on this by fluttering his eyes and shaking his head. He looked at me with a smirk and I knew where I should be sitting. We hugged lying down.

I propped myself up on one elbow and asked, "How long does it take for this stuff to work?"

He smiled maliciously, "I guess we'll find out soon enough." The pressure of his fingertips on my temples helped ease tensions, and I could feel each muscle group loosen its vise.

"Yeah, Daddy," he crooned.

Still not comfortable with that reference, I jerked with a spasm.

"Oh, Stone, you've got to get over yourself." He applied his tongue again like a massage tool. "You're the perfect daddy." His hand held my jaw so that I could not speak. "I just have to teach you how."

My instinctive reaction would have been to toss the kid across the room and pummel him with both fists. I tried to fight that urge, and I went rigid again.

"Let go," he suggested.

"I can't, Jeremy." His name is chocolate candy in my mouth. A rather large lump went down with a hefty swallow. "I've never… had sex before."

"I know," carried some annoyance. "It's about time, don't you think?" His smile conveyed the consoling I needed.

A swelling in my crotch distracted both of us. He slowly slid his hand down my chest. My whole body wanted to resist, but one particular area wanted to cooperate fully. When he got down to the hard part, he looked at me and went, "Ding!" like a toaster oven. "It's ready."

There was not one other person in the entire world that could have accomplished what Jeremy did. For once, I knew what it was like to let down my guard so far as to let someone else touch me in an intimate way. Like he said, it's about time.

Watching him disrobe got me even more excited. By the time he was completely naked, I just wanted to make love to him, this very special child-man, but I just didn't know how.

When I started to undo my pants, he interjected, "Wait! Let me do it." Using only his mouth, he opened my pants and got my shirt over my head. His hands caressed me while he put on this display of oral calisthenics.

Once I was totally naked, he started kissing and licking me, like the previous night. This time he did not avoid the middle. Jeremy licked and teased, apparently delighting in the sweet torture. When he finally applied his mouth to my waiting member, the sensation intensified and I felt like it would end quite soon. He would not allow that to happen, maintaining the fervor without tripping the switch. I finally understood what all the fuss was about.

After a few minutes of pleasure and agony, he retrieved a few items from his discarded pants. Holding one side of the plastic package between his bared teeth, he ripped it open and the rubber fell onto my abdomen. After spitting out the wrapper, he applied the condom to me. When he rubbed lubricant on, I felt like the end was near again, but he would not allow that.

He positioned himself above me and face-to-face. A grimace formed as he lowered himself onto me. His murmuring, "Not yet" helped keep me from going over the edge.

It took a few stops and starts, but he eventually managed to be sitting on me entirely. The grimace became a grin and, "Oh, yeah," flew from his lips.

It felt repulsive and energizing at once. To be inside another human being seems so complex and intimate. But who better than the person you value most in that moment.

He rocked forward and kissed me gently, licking my lips with his tongue. Once again, the fire crackled and the moment approached. "Not yet," he whispered as he started grinding his hips into mine. The moaning intensified, each "Oh, yeah" and "Fuck me, Daddy" getting louder and louder. I prayed the music from the television masked the noises. If not–oh well. This is San Francisco.

He continued my first lesson: gyrating, undulating, writhing. My responsibility consisted of lying still and appreciating the experience. About once a minute he brought me to the brink, only to let the overwhelming lustful sensation subside.

With a loud, "Shit!" Jeremy's body convulsed and spasmed. His boyish erection aimed spurt after spurt onto me, and I tensed with the uncomfortably moist sensation of having someone else's semen on my chest and neck.

Once his contractions ceased, he fell forward and shoved his talented tongue down my throat against my partial objection. The instant our tongues met it was my turn to scream and thrash. The most powerful eruption of my entire life poured into my intimate friend. The entire universe contracted into my skull, and I felt certain that I would stop breathing and lose consciousness.

Then the all-too-short final thrill portion of the hot long ride ended. I worried that maybe I had killed him. When his sweet face smiled wearily I knew he was okay.

We hugged each other passionately, breathing deeply, fast-paced in counterpoint to LeAnn Rimes's nasally twang. The world could have ended at that moment, for all I cared. I had completed my final mission and there would be no more.

It took over 60 years, but I finally lost my virginity.

Chapter Ten

Tuesday

THIS morning I woke in Jeremy's arms. I hadn't expected younger gay men to be so affectionate. I lay thinking about the possibilities and options. He probably wants me to stay in San Francisco to be with him. That would be interesting. Then again, he might want to go back to Indiana to be with me. Slim chance of that. He already escaped the Midwest once; I can't imagine he'd subject himself to that again.

More than likely he'll just toss it up to experience. It was nice meeting you. Keep in touch. Write you soon.

So, what do I want out of this? I don't really know. That makes it even more difficult to prepare for the eventual disappointment. And there will be disappointment. There always is. Two people can never want the same thing simultaneously over time. It's impossible. If Dad hadn't died in the line of duty, I was pretty sure that Momma would have divorced the inflexible, self-centered jerk. He was a hero, yes, but more so in his own mind. Dad was definitely a my-way-or-the-highway kind of guy.

I have worked very hard not to turn out like that. My staff regarded me as more of a gentle steward than a tyrannical bastard. At least that's what I heard.

The young man whose arms surround me wants a daddy. I would not feel comfortable in such a parental role. Maybe there is room in this game to be more like a caring friend than a controlling father.

If I am giving this much thought to such a possibility, I guess it means I want to invest the time to seeing if there is some chance that Jeremy and I could really be a successful couple.

So what is wrong with that? Just because I'm twice his age and I've never had a relationship in my life. He seems like a sweet kid, but I've only known him for two days. I wonder if he feels the same.

He does keep saying I'm the perfect daddy. That's flattering in one way but insulting in another. Sure, I'm over 60, but this is my first adolescent romantic adventure. I guess I want to approach it like a lovesick teenager, not a stale, jaded senior.

"Daddy?"

I shuddered.

"Stone?"

"Yes?"

Jeremy started massaging my neck and shoulders. "How long will you be staying here in San Francisco?"

Good question. Now that I've completed my mission, I'm on my own time. I could leave today or I could wait until Friday, my original planned departure date. Henry's list is just about finished.

"I don't," I had to clear my throat first, "I don't know. Why?"

"Just wondering." He hugged me. It felt like home.

"Don't you have to work today?"

"Nope."

"Don't you ever work?" I rolled over to face him, taking him in my arms.

"Thursday, Friday, Saturday nights." He smiled and it made his nose move even farther off-center.

I smiled. "Nice schedule. Where do you work?"

The smile faded. "Oh, a sex club called Eros."

"Eros?"

"Yeah. You heard of it?"

I sat up. "My friend Henry gave me a list of things to do while I'm here. Eros is one of them."

"I could give you a free pass."

"No. No." I swallowed. "I don't think I'm ready for something like that."

He reached up with one hand and suggested me back down to the bed. "I think you're right," and the smile reappeared. "Who's Henry?"

"Oh, he's one of the guys on the police force I used to work with. It was Henry who first talked to me about being… gay. He recognized what was going on. Guess it takes one to know one. So they say. Anyway, Henry is about one of the only friends I have."

"Sounds like you're lucky to have a friend like that."

"Lucky. Sometimes." I rolled away from Jeremy. "He's constantly pressuring me to do things I'm not ready for."

A tickling finger found its way to my navel. "Excuse me, Mr. Former-Secret-Service-Ex-Chief-of-Police, but if you always waited until you were ready to do stuff, you'd never do anything at all!"

Ouch. That stung. Mostly because it's true. Time for a quick subject change. "So, what's the club like?"

"Why don't you come by and find out for yourself?"

"Can't you just tell me?"

He paused, "Yes, I guess I could."

I waited, but he wasn't speaking. "Well?"

"Well, what?"

Fired by frustration, I rolled over, pinned him on his back and blurted, "Tell me about the fucking sex club!"

His bright green eyes flashed. "Oh, Daddy. You're hot when you're angry."

"I'm not angry!" I roared unintentionally.

"Mmmmmm," purred Jeremy.

His arousal poked my thighs. I wondered/worried whether I would be able to respond in kind. How long does Viagra stay in your system?

His bony fingers did some checking, and we were both pleased with the results. Either I still had some of the medication in my system or things just worked on their own after last night's priming.

"Mmmmmm," purred Jeremy.

We repeated last evening's lessons, a bit hastier, with less passion, more matter-of-fact. It didn't quite match the summit of the first time, but it sure was better than waking up alone.

— ◆ —

"What would you like to do today?" he inquired.

"Aren't you getting sick of me yet?"

His gazed morphed into a soft smile. "I don't think that's going to happen for quite a long time."

My need for privacy frequently pricks at me. I figure other people have that same need. Perhaps not all people.

"You still haven't answered my question," he persisted.

"Which one?"

"Oh, let's start with 'How long will you be staying?' and work from there." His head rested on his balled-up fists.

"My original plan was to go back Friday, but I've toyed with the idea of leaving sooner."

"Why?"

How to explain. "This place is not what I expected."

"It never is."

"And," I continued, "I have felt so out-of-place. I just want to go back home."

"Listen to you," he pointed. "Big Little Old Man doesn't like San Francisco and wants to go home. Hey, Dorothy! Click your heels and repeat after me, 'There's no place like home. There's no place...'"

He stopped abruptly when a pillow hit him in the face. Laughter erupted from it and he pulled the pillow away. "I'm sorry, but you're not in Kansas anymore."

"Indiana," I corrected.

"Oh, you're hopeless." His hands flew up without destination. "Haven't you ever seen...? Oh, never mind." They dropped down.

I found his annoyance endearing, and my heart softened further. "Of course, I have found one thing worth staying for."

"Yes?" The smile returned.

"Anchor Steam Beer." The same pillow hit me.

— ◆ —

We showered and I took him to Squat and Gobble for breakfast. The shirt I lent him engulfed his slight frame, and, seeing it on someone else, I realized that my wardrobe could probably use some updating.

As he forked at a vegetable crêpe, he turned tour guide again. "Do you want to see the Redwoods today? We could go up to Muir Woods."

I guess I should do some sightseeing here before condemning the place. "Sure. That sounds like fun."

"There are trails through the forest. We can have a long walk." He smiled mysteriously, perhaps reminiscing about a previous adventure.

As we walked back to the motel, I took a big risk and grasped his freely-swinging hand. His head turned to me, grinning. "Good Daddy," he sang.

I'm doing it. I'm walking holding hands. With someone I care about. It felt better than I had hoped. I smiled and cried a little.

The drive up took us through the Pacific Heights section of San Francisco. Giant mansions plopped atop of a broad ridge, neatly aligned along steep grid blocks, peered down at us with disdain as we passed.

Driving across the Golden Gate Bridge is an experience we all dream about. The bridge itself isn't that different from other suspension bridges, but it's the dramatic setting of the span that captivates people. Connecting two reluctant, craggy points with its majestic arch, joining alien worlds, foreign countries. The striking differences between where you've come from and where you're going. Leaving the built-up, civilized cacophony of San Francisco and arriving in the serene wilderness of Marin marks the contrast.

Continuing on, we picked up the Coast Highway, following its twists and crooks through the countryside. At points, breathtaking vistas–acres of scrubby valleys or glimpses of the broad ocean– opened up and surprised us. Jeremy had to keep reminding me to stay on our side of the road.

Muir Woods is nestled deep in the redwood forest. A Zen-like calm descends as you enter the tall cathedral of trees. Walking paths escort you through the main part of the park, and hiking trails for the adventurous lead off from time to time.

As we began our sojourn, Jeremy attempted to take my hand. I flinched, pulling back.

"What's wrong?" he tilted his head to the left.

"Not in public," I admonished.

"Excuse me," punctuated Jeremy, "But weren't we holding hands in public this morning?"

"That's different. That was in San Francisco."

"What are you so worried about? That someone will see you?" He pointed at some of the other visitors. "Do you know any of these people? Are we ever going to see them again? Think someone is going to beat us up? Hello," he's starting to get annoying, "Weren't you the chief of police?" He stopped and stared up at me, hands on hips.

While his delivery style is insulting and off-putting, the logic of it makes tragic sense. I grabbed his hand forcibly, squeezing it tighter than necessary and dragged him along. "Happy now?" I asked with a smirk.

We meandered together under the canopy of ancient redwoods. Holding hands. In public. Nerve-wracking as it was, it validated our feelings and expanded my sense of pride. After a while, it didn't even faze me when other people looked at us with dour judgment.

Jeremy asked me to tell him about some of the adventures I had as a police officer. Astutely he avoided questions about my Service days. I hadn't really thought much about the police stories lately, and the telling of the tales excited me as much as him. Once I got started, case after case blended together into a tapestry of justice for Northwestern Indiana. The bit about the drug dealers at Brittany's amused him most.

Reliving my former glory brought life and zeal to the uniformed mannequin that I allowed myself to become. As Jeremy delighted in each vignette, I kept thinking of the self-imposed oppression I had tolerated.

I looked at young Jeremy through a different lens. Here is a man who accepted his true nature at an early age and challenges those around him to accept it as well. That takes more courage than I ever had. Facing loaded weapons and hostile crowds was far easier than confronting my own personal feelings.

He's so right. I was a goddamned chief of police. What do I have to fear from the narrow-minded opinions of others?

A deep breath of magic forest air invigorated me. I stopped and hugged Jeremy tightly to my chest.

"Well," he mumbled into my elbow, "I don't know what this is about, but it sure feels good. I can hear your heart racing." He looked up wide-eyed.

I looked down and whispered, "Thank you."

Without requesting an explanation, he smiled, jutted his chin and nodded his head.

For the next few minutes we walked among the trees, hand-in-hand, not speaking. When we arrived at the out-of-place gift shop and snack bar, I realized how hungry I had become.

Jeremy told me his story while we nibbled on pre-packaged treats and sipped sodas. He escaped Ohio as soon as he turned 18, tired of being beaten up and hassled for being gay. The same beasts who lambasted him in public welcomed his warm mouth and tongue in private.

By the time he arrived in San Francisco, he had designed his entire destiny: to be an openly-gay country-western singer, find the perfect daddy, live happily ever after. Never went to college. No desire for any kind of higher education.

All in all, the afternoon gave us the chance to know more about each other, for me to grow more fond of this little boy with big dreams. I don't know when I've felt more connected to another human being, unlikely as the pairing may have been.

— ♦ —

Dinner occurred in a small village named Sausalito. The restaurant overlooked the Bay and we chatted and ate freshly-caught seafood while the sun set.

Crossing the Golden Gate Bridge at night is not as picturesque as in the daytime, but I enjoyed it all the same, until I had to stop and pay the exorbitant toll.

Jeremy directed me to his place so that he could get a change of clothes and some personal effects. As his roommate worked evenings, I got to see it this time.

The common area of the old, railroad-car style flat practically sparkled from over-cleaning. Not one pillow or piece of furniture caught your eye as being out of place. No dust on the well-watered houseplants.

"This way," he commanded, and I followed him down the narrow central hall and into a pigsty with windows. Posters and ads cut from magazines clung lazily to the wall. Piles of clothes covered the bed and a chair. Jeremy tossed items around until he filled a small backpack and announced, "Ready."

Walking back to the front door he waved his free hand about, indicating the cleanliness and order. "One advantage of having an obsessive speed freak for a roommate. Just don't put something in the wrong place or she'll write you a two-page memo detailing the expectations of proper object placement."

Back at the motel, I opened the door and it looked like I had just returned to Jeremy's mess of a room. Strewn about, my clothing similarly decorated the place, hanging from the lamp and dangling from the bed. The suitcase writhed, empty on the floor. Good thing I had brought the gun with me.

"I think you'd better go," I advised Jeremy, peering in cautiously.

"I think I'd better stay." He placed his backpack on the dresser and proceeded to pick up my stuff.

Transfixed to the spot, I just stood and observed. Who would do this? Top Dog? What was he looking for? The door appeared undamaged–no forcible entry. Someone who had a key or knew how to work a lock. Very professional. But then they threw my belongings all over the place. Very amateur. They obviously wanted me to know that someone had been here.

When I finally unfroze and stepped in to assist, I heard knocking on the still-open door. A middle-aged, Indian-looking man stood there gawking at the scene.

"Yes, may I help you?" I asked.

"Yes, sir. I am noticing that you are having a guest every night, but you are only been paying for one people. Do you intend to have paying for two peoples?"

Of course. I had a reservation for only one. Who knew I would find a second? "Please add it to my bill. I'll settle with you on the way out."

"Thank you very much. Good night, sir." He turned to go.

"Wait, please," I called out.

He paused, "Yes, sir?"

"Did you happen to notice someone else entering my room this evening?"

Without thinking about it, he hastily replied, "We do not pay attention to the peoples going and coming. Please remember to pay for the extra people charge before you leave."

"Thanks anyway." I closed the door and started to assist Jeremy with the clean-up.

"I'm sorry." He tried to comfort me.

"About what?" My mind continued to obsess about the break-in.

"That this happened to you." He waved his hands around the room. "But doesn't it usually mean you're on the right track and that you've upset the bad guys?"

Bad guys? There are no bad guys in this story. I stood silent in contemplation.

"If you still want me to go, I'll understand." His puppy eyes waited for the response.

If there were harm to come, I certainly wouldn't want Jeremy to be here. But if he truly wanted to be part of my life, this is one facet of it too.

Time for him to show his hand. "What would you like to do?"

"It's a little scary here, but I feel safe with you." Hug. Big hug.

After we finished cleaning up, we cuddled in bed and watched Leno together.

"Who do you think did it?" He looked at me expectantly.

"I'm not sure."

"I'll bet it was Top Dog. He sounds wicked."

"Could be." Felt like it was time to go home. "Now, shut up and hold me."

Chapter Eleven
Wednesday

What little sleep I got suffered from spates of paranoid dreams. Pursued by terrorists, snipers and shrapnel-laden bomb blasts, I woke with a jump all too frequently. Jeremy purred in his sleep, and I wiped off my sweat from the latest nightmare.

Trust would not come easy now. Each person would have to prove themselves again, starting with my young bed partner. He was far too nonchalant last night, accepting the break-in with uncharacteristic grace. Could he possibly have been sent by Top Dog to observe me and report? I did react rather badly after he asked for weekly updates. Perhaps this is his way of monitoring things since I might not be as compliant as he would like.

The embarrassing scene on the plane probably has something to do with it. He wants vengeance. My head on a platter. The very last word.

Soon I'll be able to report off to him and be done with the whole affair. His little plan didn't work out like he thought it would. The "Last Great Hope" turned out to be a transsexual, skinhead neo-Nazi. No need for me to add fuel to the fire. The universe has dealt with him in its own way. I just feel sorry for Chrissy, who could have had a totally different kind of life if Top Dog hadn't meddled.

Now what? Where next? Is there a double agent in my bed? His affection came too quickly, almost pre-ordained. How could anyone decide on the love of their life just by looks? It's not possible.

When I rolled over to check on him, he exhaled loudly. So innocent, so trusting. Very childlike. I never thought I'd want someone else invading my life, but if I had to choose, I think it would be someone very much like him. Someone who looks up to me, someone who needs me, someone who adores me, someone who appreciates me.

I think I love him, and I'm disillusioned with myself for it.

It's time to go back home to Indiana. Somebody is after me, and I don't feel safe here. I've got to dump Jeremy, make flight arrangements and settle with the motel. I'll have to come back to

San Francisco again when I'm really retired. I guess mixing pleasure with business didn't work out so well after all.

"Somebody's deep in thought this morning. I can hear the gears rattling."

Jeremy lay there, staring at me. He smiled a little.

"Still going over last night? You're probably suspicious of me now. And you have every right to be. I would be in your place. I also know there's nothing I could do or say that would make you feel any different. Perhaps I should just disappear for a while and give you some space."

That sounds good. We've spent the last few days together and I'm beginning to feel the ill effects of not having my accustomed privacy.

He climbed out of bed and headed for the bathroom. The sight of his naked body distracted me momentarily.

"Yeah. That sounds good. I've got some calls to make."

Over his shoulder he posed, "Airlines?"

"Yes, as a matter of fact." How did he know?

As if he continued to read my mind, "So Midwestern."

"What's that supposed to mean?" I shouted toward the bathroom.

I heard a flush, then his voice, "At the first sign of trouble you curl up in a tight little ball and head home, where it's safe. So typical."

I really wanted to slug him. How dare he dismiss my feelings like that. He may be insightful, but he sure is insensitive. Maybe it's best we have some time apart.

"Is it okay if I shower first?"

"Sure. Fine."

During the next few minutes I reviewed the events of the last few days again and again, coming to the same logical conclusion. Time to go.

I packed everything except what clothes I would need today. The suitcase was still quite heavy. He stepped out of the bathroom and began to get dressed.

"I could drop you off on my way to the airport. I'll just need a few minutes to get ready."

"Take your time," he said, pulling on a sock. The expression on his face defied easy description, but I guessed abandonment figured in there somewhere.

The warm water washed over me as I stood in the shower. I thought back to the other night when Jeremy rudely introduced himself. The nagging thought that I may have passed up a once-in-a-lifetime offer surfaced again, and I had to process this anew. If I leave Jeremy behind in San Francisco, would we be able to continue our relationship from afar? Or even in the future down the road? Probably not. He's young. He won't have any problem finding another partner. Me, on the other hand...

As I dried my hair—my gray hair—my gray, thinning hair—I kept catching glimpses of myself in the mirror. My body is still in fairly good shape for someone my age, but how long is that going to last? How long does anything good ever last? When was the last time I had anything really good?

I can't believe how quickly I jumped to suspecting him, but that's what I am trained to do. He's just a naive kid from Ohio with unreachable dreams. Who says he loves me. Might be one of Top Dog's boys, but that seems extremely unlikely. Every sense I have about the lad tells me he is just what he says he is. Besides, Top Dog likes them hunkier and prettier.

Walking back to the bed with just a towel, I found Jeremy sitting sulking, dressed and ready to go. Like a whipped puppy.

"How would you feel about a trip to Indiana?"

His pout flipped to a smile. He jumped up and hugged me. "You really mean it?"

He let me go and I just stared at him.

"What am I saying?" he gawked. "That's exactly what I wanted to hear!" The subsequent hug carried so much energy there probably wouldn't be any need coffee this morning.

"Let me make that call," I said when he finally eased up. The smile on his face caused the end of his nose to point to seven o'clock.

In a matter of minutes I had arranged two seats (one aisle, one center) on the late-morning flight to Chicago. Jeremy's smile had not faded. Stirrings in my groin felt good, but that would have to wait.

"We'd better get going. Our flight leaves soon. Do we need to stop at your place on the way so you can get some things?"

"Nope. All ready to go." He patted his backpack.

"You mean you packed hoping to go with me?"

He shrugged with a smirk, "Call me optimistic, but I wanted to be prepared for anything."

My eyes glanced briefly at the ceiling, and the stirring down below kicked up a notch. "Let's go." I lugged my overweight bag and headed out.

Jeremy went across to Peets while I settled with the motel. He returned with coffee for me and hot tea for himself.

"Didn't like French Roast?"

He held up the cardboard container, "Not my cup of tea." He sipped gingerly.

We drove directly to the car rental agency, hopped on the shuttle train and took the escalator down to the flight gates. I got us checked in and we had about five minutes to spare.

"Good timing," I offered.

Jeremy nodded his head. His attention appeared to be fixed on a rather attractive man sitting a few rows away. It was Agent Hank. Back from Japan, I guess.

The announcement to begin boarding boomed around us. I felt an unexpected hand on my shoulder and feared Top Dog's unwelcome presence.

"Looks like you're not leaving your heart in San Francisco," came from a familiar voice, but, thankfully, not the one I feared.

Jeremy and I looked up at my favorite flight attendant. We all smiled.

"See you on board, Gorgeous," and he minced through the door to the plane.

"I can't take you anywhere," Jeremy mugged.

Not knowing how to respond, I went with, "What can I say?" and held both palms up.

As we boarded, I kept an eye on Hank Hunk, expecting my old boss to pop out of nowhere, which made the acid from the coffee churn in my stomach. We got to our seats without incident, and the one by the window remained empty.

No sign of Top Dog, Hank ended up six rows ahead of us. It wasn't until the plane was in the air before I could finally believe that the old bastard would not be joining us this time. Maybe Hank is acting as minion.

Many of the other passengers looked Chinese. This is probably the return flight from Shanghai. That explains the presence of the same attendant.

Squeaky wheels announced the arrival of the beverage cart. A cold bottle of Anchor Steam landed on my tray. I smiled.

"And what will Junior be having today?" he queried as he handed us bags of Goldfish.

Jeremy giggled and requested a Coke. He also wanted head-phones. The movie would be "Spiderman," one of his favorites.

Even though the attendant did not charge us for anything, I managed to slip a ten into his pocket.

The first swig of bitter brew sent shock waves through my body. Jeremy had not yet experienced me with my beer, and his eyes inflated. Then he put on the headphones and watched some coming attractions.

Every couple of minutes I looked around the cabin to see what Hank might be up to and whether Top Dog had appeared out of nowhere. The agent just watched the movie, and no sign of you-know-who.

Finally, I tilted the seat back to relax a bit. The beer tasted just as good as the first time. I hope I can buy this stuff at home.

Once the movie got underway, I allowed myself a much-needed nap. Up until this moment, my mind had been racing around the implications of bringing a young man home with me from San Francisco. Who is he? A long-lost relative? I could easily lie to cover up our true relationship. But why? Too many years of false-hoods had already accumulated. I was the chief of police. They'll just have to deal with things the way things are. That's all.

But is Fort Dyck, Indiana, ready to accept its former chief, a direct descendant of the town's founder, as an openly-gay man? That's a question we can't answer on an airplane thirty-something thousand feet in the air.

— ♦ —

"Turkey or roast beef?" The attendant shook my shoulder again. "Lunch time, Sleeping Beauty. Wake up, now," he invited, smiling.

Having become twisted in the seat I had to readjust myself, giving me time to think. "Uh, turkey, please."

He handed me a tray with a sandwich and some other yet-to-be-identified objects. "I figured you more to be a beef man." His eyebrows peaked as he unlatched the brakes and moved on.

Jeremy smiled as he munched on his lunch. The sandwich looked just as unappetizing out of the wrapper.

"How was the movie?" I asked.

"Good. I had wanted to see it again, but I couldn't afford it."

"Couldn't you get one of your other boyfriends to take you?" I teased.

He scowled. "I have no other boyfriends."

"I see," and I smiled a smile I've never smiled before.

A hand on my shoulder startled me. I shuddered.

"Sorry. Stone, isn't it?"

After closing my eyes and exhaling noisily, I looked up to see Hank's beautiful face.

"Hello, Hank. Where's your old master?"

The young agent's face turned quizzical for a few seconds and then he chortled. "Oh, he's back in D.C. already. I stayed a few days in San Francisco visiting. Who's your friend?"

I pointed to Jeremy, "Hank, this is Jeremy."

My new boyfriend reached up eagerly to shake hands with the handsome hunk.

"Nice to meet you," Hank purred.

"Same here," Jeremy volunteered.

I couldn't tell whether the sharp pain in my gut could be attributed to the lunch or this exchange. There's no reason for me to be jealous. Yet.

"See y'all later," and he sauntered back to his seat.

"You just know everybody," Jeremy taunted.

"I've been around."

"More than I would have guessed."

I waited until Hank sat down to continue. "Jeremy, that guy works with Top Dog. The last time I saw him, the two of them were headed to Japan together."

"So?"

I checked again to make sure the agent was still in his seat. "It's a bit of a coincidence that he's on this flight with us. It originated in China. He had been in Japan."

"He said he spent some time in San Francisco. You're being paranoid."

"With good reason."

"He's just a pretty boy. I don't think he's very threatening at all."

My head snapped toward Jeremy. "Not to you."

"Oh, calm down," he whined, "I'm not interested in play toys. I want a real man." He squeezed my hand with a vengeance.

$$-\blacklozenge-$$

The rest of the flight I remained vigilant and fidgety. The plane taxied in to the gate around 4:30 Central Time. I tried to keep an eye on Agent Hank as we deplaned, but I lost sight of him after about a minute.

"What are you looking at?" Jeremy inquired.

"Nothing."

I didn't see him at the baggage claim either. Jeremy had carried his backpack with him, but I continued to be weighed down by my hefty suitcase.

As we stood on the platform waiting for the shuttle, the late-afternoon sun created a glary haze. Seemingly out of nowhere, a red, jeep-like blur jumped the curb and slammed my bag. Luckily, its mass kept it from going too far, but I think it may have left a dent in the vehicle's front fender.

"That was freaky!" Jeremy squealed. "Are you okay?"

"Yeah. You?" I started to collect the various items that had fallen out.

He grabbed a pair of errant underwear and handed them to me. "For the moment. Do you think this is connected with the incident from last night?"

"Not sure," I mumbled. "Still want to come home with me?"

"Nothing else in the whole world I would want right now." His smile touched me in both warm and alarming ways.

We only had to wait about ten minutes for a shuttle going in our direction. Again, sharing it with a family headed for Gary.

Even after we loaded our bags and sat securely in the van, my heart continued to machine gun and the suspicion gland would not quit. I kept running through the list of possibilities, and nothing made any sense.

"Forget it," Jeremy whispered, "You're not going to catch any crooks today." He looked up at me with a reassuring smile and grasped my hand.

At first instinct I wanted to pull away. He tightened his grip and I couldn't.

"What are you afraid of, Chief?"

I snatched my hand back and snapped, "I told you not to call me that."

"Yeah, you're not acting like much of a chief anyway," he trailed off.

Not wanting to be one-upped by this upstart pup, I grabbed his hand and held it firmly until we had to let the other folks out in Gary.

— ◆ —

All through the rest of the trip, I kept worrying about my house. What if someone broke in there as well? Henry was supposed to be watching it, and he certainly would have tried to get a hold of me if anything was wrong. But what if the trespassers waited until Henry left? They could have easily gotten in.

"You're worrying too much." Jeremy patted my hand trying to comfort me. It was going to take more than hand patting to calm me down tonight. "I'm sure the friend who's watching your house wouldn't let anything happen to it."

Sometimes it's good to have a second person around to strengthen your link with reality. Jeremy's resoluteness certainly has helped to keep me calm. It would have come in handy to have had this kind of support through the years. Shame it didn't come until after I retired.

"Hey, don't you have to be at work this weekend?" It just occurred to me.

"Pfft," he buzzed his lips. "That place doesn't need me," he whined. "I should call them from your house, though."

"Okay. Wouldn't want you to jeopardize your job."

"Oh, I don't really care too much about them. And they don't care too much about me either."

I just glanced at him with arched eyebrows and left it at that. With an attitude of superiority like his, they probably wanted him gone anyway.

— ◆ —

The driver followed the directions I gave him, and we pulled up to my place. A squad car waited out front and my chest collapsed.

"Okay," Jeremy whispered, "Now you can worry."

As we unloaded our bags, Officer Petroni approached us. "Hey, Chief. We got a little situation here. Nothing real bad. No forced entry. Very clean. Doesn't look like anything's been stolen, just roughed up a bit. I've called Henry. He'll be right over."

Petroni grabbed my suitcase and nearly toppled over from the unexpected weight. "Geez, Chief. Feels like you took the whole house with you here." He went up on the porch and opened the door for us. "Come on. It's okay."

"Welcome to my home," I murmured to Jeremy as we walked in. My favorite chair lay on its side, the TV had been moved, cupboards left open, drawers hanging out.

"I think you should fire the maid," Jeremy whispered to me, trying to be cute. The situation did not call for cuteness, and I shot him a stern glance.

Petroni dropped the bag in the middle of the living room. "Oooof. That's heavy. We already checked for prints. Nothing doing. You can start putting things back together now."

"Thanks, Officer," I admonished, clapping him on the shoulder.

As he passed through the door, Henry's Honda pulled up. He bounced out and ran inside. "Stone, I'm sorry. I tried to call you earlier, but they said you left this morning. What–?"

Henry stopped abruptly when he caught sight of Jeremy.

"My, my. I guess you took my advice after all," he quipped.

"Oh, shut up!" I snapped. "This is Jeremy. Jeremy, this is Henry."

They shook hands gentlemanly and Jeremy added, "Nice to meet you. I've heard so many things about you," with a sparkle in his eye.

Henry shifted his flustered gaze to me and then back to my new friend, "Can't say I've heard anything about you."

We all chuckled. They looked at each other and smiled.

Henry grinned at me. "Let's grab something to eat at Monica's. You can come back later and clean up. I'll get to know Jeremy a bit better and it'll give Darlene something new to talk about."

We climbed into Henry's car, me in front, Jeremy in back. As he pulled out, Henry asked, "So, at which of those places did you guys meet?"

Jeremy squinted, "What is he talking about?"

I exhaled heavily. "Before I left, Henry gave me a list of places I had to go to while I was in San Francisco. He thinks we must have met at one of them."

"Did we?"

"No. Wait, yes we did. Beck's was one of the places."

"Darn, I was hoping it would have been Eros," Henry bleated.

"I couldn't get him to go there," Jeremy contributed. "It's where I work… worked… and could have gotten him in for free."

Henry pulled his car into the parking lot. "He's an old fuddy-duddy."

Jeremy glanced up at me, "I don't think so."

"Awww, young love," Henry teased as he got out.

— ◆ —

Our usual table seemed different with three people instead of the customary two. I felt invaded, even though it was just Jeremy. Darlene's expression bridged surprise and glee.

"New officer?" she preened.

Henry blasted, "No, it's Stone's new boyfriend," before I could say anything.

"Very funny, Henry," Darlene and I responded simultaneously.

She chuckled coyly and dropped three menus on the table and turned away with, "Be back in a minute to get your orders."

I stared at Henry, smoldering.

"Ouch! Don't stare so hard, Stone. It worked great. Darlene doesn't have a clue."

"That's not saying much," I countered.

We all giggled as she came back.

"What's so funny?" she scolded.

"You wouldn't understand."

"Whatever, Henry. What do you want?"

Henry and I got our usual fare. Jeremy went for a plain cheese thin-crust pizza. I had forgotten about his unusual eating habits. Henry looked over when he started licking his fingers.

"That's kinda cute. Bet it comes in handy."

We introduced Jeremy to Darlene as a relative visiting from California. The scowl on his face informed me didn't much like the idea of being relegated to relative status, but this is still a small town and I'm just not ready to make that big splash yet.

With all the recent activity, I felt suddenly drained. I asked Henry to drop us off. He paid for our meals and could not leave without one final jab at the waitress.

"Here, Darlene," he handed her a few dollar bills. "Put this toward your Keep Fort Dyck Blonde campaign."

"Goodbye, Henry. Good night, Jeremy. See you again soon, I hope," she winked.

When we got into the car, Jeremy reflected, "She sure is aggressive–and clueless."

"And popular," Henry added. "It works for her."

When we got back to my house, I asked Henry to wait a minute. Jeremy and I walked inside, and I went to the suitcase.

"What's that?" he asked, looking at the greeting card I had pulled out.

"A little something for Henry," I responded. Jeremy grinned. "I'll be right back."

Henry rolled down the window and I handed him the card. "What's this?"

"What you requested. Take a look."

He pulled the card out of the envelope and quickly slid it back in. "Stone!"

"What?"

"Nothing. You do like me. Thanks." He drove off wearing a big smile. With more than a bit of trepidation, I went back into the house, not knowing what to expect.

Nothing had changed. Still the same mess we had left an hour ago. Jeremy stood in the living room. I peered into the den, expecting the worst. Everything was fine. Nothing had been touched.

The computer started right up. "Make yourself at home. I've got to send an e-mail."

Jeremy looked around tentatively. "Okay." I would guess the chaos of the place did not appear very inviting.

After booting up, I logged on, singing along with the modem, fearing an onslaught of messages. My mailbox indeed overflowed, but it was getting late and we had some clean-up work to do before bed.

I ignored the unread messages and composed one to Top Dog. "Mission complete. Problems. Let's talk. Stone." Sent it on its way and logged off. I'm guessing I'll be getting a call very soon.

"You sing to your modem?" Jeremy accused when I returned to the living room. He had been restoring items to their proper places. Most of them were in the correct spots.

"Not *to* it, *with* it. There's a difference." I walked around, rearranging the few objects that were out of place.

"Whatever. How did I do with your stuff?"

"Very well actually. I'm impressed."

"Thank you, Daddy."

I shuddered, very much like the first taste of an Anchor Steam. Before I had a chance to tell him how unnerving it felt to be called "Daddy," the phone rang.

"I'll take care of you a bit later, Young Man." He smirked; I picked up the phone. "Hello."

"Guess who?"

"Mother!" I mocked. "How nice to hear from you beyond the grave."

"Knock off the crap, Stone. What problems?"

"Don't you already know?"

"Don't play games with me! How would I know?"

"Didn't you send a 'clean-up' detail after me? I've had my belongings tossed about twice this week."

"No, Stone," Top Dog intoned, "I haven't had anyone on you."

"Are you telling me you didn't have one of your inferiors try to scare me? I saw Agent Hank on the plane. And somebody tried to run me over at the airport."

He paused. "No. I just got back from Japan. I have no clue what you're talking about. At least you know someone else loves you."

I wanted to say "Fuck you!" to the bastard, but he'd probably get off on that. "Yeah. Right. I'll handle it."

"So, what's your good news?"

I told Top Dog everything I could about my journey. He listened intently, tossing out monosyllabic acknowledgments along the way.

When I finished, he politely said, "Thanks for all you've done. I'll take over now. Thanks again, Stone. Sorry to be such a pain in the ass."

He wishes he could be a pain in my "back there." We hung up.

"You're shaking," Jeremy observed.

"Oh," I hadn't noticed. "Dealing with him is never… easy."

"I'm sorry." He grasped my hand. "You were about to discipline me, if I remember correctly." His naughty grin begged for attention.

The phone rang again.

"My, aren't you popular this evening?"

"Hello," I said into the receiver with a modicum of trepidation.

"Stone?" asked a gruff voice.

"Yeah?"

"Chrissy."

Didn't make the connection immediately. "Who?"

"The Kennedy kid," she rasped.

"Oh, yes."

"I wanted to let you know that I'll be coming to visit you tomorrow."

"Tomorrow? All the way from California?" I squeaked.

"I need to talk to you."

"Aren't we talking now?"

"I mean face-to-face."

"Oh."

"Yeah. There's something I want to discuss with you."

"Okay." Now I was at a loss. "Um, do you need my address?"

"No, we got all the information we needed."

"'We'?"

"My people. Oh, sorry about messing up your stuff. Just had to check you out, you know."

"That was your people?" Partial relief, partial disbelief.

"Yep." Said with pride. "See you tomorrow, Stone. Get some rest, you're gonna need it."

"What's that supposed to mean?"

"You'll find out tomorrow. Good night, Stone." Click.

"Wait!" I yelled to the dial tone. As I placed the phone back, Jeremy looked up with questioning eyes.

"You're shaking again, Honey." He braced my arm. "What was that about?"

"It was Chrissy, the brick we met in Paradise."

"The Kennedy kid?"

"Yeah. That's the one." My mind started flipping through possible scenarios of why she wanted to see me.

"What did she want?"

"Good question. I don't know. We'll find out tomorrow. She's going to pay us a visit."

"We better get this place cleaned up then."

"I don't know why. It was her people that messed it up."

His eyes opened wide. "Not Top Dog?"

"Nope. Come on, let's get to work. Leno comes on an hour earlier here. Remember?"

"Leno? I had other things in mind," he grinned, "Daddy."

I closed my eyes and gritted my teeth in hopes the exertion of putting my house back in order would exhaust the young pup.

Chapter Twelve

Thursday

AFTER last night's activities, straightening up followed by spontaneous-combustion sex, I had hoped I would have been too exhausted to dream. No such luck. Between the time I finally calmed down enough to fall asleep and the sunrise awakening this morning, I had been to Dallas twice, Nazi Germany at least once, plus my house burnt down. Jeremy continued to sleep in contented silence. I don't know how he does that.

Not wanting to disturb him after all the help he gave me yesterday, I snuck out to the kitchen. As I opened the swinging door, my nose detected the aroma of fresh-brewed coffee. How could that be? I hadn't set it up last night. One cup worth waited anxiously for me in the carafe.

As I poured my morning life blood, I realized I must have made the right choice bringing Jeremy here with me. It went against almost everything I knew, but felt right in almost every way. It was a big gamble, and I never gamble.

"God, your slurping could wake the dead," Jeremy droned from the doorway, hand over one eye.

"And good morning to you too," I chimed. "Thanks for setting up the coffee."

"You're welcome. I'm going back to bed."

"Shall I join you?"

"Not after you've had caffeine, thank you." He turned and let the door swing closed.

Hmmm. It stung a bit at first. He hadn't turned down advances before. Had I done something to offend him? He is out of his element and probably didn't realize how it sounded. Just needs some more rest, that's all.

A stack of mail on the table looked foreboding, but I went through it anyway. A few bills, mostly junk mail.

After I unpacked the suitcase, I put it back down in the basement despite the nagging feeling that I would be using it again soon.

Downstairs I saw some footprints in the dust on the floor. They appeared bigger than my size nines, and the waffle patterns did not match any of my shoes. Without consulting the police, I swept away the dust, removing any trace of evidence.

Back upstairs in the kitchen, I needed some diversion to take my mind off of the slightly illegal act I had just performed. In case Jeremy might be hungry on second rising, I whipped up a batch of dry-mix pancakes.

The door swung in and his groggy face appeared. "Mmmmm. Something smells good."

"Pancakes," I offered, "Want some?"

"Do you have any syrup?"

"Sorry, fresh out. Haven't had time to get to the store. Been kind of busy." I placed a few pancakes on a plate and set it on the table for him.

"Forget it. I can't eat pancakes without syrup." He started out.

"Can you try? I made these just for you."

His shaggy head shook side to side. "Thanks anyway," and he pushed through the door.

Instead of throwing the plate at him, my first instinct, I grabbed one cake and shoved it in my mouth. I wasn't hungry, but I didn't want to waste food either. Not much taste to it. Probably needed syrup.

So, what's going on with Jeremy? He's been rather unpleasant and grumpy so far this morning. I can't think of anything I might have done to offend him.

The door swung open again. "Do you have any tea?"

"As a matter of fact, I don't."

"Great." The door closed.

Who is this person I let into my house? He looks like the captivating young guy I met in San Francisco but acts quite differently.

When I went to the living room, I found him stretched out in my lounger, wearing my robe, watching my television. I walked over to the set and switched it off.

"What'd you do that for?" he cried.

"I want to know why you've been so goddamned unpleasant this morning."

He sat the chair upright but looked down at his bare feet. "I don't like the way you're treating me," he muttered.

"What?" I exclaimed. "What part of paying for your trip here has been so horrible? I'd like you to tell me."

When he angled his head up, it accentuated his off-center nose. He grasped his pointed chin with one hand. "I wanted you to be more of a daddy to me. That's the image I had in mind for you. I don't think you get it."

"Okay. Fine. If it's 'daddy' you want." I breathed in then erupted like a drill sergeant, "Get your sorry ass out of my chair, get into the kitchen and eat the fucking pancakes I made for you, with or without syrup!"

He smiled faintly. "Yes, Daddy." And he marched through the door back into the kitchen.

I don't get it. I thought he would appreciate being treated with respect, after all the stories he told me about being abused. How was I to know he would want me to continue the mistreatment?

Back in the kitchen, he sat chomping away merrily on the dry, tasteless cakes. He looked up and smiled.

"How are they?" I asked.

"Really bad," he answered.

"Yeah, I know." I tried to think of something a daddy might say. "Well, eat them anyway."

"Yes, sir," the young man responded happily.

I watched as he ingested my hapless cooking. "I thought I would take you around Fort Dyck today and show you the sights."

"That shouldn't take very long." He popped the last bit of pancake into his mouth.

"We'll walk."

He stopped chewing and looked up at me. "Good," he patted his abdomen, "I'll need to work off those lead-belly pancakes."

I managed to arch one eyebrow. "You mean you don't like your Dad's cooking?"

"Not 'Dad,'" he whispered, "It's 'Daddy.'"

"Oh, sorry."

"And don't apologize. Daddy is always right."

"I like that part."

He grimaced then paused. I just looked at his adorable face while he put his thought into words. "When will you be able to tell people who I really am and not some made-up story about a visiting relative?"

"Is that what's really bothering you?"

"Kind of. I would like to hear you acknowledge our relationship openly." He put the plate in the sink.

"What relationship?"

Jeremy swung around to face me. "Come on, Stone. Don't tell me you don't consider us in some kind of a relationship."

Frankly, I didn't. "We haven't even known each other a week. How do we know where this is going? I need some time before I can make that kind of important decision."

"You mean I'm going to have to live under your scrutiny until you decide whether or not you can handle this relationship? That's not fair. What is your heart telling you?"

The robe slipped open revealing a bit of his fired-up, smooth body. Distractions.

I swallowed and responded, "I can't just make my mind up like that. You have to let me absorb all this before it makes any sense."

He closed the robe and tied the waistband. "And how long is that going to take? Days? Weeks? Months?"

"Years, maybe. But if you're as committed as you say you are, then it shouldn't be a problem."

He crossed his arms. "It's just not fair if I accept you unconditionally and you put me under a microscope."

No, I guess that isn't really fair. My heart says go-go-go, but my mind says wait-wait-wait. "Daddy says 'tough'!"

The corner of his mouth shifted up slightly. "Yes, sir," he mumbled.

So, that's how this works. I just have to say "Daddy" and he obeys. Like a twisted version of Simon Says.

He walked over and hugged me. "I'm sorry, but you wouldn't acknowledge our relationship and then you weren't acting the Daddy. I guess I could deal with one or the other, but not both. Thank you for listening to me."

I looked down. "You're welcome. Now, clean this mess up and get yourself ready to go for a walk."

"Yes, sir." He let go and started to clear the table.

I walked into the living room, plopped down in my chair and watched morning television. It's almost how I envisioned married life would have been. This might not work out so bad after all.

A bright, sunny Indiana summer day awaited us outside. Not too hot for late morning, few clouds, tolerable humidity.

I wanted to show Jeremy where I had worked, and I headed us toward City Hall. As we walked up Second Street, he pointed at the Lake County Calvinist Church across the way.

"Is that where you go?"

"No, my family is Dutch Reformed. That one's up another block." I pointed north. "We'll pass by it too. Feeling the need to worship this morning?"

"Not really," he smirked up at me, "All my prayers have already been answered."

Oh brother. He can be so sappy. Sometimes it's difficult to tell if he truly believes the things he says.

Not knowing how to respond to stuff like that, I just pretended I didn't hear it. And lucky for me, he did not elicit a response.

We turned right on Duncan and I could see my old home away from home at the end of the block. Part of me wanted to turn back and part wanted to run ahead.

"There sure are some nice houses around here."

"Yeah. Most of them are over 100 years old."

"And they're still in good shape. Just like someone else I know," and he patted my butt. I jumped.

"Hey! Knock it off! This isn't San Francisco."

"Yes, sir," he chimed.

We stood across from the squat old building where I had held court for many years. Officers waved to me as they went in and out.

"Aren't you going to take me inside?"

I hadn't planned to. I didn't want to. It would be too much trouble explaining Jeremy's presence.

"Maybe on the way back."

"Chicken."

"What did you say?"

"Chicken. I was thinking out loud what I wanted for lunch."

"Yeah, right. After all those pancakes you just ate."

"Walking makes me hungry." He licked his lips at me.

"Stop that!" I commanded with a squeak.

"What are you so afraid of? That someone will find out you're gay?"

"Shut up!" I roared and walked away briskly.

"Fine. Leave me in your little hamlet alone and unguarded. Left to be bashed and beaten by Darlene's redneck boyfriends." He turned and walked the other way.

I stopped and wheeled around. "Get over here now!"

"Is that an order?"

"Yes!"

"Okay, Daddy," he boomed.

I'm sure my face was already red from all the yelling and it couldn't have gotten too much redder from the embarrassment. I walked ahead and stopped when I realized I had reached the old Dyck House. Kids in costumes practiced their Dutch Days pageant on the front lawn.

"Oh, I remember this part," Jeremy remarked as he approached. "Is this the weekend?"

Adults ordered the young folks around. "I guess."

"Goody. I'll get to see it again. Maybe I'll stay awake this time."

It is pretty monotonous stuff. Unless one of your kids is in it.

I turned to face him. "Are you going to behave yourself now?"

"I'm bucking for a spanking."

Even though my mind filled with images of his cute buttocks, I managed to say, "I think you'd get too much pleasure out of that. It would probably hurt more if I refused to spank you."

He smiled. "I think you're catching on."

We walked past the grand old residence as children who had no idea of what they were saying repeated the same old script. The dry, dull history of my incredibly boring ancestors.

I gave Jeremy an abridged synopsis of the story. He thrilled at Old Cornelius and his polygamy.

"Do they re-enact that? I don't seem to remember that part of the story."

"No, they conveniently leave that part out."

"How do they account for all the women he brought with him?"

"Cousins." I intoned.

Thursday

"Not whores and concubines?"

"Shut up!"

"Yes, Daddy," preceded a devilish smile.

We turned up Sixth Street and I pointed out Henry's place. It had been built about fifteen years ago, after the previous residence had burned to the ground following a kitchen fire.

"I think your place is nicer."

"Thanks. Me too. I don't like these newer houses."

"He still has a Gore sign in his window."

"Henry doesn't give up very easily."

"I guess not."

Eventually we got to Jon's Drive-in, a relic from the 1950s. The kind of place where the carhops used to roller-skate up to take your order. The siding had nearly rusted through in a few places and the paint had faded to pastel.

"What's that place?" Jeremy asked, pointing at Jon's.

Caught reminiscing about cruising up with the family in my dad's Oldsmobile convertible, I shook off the memory and replied, "An old drive-in. Still hungry?"

"I doubt they serve chicken there."

He's right about that. The menu hasn't changed in 50 years: burgers, fries, shakes.

"What about that place?" He pointed at Brittany's.

"Brittany's? The drug hang out? Henry was supposed to have busted them while I was gone."

"Cool. Let's go there."

Thinking of my last encounter, I didn't really want to. "You're kidding."

"No. I'm fascinated. I didn't think I'd see something like that out here in the corn fields."

I rubbed my eyes with a hand. "We can go in, but I don't want to eat there."

"You're such a poop."

"Just wait. You might come to the same conclusion."

Inside, Winnie whittled her nails unhurriedly with a hunting knife. Only one other patron sat at the grimy counter.

After finishing the nail she was working on, she nonchalantly looked up, "Can I help you boys?" She seemed drawn to Jeremy.

"Just looking," I said. The waitress must not have been looking at me because I am fairly certain she would have remembered me from the other evening.

"We're from the DEA," Jeremy bluffed.

My head snapped in his direction.

"Get out of here," she ordered.

"Jeremy," I cautioned.

"Get out of here," she repeated.

"Wouldn't want to eat in this nasty old dive anyway, honey."

Once we got outside, I blasted him. "What do you think you were doing in there?"

He shrugged. "Just having some fun."

"I don't think you understand how dangerous those people might be."

"What's she going to do? Freeze me to death with her icy personality?"

"Her friends don't play with toy guns. They are real, wanted criminals."

"Whatever." He brushed it off. "Are those golden arches over there?"

Yes, even Fort Dyck has a McDonald's. We walked down U.S. 41 and into the chain store. Jeremy ordered the chicken sandwich he had mentioned earlier. I got a Big Mac.

– ♦ –

You can't go directly from there back to my place, and we had to walk along the State Route. When we got to the Donut Hut, one patrol car sat in the parking lot.

"That's classic," Jeremy mused, pointing at the black-and-white.

"The place would probably go out of business if Henry left the force."

Jeremy chuckled. The door opened and, oddly enough, Henry stepped out holding a bag in one hand and a cup of coffee in the other.

He held up the bag and smiled. "Got a little something for the boys. You guys want a lift?"

"No, we'll walk. Thanks."

"Okay, Stone, but it looks like you have some company waiting for you at your house."

Company? How could she have gotten here so quickly?

Henry got into the patrol car and drove off. We picked up our pace.

Jeremy looked up at me, "You think it's the Princess Kennedy already?"

"Guess we'll find out when we get there."

I didn't know whether to feel honored or frightened. Why is she singling me out? Maybe she wants revenge. That's why she had my place sacked. Now she's here to do it in person. What did I do to deserve this?

We started walking faster, turned up Second Street, and when we got to the corner of Grant, I could see a rental car parked in front of the house. As we approached, I could also see that the car was empty. The fuzz on the back of my neck tingled.

Jeremy looked up at me questioningly, and I put a finger to my lips. This was no time for jokes. I had left my gun at home, not expecting to need it in my own home town.

I surveyed the front porch. Empty. To add to the dramatic tension, the spring on the screen door squeaked as I opened it. With my heart pounding, I turned the knob of the front door. I could hear the television, then it switched off. Someone was definitely in there. The tang of cigarette smoke nipped my nose. I motioned to Jeremy to wait on the porch.

Slowly, I pushed the door open with my foot, just in case I needed both hands. Seated in my favorite chair with a smug grin was Top Dog.

"You Midwesterners should really learn to lock your doors," he chided and then took a drag off his cigarette.

"What are you doing here?" I barked.

"I was just in the neighborhood. Thought I'd stop by. Didn't think you'd want me sitting out front, so I let myself in. You have an ashtray?"

"No, I don't," I replied, waving the swirling smoke away with my hand. "It's okay, Jeremy," I yelled out, "Come on in."

"Jeremy?" Top Dog mused, shaking his ashes to the floor.

The door opened and my young friend entered cautiously. I introduced him to the old bastard. They shook hands.

"You've got good taste, Stone." He smiled.

"What do you want?" I was in no mood for his sadistic games.

"I told you, I was just in the neighborhood, Stone."

"Cut the crap. What's going on?"

Top Dog's eyes opened wide. "Well, who do you have to fuck to get a drink around here? I hope it's him," he pointed at Jeremy.

The young man giggled, unaware of the old man's predilection. I shot Jeremy a stern glare, and the smile disappeared.

"How 'bout I get us some beers from the kitchen," Jeremy offered.

"Mighty kind of you, sonny. You old enough to drink?"

As he passed through the swinging door, Jeremy slung a stinging glance at the old bastard.

"Did he follow you home from San Francisco? Think your mommy will let you keep him?" Top Dog laughed a hearty haw. "Nice place you got here. Too bad it took so long to get an invitation."

"What are you talking about? I didn't invite you."

"No, you didn't. I invited myself," and he let fly another peal of laughter.

Jeremy returned with three bottles of Milwaukee's finest and handed one to each of us.

"A toast," Top Dog raised his, "To success!"

Jeremy and I exchanged puzzled looks. "What success?" I asked.

Top Dog stared at me with his cold, fiery eyes. "You completed your mission and located the child."

As Jeremy and I sat on the couch I said, "Yes, I did, but I didn't expect you to be so happy about the news, though."

"And I hear you're having a visitor today."

"News travels fast." I took a swig of the beer. Nowhere near as good as Anchor Steam.

"I was hoping to meet this very special person."

Oh, so that's it. The only way he had to connect with his creation was to tap my phone and wait in my chair.

"I don't know when she'll arrive," I stated.

"That's okay. I can wait." He took a sip of beer. "Do they deliver pizza in this backwater burg?"

                    Thursday

As if on cue, a vehicle pulled into the driveway, and we all looked out the window as one. Chrissy stepped from the passenger side of a red jeep with a dent in the front fender. She checked left then right, and strode to the door.

"Stone!" she bellowed. No knocking for her. Dressed in camouflage fatigues topped with a green beret, she stood outside, waiting to be received. At least she didn't just let herself in and flop down in my chair, like some people.

"Sounds like you have company, Stone," Top Dog taunted.

"Yeah." I walked to the front and let Chrissy in.

"Stone," she barked as she entered.

We all stood together in my living room: me, my boyfriend, my old boss, his creation. A real classy photo op.

"Chrissy, this is Jeremy," they nodded to each other, "And this is..."

"Wait! Don't tell me. I think I know who this asswipe is!" she roared. "Yeah. It's that guy you told me about." She poked a stubby finger at Top Dog. "If it weren't for you, shit head, I'd be sitting on a yacht off Hyannis Port drinking cocktails with the rest of the Kennedys–and my *penis*!" she spat the last word at him.

Top Dog held out his hand to shake. "I'm so happy to finally meet you," he crooned. "This is a wonderful opportunity."

Chrissy refused to take his hand. "Get the fuck out of here, mister! I don't want to see any part of you, except your backside leaving."

"Can I at least have a chance to explain?" he backpedaled. It gave me joy to see someone finally boss him around.

"Get the fuck out! Now, motherfucker!" She removed the beret, revealing the swastika tattoo. Top Dog's eyes bulged in horror. Chrissy casually tossed the hat on the end table and then stared down the old bastard. "What the fuck are you waiting for? Get the hell out of here!"

Without another sound, Top Dog put down the beer and walked toward the front door. I could sense the gears turning. No one gets the best of him.

"If you want some good pizza, try Brittany's over on U.S. 41 and Lincoln," Jeremy suggested.

I almost spoke up to correct the situation, but realized his mischievous ploy before I said anything. I just smiled at him and he smiled back. He's a smart kid. Unpredictable at times, but smart.

After Top Dog's car pulled away, Chrissy spoke, "Good. Now that the bastard's gone, let's sit and chat."

Jeremy looked at me for a cue. I shrugged and stuck my lower lip out a bit, and we sat again on the couch. Chrissy commandeered my lounger. She pulled out a cigar and lit up before I had a chance to object.

"Nice place you have here," she puffed while looking about.

Not sure of what else to say, I went with, "Thank you."

She picked up the beer Top Dog had left, wiped the opening with her sleeve and took a big swig. "This ain't too bad either."

Jeremy and I exchanged quick glances. He hunched his shoulders a little. No help there.

I looked over at the rather large person in my favorite armchair puffing away on a stinky cigar. "Is there something you wanted to talk about?"

Laughter rang through the house as Chrissy opened her mouth wide and leaned back. "Stone, you crack me up. Two-thousand-mile trip. No chit-chat. Right down to business. Let's get to it. You want to know why I'm here, yes?"

A second went by before I realized she was waiting for me to respond. "Yes. Yes, I do."

"Sure," she punctuated with the cigar. After a big swallow of beer she continued, "When you came to see me in California, you tried to tell me that my birth parents were John and Jacqueline Kennedy. Right?"

"Yes."

"John Fitzgerald Kennedy?"

"Yes."

"President John Fucking Fitzgerald Kennedy!?"

I could do without the obscenities. "Yes."

"Hmmmm. And your boss thought he could keep me safe by having me adopted out under a fake name?"

"Yes."

"So the Walshes–lucky bastards–got me, and the rest, as they say, is history."

"Yes." I couldn't think of anything else to say.

"Fuck!" Chrissy erupted. I started to worry that my neighbors would get alarmed, but then I realized the jeep parked out front had probably already given them a case of nerves.

She threw her head back and sucked the remains of the bottle in one swoosh. "I need another beer, pipsqueak."

"Sure." Jeremy practically flew into the kitchen.

Chrissy looked at me, and I could see what looked like a small tear in her left eye. "Tell me about my parents, Stone."

My heart choked and coughed. This brash, overblown skinhead now wants to know about mommy and daddy.

"Well," I searched for words, "That was a long time ago. It's hard to remember everything."

"Just give me a few choice tidbits that other people don't know, something I didn't read in school books. You get me?"

I scratched my head and started with, "I have to be honest with you and say that I really didn't care much for your father. Not because of anything he did to me. He always treated me–and all the other Agents–with utmost respect. Took the time to learn all of our names and always addressed us personally. It's just that he was so darn liberal."

She grinned. "Can't say I'm too keen on that either."

Jeremy returned and handed Chrissy a bottle. She looked up at him and smiled.

"You're all right, pipsqueak. Not bad at all." She turned to me. "You got good taste, Stone."

"So I hear," and I emptied my bottle. "Your mother was a class act all the way. She knew what your dad was out doing behind her skirt, but she went right on being the absolute best First Lady she could be."

Chrissy clucked her tongue. "It's still difficult to believe this stupid switch-the-baby thing. Doesn't make sense. Doesn't seem right."

"She was also a great wide receiver."

"Football?" accompanied by a puff on the cigar.

"Up at the compound. With the rest of the clan. Used to play on the big lawn. I tackled your dad pretty hard once and then realized what I had done. Sacked a guy with a bad back who also happens to be President of the United States. I tried to apologize and he just laughed. 'Relax, Stone. It's just a game,' he said."

"I certainly didn't get to play any football with the Walshes." She took a swig of beer. "They didn't want their precious little girl to get hurt. Fuck, I wanted to climb trees and punch guys out, just like the other boys. No, I had to sit and listen to their loud-mouthed, liberal friends wailing about their bleeding-heart causes. Waaaah, waaaaah, waaaaaah," she imitated wailing, "Bunch of cry-babies. Made me want to puke."

"But you got to know some very famous people."

She shot a glance back at me, "And so did you," one eyebrow went up. "Doesn't mean we have to like 'em." Another slosh of beer.

"That's certainly true." I turned to look at Jeremy. He appeared entranced by our interaction. "What made you get involved with this supremacy movement?"

Chrissy nodded and then puffed on the cigar. "Good question. I got to the point of hating the Walshes so much for what they did to me and what they put me through, I wanted to do something that would make them really, really upset. I wanted revenge. Sweet, sweet revenge. So, I joined up with Aryan Nation, figuring it would be about as far away from their beliefs as possible. After a while I realized that stuff started to make a lot of sense. But even they were a bit liberal for me. So when some of the guys broke away and started Kinder von Hitler, I went with them."

"Do they know you're not really a woman?" Jeremy broke his silence.

"Do you know you're not really a man?" Chrissy spat back.

"Excuse me?" Jeremy blinked in disbelief.

"You take it up the ass, little boy. Not very manly," and she puffed a cloud of smoke from the cigar.

"I take it like a man, thank you very much," Jeremy retorted. I stifled a smile.

Chrissy cackled. "You're all right, kid."

"Gee, thanks," he muttered.

"So, what brings you to our neck of the woods?" I asked, trying to move things along.

"Oh, enough small talk. Back to business now. Okay. Stone, old man," she sucked and puffed, and then stared right through me, "I want you to work for me." Cigar ashes flittered gently down.

"What?" Her request caught me off guard. The smoke started to sting my eyes, and I could feel protective tears forming.

She smiled. "I'm making a run for our new congressional seat, and I want you to be my personal bodyguard during the campaign."

So many questions hit me all at once, overwhelming my thoughts, and my eyebrows raised to their highest position. What have we unleashed?

"My people have been wanting a representative seat for quite a while," she continued. "The information you have provided me has given us hope. With a name like Kennedy to go with, I can't lose."

So many questions. Many, many questions. Where to start? "Umm, why me?"

"Umm, why you?" she mocked. She shook her slightly tilted head and responded, "You're the only one I can trust who's not in my group. How's that?"

"What about those goons you left out front?" I pointed toward the jeep.

"You said it: they're goons. I need a respectable presence for inside work. They can stand guard outside; you'll be with me."

I looked at Jeremy. He raised one shoulder, giving a non-verbal indication of not knowing what to say. "What if I refuse?"

"You can't." She took another stinky drag. "You owe me."

Jeremy breached his silence, "Why does he owe you?"

Chrissy's head rotated slowly on its short neck. "I wasn't talking to you, pipsqueak." She smiled in a slightly-menacing way. "I'm giving your boyfriend here a chance to redeem himself."

"I don't need any redemption today, thank you."

"My father died because of you," she accused, driving a two-foot, rusty needle through my chest. Any resolve I had mustered now crumpled.

"Isn't it too late to file for candidacy?" Jeremy asked.

"Sure is, pipsqueak. But I'm running as a write-in candidate, for your information. I'm counting on the Kennedy name recognition factor."

That brought me back. "So, you believe me now?"

"Doesn't matter what I think. It's what we can get the public to believe that matters."

She's not stupid.

"Especially with you there by my side to corroborate the story." Another slow puff. "With all the recent terrorism and shit, I think most people are ready for some White Supremacy." She banged her free hand down on the arm of the chair.

"But it's so hateful!" Jeremy cried. "Your people hate just about everybody."

Chrissy narrowed her eyes as she stared at him. "It's not just about hate, pipsqueak. I don't think you understand. It's about protecting the rights of citizens. We gotta start cleaning up this country before it's not worth saving anymore."

Scary to think what her idea of "cleaning up" would be. An ultra-reactionary skinhead neo-Nazi using the Kennnedy name to get elected. It's almost laughable. Unfortunately, she had me by the balls of old guilt, and my usually-sharp, instinctive defenses went numb. I figured she'd never get elected on that platform, and I'd be off the hook in a few weeks.

"Okay, I'll do it," and with that, Jeremy's jaw dropped. "But you have to tell me the real reason you want me specifically."

"I already told you," she puffed.

"You told me part of it, yes, but I don't believe that's the whole story."

She smiled that malicious smile again. "You're good, Stone. That's why I like you." She poked the cigar butt at us. "And I think you, more than most people, can understand some of what I've been through." She winked. While I suppose it was intended to be endearing, I shuddered.

"I think you're also struggling with your own identity issues," she went on, taking a puff every so often. "When you told me that crap about looking in a mirror and not identifying with the image, I figured you might understand my problem. I'm a freakin' man trapped inside a goddamned woman's body, and I'm royally pissed."

We all exchanged glances and tried to guess the others' thoughts. Chrissy smiled wide.

"You're a big faggot trapped in a law man's body." She pointed at me with the cigar hand. "At least you got a dick to play with. All I can do is eat pussy." More smiling. "Man, do I love to eat pussy."

Just like your father, I couldn't help thinking.

Her smile dropped. "But I'll never, ever get to fuck anyone. I'll never have the same chances as any normal guy, because my dick got lopped off by some stupid ass doctor, and they made me look like a fucking girl!"

Blood rushed to her forehead, illuminating the swastika. Veins on either side throbbed in rhythm. Sweat meandered down her face.

Chrissy just stared at me through slit eyes and nodded. It was JFK deciding to hit the Bay of Pigs, launch a moon rocket, stand firm against Krushchev. *Ich bin ein Berliner*. Out of the ashes of the American Camelot rose a phoenix of a much paler color.

"We got you on a flight tomorrow." She reached into a pocket, pulled out two tickets and dropped them on the end table. "My first public appearance will be this Saturday at a local school in Paradise. Do you want us to supply you with a weapon, or do you want to use your own?"

I tried to think of where I had left my Baby Glock. "I'll use my own, thanks."

"Okay." She stood up and swigged down the rest of the beer. As she put the bottle down, she retrieved the beret and placed it on her head. "Some of my people will pick you up at the Sacramento airport tomorrow."

"It's too late for me to arrange a shuttle now. They need 24-hour notice."

She patted me on the shoulder. "All taken care of, old man. Get packing. See you tomorrow."

As Chrissy strode to the door, her demeanor, her swagger, commanded attention. So self-assured.

"Gentlemen," she turned to acknowledge us, then opened the door. Chrissy looked back, "Hey, pipsqueak, that was a cute bit, sending that old bastard to Brittany's." She smiled, turned and left.

We stood staring at each other as we listened to the jeep pull away. I had no idea what to say. Did I just agree to serve and protect the new anti-Christ?

"I really want to ask you what you think you're doing, but I'm afraid you don't know," Jeremy looked up with one eye squinting.

"Yeah," was all I could say.

"I can't believe that you're going to put yourself in harm's way for this freaky fascist hate-monger." He started to get worked up.

"She stands for everything I'm against, and I just can't understand where you're coming from."

"No, I don't think you can." Not that it was any easier for me either.

I needed some distracting activity and started to clean up the mess left behind by the two smokers. Jeremy and I worked together as a team until another car pulled into the driveway. We looked at each other with a *what-now?* expression.

Outside, I could see Henry walking up to the door. I went to let him in.

"Pheww!" he remarked, waving his arms around. "Who's been smoking in here?"

Not knowing how to fully explain it, I just said, "It's a long story."

"Tell me over dinner." He pointed his thumb toward the car, and we both moved robotically out.

— ◆ —

"Holy shit!" Henry blurted when I had finished telling him the story over a giant pizza at Monica's. There was no reason to withhold any information now. Chrissy would be going public in two days.

"No wonder the freak's so angry. No cock. Probably never had an orgasm in his entire life. I'd be fucking angry myself." Henry held nothing in reserve.

"More like lack-of-fucking angry," Jeremy contributed.

"So he/she rebelled against her ultra-liberal parents and became a white supremacist." Henry missed his calling. He should have gone into psychology. "And now that you told her about being the long-lost child of the Kennedys, she's running for public office." He cracked up with laughter.

Darlene rushed over, "Henry, if you can't keep it down, I'm going to have to ask you to leave."

"Sorry, Darlene, we're just having a good time."

"You want another Coke, Jeremy?" she fluttered her eyelashes futilely.

"Yes, please." He held his glass out for her, and she smiled at him as she took it. "Totally clueless," he whispered after she was out of earshot.

"I can't believe you're going through with it, Stone." Henry swiped the last slice of pizza without asking. "You must be harboring a shitload of guilt to get roped into something like that."

"Somebody's hungry tonight," Darlene teased Henry as she set down the full glass. "You boys want another one?"

"I'm not very hungry," I managed to say.

"Me, either," Jeremy agreed.

"I think I'm about full," Henry announced. "Just bring me the check."

"Henry," I started to object.

"Forget it, Stone. You guys are so entertaining. Besides, aren't you on a retirement budget?"

"Whatever, Henry." I guess I'm not comfortable when he pays for all three of us two nights in a row. "Let me get the next one."

"Okay, you're on." He started to pull some money out of his pocket. "Hey, do you guys need a ride to the airport tomorrow?"

"Thanks, no. Chrissy arranged everything. We've got to get home and start packing."

"You've got to start packing," Jeremy piped in. "My shit's already packed." He and Henry chuckled together. I guess I'm not finding things so funny.

We got up and moved to the door. Henry settled with Darlene, continuing his teasing, I'm sure, but I wasn't paying particular attention.

He dropped us of in front of the house. "Wish I was going with you guys. Good luck, Stone."

"Thanks."

"Thank you, Henry," Jeremy smiled shyly, and for the first time I felt a burning pang of jealousy in my chest.

— ◆ —

Inside, I headed directly for the suitcase. It snickered with amusement as I retrieved it once again.

Jeremy had flopped into the lounger, absorbed in some documentary about penguins in Australia. Just as well, because I didn't feel like talking anyway.

Since I anticipated being away just a few days, I only packed a few sets of clothes, including my dark suit and the gun. At least the bag wouldn't be as heavy this time.

Given today's events, I anticipated a minefield of dreams later tonight. This might be the stupidest thing I've ever done, and I'm being motivated by guilt over some incidents from 40 years ago. But maybe it will give me a chance to finally assuage the unre-solved feelings and give these ghosts a proper burial.

When I finished the inventory a second, or maybe third, time, I closed the suitcase, and noticed Jeremy standing by the bed, watching me.

"Oh. How long have you been there?"

"Umm, not long."

"Get tired of penguins?"

"No. Just wanted to see how you're doing." His lowered eye-brows conveyed concern.

That felt nice. I walked over and hugged him lightly. "I think we'll be all right," I whispered.

"We?" he trumpeted. "Is that the royal 'we' or are you finally starting to include me in your personal thoughts?"

I looked down at the tip of his crooked nose and commanded, "Daddy says, 'Shut up' now."

He smiled and hugged me hard.

Chapter Thirteen

Friday

As predicted, my numerous dreams ended in various catastrophes. Fires, bombings, shootings, riots. The only thing missing was me being nailed to a large, wooden cross.

Of course, Jeremy slept in silent slumber. Smiling. I wake in cold sweat. He's lost in pleasure.

My goodness. I just realized this is the first time someone else has ever slept in my bed. The momentous occasion passed without fanfares and balloons. No flares, no drum roll. Hmmmm. Why couldn't something like this have happened before now? While it would be more delightful to spend the rest of the day lost in contemplation of this event, I do have obligations.

The shuttle will be here in a half hour. As much as I hate waking him, he's going to need the time to get himself ready.

"Jeremy," I cooed, gently nudging him.

He rolled over.

"Jeremy," I said aloud, hoping to get through to him.

Nothing.

How I wish I could have a night's rest like that. Perfect, peaceful, solid sleep.

"Daddy says it's time to get up." The trump card worked.

One eye, then the other, slowly opened to the dim dawn of day. He smiled at me and swallowed.

"What time is it?" he asked with broken voice.

"Five o'clock. The shuttle will be here in half an hour."

"Let me sleep for fifteen more minutes. You shower first."

He sure is bossy for someone who's supposedly looking for a daddy. I bent over and kissed him lightly on the side of his nose.

"I'll be back in ten minutes."

"Fifteen."

"We'll see."

Even though I didn't need to, I climbed over his floppy body to get out of the bed, jostling him from side to side. I stood and looked down at the crumpled young man.

"You're mean," he offered. "Go shower," he ordered.

"Hey! Who's supposed to be the daddy around here?"

"You are. Now, go away and let me rest."

In the shower the warm water washed off yesterday's residue. I wished I could just as easily cleanse my conscience. Carrying around 40 years' worth of guilt is no easy task. The job I am about to undertake will not change anything that's already happened. So why bother? If this minor sacrifice can remove just one brick from my wall of shame, I will feel like I've accomplished something.

Once again the kitchen smelled of fresh-brewed coffee. I'm beginning to like having a slave boy around.

After sucking down the morning mud, I returned to the bedroom to apply further motivation to Jeremy. Much to my surprise, he was dressed and ready to go.

"No shower today?"

"No. I'll wait until we get there," he mumbled, lacking in energy.

"Okay."

I finished getting dressed, and he sat watching me from the bed. A horn tooted out front, and we looked at each other expectantly. I walked over and hugged his shoulders. "Come on, sleepy head. You can nap in the shuttle."

We carried our bags out front, and a tall man in a blue turban stashed them in the rear of the van. We climbed into the back seat and settled in for the ride to Chicago.

Neither of us slept on the shuttle ride. The driver turned on the television for us and we watched the morning shows. In Gary we stopped to pick up a young fellow in a business suit. After a brief nod of acknowledgment, he secluded himself in the other seat with *The Wall Street Journal*.

Inside O'Hare we got left at the appropriate area for our airline. Not my usual one. Guess I won't be getting free beer today.

I checked in my bag. Jeremy would carry his with him.

We made it through security okay, but it took a few minutes to deal with the gun. Apparently, this airline is not used to having passengers who carry firearms.

This airline's gates are also farther away, and it was quite a walk. Eventually we got to our gate with only a few minutes to spare.

Our flight had one stop in Las Vegas. Neither of us had ever been there, and we didn't know what to expect.

We took off a few minutes late, without any explanation from the crew. Their in-flight magazine held my interest for a while, but Jeremy fell asleep promptly.

After a few minutes of continuing contemplation, I couldn't hold my eyes open either, and I succumbed as well. We both woke as the plane began to make its approach into Las Vegas. Jeremy wanted me to look out the window at all the fancy hotels, but, of course, I wouldn't. He warned me he would be having chicken again for lunch.

Inside the terminal, just as I had feared, stood rows and rows of slot machines. Jeremy wanted me to try my luck, but I am adamant against gambling.

"It's a big waste of time," I told him.

"And we have time to waste," he retorted.

Our flight to Sacramento wasn't leaving for about an hour. I started to walk toward the snack bar, when something caught Jeremy's attention.

"Look, a Spiderman slot machine! I have to play that."

I stopped walking. "Fine. Go ahead. I'll wait over there," I pointed to the snack bar.

He looked up with the puppy eyes. Then I knew something was coming down.

"I need some money, Daddy," he pleaded.

"No." That was easy.

"Please."

"No."

"Please, please, please, please, please, please."

"No."

"Whatever I win will be yours."

"No." I made the mistake of looking down at the you're-breaking-my-heart expression. After grunting my displeasure, I took a twenty out of my wallet and handed it to him.

"Thank you, thank you, thank you, thank you." He grabbed my hand and started pulling me toward the blinking lights.

"I don't want to," I tried to say.

"Please be with me," he whined.

Against my desires, I stood there as he fed the bill into the hungry machine. He reached over and pulled the handle. I wanted to look away, but I couldn't.

Fives, sevens and spider webs whooshed by on the reels. Nothing.

"You want to pull the handle?" he asked.

"No." It was bad enough just standing this close.

He pulled it again and again, delighting in watching the spinning reels. After a few minutes he looked up at me, pouting.

"All gone already?"

"No. There's enough for one more time. I'd like you to do it."

"No. You go ahead."

Again he glanced up with that hurt look. He wants me to share his enthusiasm. Might as well ask me to look out a plane window.

"Let's do it together," he suggested.

"Oh, all right." The sooner it's over, the better. Twenty dollars had bought us about twenty minutes of amusement.

I put my hand on the plastic ball and he covered mine with his. It was warm and sweaty. Together we pulled the lever down and the wheels began to spin. I looked over to the snack bar to see what might be edible.

All of a sudden I heard loud beeping noises, and lights on top of the machine flashed. Jeremy yanked on my hand and pointed to the glass window of the machine. Three spider webs lined up in the display.

"Is that good?" I yelled over the noise.

He smiled and pointed to a panel on the machine that indicated three spider webs and the number 1,000. Had we won a thousand dollars?

One of the airport agents approached us, asked to see identification, then requested us to wait for him to return. Jeremy grinned and grinned.

"I just knew Spiderman would come through for me."

"What did we win?"

The agent returned and handed Jeremy two hundreds, two twenties and a ten. Then he stuck a key in the machine and watched as Jeremy pulled the handle one last time. Nothing.

"Two hundred and fifty dollars? I thought it said a thousand."

"A thousand coins," he explained. "This machine takes quarters." He handed me a twenty. "Here's your original investment. Let's get some lunch. I'm starving."

"Wait a minute. Didn't you say whatever you won would be mine?"

He mocked an unknowing face. "I don't remember saying that."

"Fine." At least I didn't lose any of my money on this gamble. "Let's get some food, but it's your treat this time."

"Sure."

We walked hand-in-hand to the snack bar. I did not notice anyone watching us.

The food we ate cost as much as it was disgusting. The lack of flavor did not surprise me. I had no hopes of finding anything with a good taste in this airport anyway.

We got onto the next flight without incident. The plane took off and almost immediately began its descent. We retrieved my suitcase and headed out into the hot, dry valley heat. It felt good to have warmth without humidity. More like getting oven roasted than pressure cooked on the East Coast.

I felt certain that the Kinder von Hitler would send us a couple of tender ragamuffins to accomplish a simple task, such as our transport. Much to my dismay, two filthy lieutenants wearing camouflage jackets with Nazi emblems approached us and bade us to follow without a word.

The jeep was not far and we all climbed in. No conversation. The only talking occurred between me and Jeremy.

Two hours later we arrived in the little town of Paradise once more. I had wondered if we were going to be guests at Pale Face Ranch, but when we got to the Honey Run Road cut-off, the jeep kept driving along the main street, Skyway.

They pulled into a motel called Wildwood and indicated, without words, to get out. We grabbed our bags and stared in disbelief. One of them pointed at the motel office and we walked toward it.

Inside, I gave my name, and the desk person handed me a room key. The place looked small, like one row of little cabins. We went to the room and I let us in.

"That was so weird!" Jeremy commented. "Aren't they allowed to speak?"

"I don't know," I responded. "I thought you were supposed to be the expert on this group. Maybe they're not supposed to talk to non-members. But they didn't talk to each other either. Maybe having their tongues cut out is part of the initiation rites."

We put our stuff down and started to unpack. The room smelled of pine and mold.

As I started to hang my good suit for tomorrow, someone knocked at the door. I patted my holster, looked at Jeremy, and then opened the door cautiously.

"Hi!" blurted a tall, pasty-faced redhead, approximately 25 years old. "I'm Arnold Zemple. Chrissy's campaign manager."

I gave him the once-over, from his coppery curls to his cordovan loafers. He looked like an over-grown college kid in a bargain-store suit. Nothing about him triggered my suspicion gland, and I opened the door further. We stared at each other for a minute. I had no clue what he might be reading in my face, but I could not shake the image of the pig from the TV show "Green Acres" named Arnold Ziffle. The pig was the smart one of the family. This might well be the same situation.

He bent forward awkwardly and asked, "Are you guys hungry?"

It wasn't quite dinnertime yet, but the crap we ate in Las Vegas required some supplementation. I glanced over at Jeremy inquiringly and he nodded. We allowed the pink string bean of a man to lead the way. He walked with a slight limp.

Just across the road is the Cozy Diner, looking rather like a ski lodge. The lowered ceiling would make the whole place feel really cramped if it weren't for the skylights, tinted sky blue and painted with cloudlike designs. We occupied one of the boxy, wooden booths in the back by the fireplace with the wall of fake stone. Our waitress reminded me a bit of Darlene. I guess there's one of her in every town. We ordered some sandwiches and sodas.

"I just wanted to spend some time with you today so we could iron out any last minute concerns you might have about tomorrow." His smile attempted to be comforting, but it missed the mark and hit closer to disconcerting.

"There are some concerns I have," I started to say.

                Friday

"I'm sure there are, but let me tell you what we have in mind first," Arnold interrupted.

The waitress arrived with our food at that moment, and we waited until she finished placing the food on the table before continuing.

"First of all," he started, then arranged his food in front of him. "Let me thank you personally for helping out with the campaign."

"The pleasure is mine," I mumbled through some fries.

He giggled nervously and continued, "When I heard who you were and what you did," he paused and looked up at the ceiling with open hands, "I was, well, flabbergasted. To have someone of your stature and gravitas on our team is quite an honor."

I would have to look up "gravitas" later to make sure it wasn't something bad. His smarmy style of speech and presentation put me off immediately. Plus, his lips had that unattractive, permanently-parched look that redheads sometimes get.

"Our Congressional district covers ten sparsely-populated counties, very large, and the incumbent has been in this seat way too long. It's fairly conservative country, and we're hoping to appeal to that aspect of the voters. The effort to get Chrissy elected has been hastily thrown together, and we're just getting up to speed now. Name recognition will be the key to running a write-in campaign." He then looked at me, perhaps expecting a response.

Not having anything to say at that moment, I just kept chewing on my food. Not as good as home, but certainly better than the Las Vegas airport.

"Tomorrow will be her first public appearance. We've notified all the media, and we're expecting quite a show. I anticipate the unveiling of the last Kennedy child to be, frankly, a circus."

"Is that all it's going to be? An unveiling?"

"Oh, no," he grunted. "Chrissy plans to announce her intention to run for Congress and outline her agenda."

"Agenda?"

"Yes, of course." He stared at me with little pig eyes like I was stupid for not knowing this. "The position of Kinder von Hitler. We believe it's time to make our beliefs known to the world."

"'We'? 'Our'? Are you part of the group?"

His expression changed from superiority to disdain. "I am not at liberty to discuss my personal beliefs." He swallowed and I could hear a distinct mental click. "When I say 'we,' I am referring to my clients."

"Of course." Sitting on the table is a plastic holder listing their dinner specials, one of which is "White Fish." How curious. "I didn't mean to imply that you're a white supremacist neo-Nazi." I said that just to see him squirm.

Arnold shifted in his seat. "I apologize for being a bit on edge right now. The compound has been besieged by the press the last few days. Ever since we put out our news release about Chrissy's real parents, reporters and news crews have been camped outside the gate, waiting for some tidbit details."

"I can only imagine." His pause gave me a chance to pose a question I had harbored. "Mr. Zemple," and it took quite a bit of concentration to say his name correctly and not call him Ziffle, "Why are we being put up at a motel, instead of staying with Chrissy?"

He shifted his position again. "We don't allow outsiders onto the compound. Besides, you're… queer."

I could feel Jeremy's hackles raise. "Is that a problem?" he shotgunned.

The slender redhead turned slightly. "Yes. For some people." His blonde eyelashes fluttered.

"Is it a problem for you?" I inquired.

His right eyelid flinched and he looked down at his neatly arranged food. "Again, I caution you, we are not here to discuss my personal beliefs." He stared at me, then at Jeremy. "May we proceed?"

— ◆ —

The next fifteen minutes consisted of Arnold going over the plans for tomorrow. The public presentation will start at eleven, followed by questions and answers. Caterers will set up a buffet for noon.

My job will be to scan the crowd, looking for potential troublemakers and protecting Chrissy from offstage. The press conference will be held at the Paradise Intermediate School auditorium. We will be picked up at ten, transported to the school and given a half hour to case it and discuss last-minute strategy. The doors will

Page 185

open at 10:45 and Arnold will introduce Chrissy promptly at 11:00.

Not a lot of details, but then there doesn't need to be. It's not like we're protecting the President of the United States.

— ♦ —

"Any other questions?" Arnold offered as he reached for a fry.

Jeremy trembled. I couldn't tell if it was fear or anger.

"Not for me. It all sounds pretty straightforward." I turned to Jeremy, "How about you?"

His eyes grew in size but seemed more glazed than excited. "May I?"

"Is that okay with you, Mr.," and I had to pause again to get it right, "Zemple?"

He finished chewing, scrunched his lips and relented, "Sure. I guess."

Jeremy put down his sandwich and proceeded to lick his fingers as we watched in amazement. "Could you," he pierced the redhead's golden eyebrow with his gaze, "Briefly outline the position of Kinder von Hitler?"

"Oh sure." Arnold relaxed his anticipatory tension. "The organization is dedicated to ensuring the safety of the citizens of this country by eliminating all foreigners–meaning those born in other countries who relocate here–and other undesirable elements." It flowed out so polished and practiced, making me wonder if he even believed or understood what he just said.

Jeremy squirmed. "What do you consider 'undesirable'?"

Without hesitating, he rattled off, "All people of color, including Arabs and Jews, and non-traditional lifestyles."

"'Non-traditional,' like 'gay'?"

"Yes, that includes gay, lesbian, bisexual, transvestite and transsexual." It sounded more like a laundry list.

I could feel Jeremy's heat rising. A storm just beyond the horizon.

"Anything else?" the pink-skinned animal squealed as he picked up the rest of his sandwich with his stubby, freckled fingers.

"No, I think that's all for today. We'll be going back to our room now. See you tomorrow." When I started to stand, Jeremy's lasers burned a hole in my forehead. His lips pressed tightly and he gripped the tabletop. "Let's go, Jeremy." Then he eased and stood up.

"Yes, Daddy," he said while looking at Arnold, who shuddered. "Until tomorrow then."

Red boy remained seated as we left the little diner. The sun had begun fade behind the tall pine trees and a slight breeze blew across the road as we walked back to our room.

— ◆ —

As soon as the motel door clicked closed, Jeremy launched into his tirade. "How can you be doing this? They're just a bunch of assholes who hate everyone who's not Christian, White and totally heterosexual!"

I calmly replied, "I think we knew that going in."

"They hate us! They hate all of us! They would kill you and me both if they had the chance!"

"They've had the chance, and they haven't killed us."

"Not yet!" He stormed around the little room, waving his arms in the air. "Once they decide we're of no more use to them," he made a gun shape with his hand, "Blam! Blam! We're dead!"

"They haven't seemed violent so far."

"Have you noticed anyone in this town whose skin is darker than ours?"

"It's a retirement community, isn't it? It's bound to be more homogenous."

"Because no person of color in his right mind would live here, next to these terrorist Nazis! The ones who tried probably got escorted out in a body bag."

"Chrissy seems to like us."

"And what's up with that? The skinhead bitch is a sexless, transgendered freak who likes to eat pussy!"

"So?"

"Don't you find that just a bit hypocritical? They say they're against 'non-traditional lifestyles,' but their leader is exactly what they hate!"

Sounds like the usual political mumbo-jumbo to me, but Jeremy's quickly reddening face indicated his inability to deal with this apparent paradox. "I know, I know."

"That makes me so fucking angry!" His pacing accelerated. "And you just accept it because you're wracked with some kind of survivor guilt trip. It doesn't make any sense!"

In an attempt to calm him down, I ignored his rantings and tried to hug him, hoping that might bring some comfort. "It doesn't always have to make sense." He pushed me away brusquely.

"I need a shower," he complained.

"I think you need something else." I grabbed the top of his pants and undid the button.

"What are you doing?" he squawked.

I pulled the zipper down. "Shut up, take off your pants, and lie face down."

"Yes, Daddy," he complied as I drew the curtains closed.

He hadn't put on underwear today, and his flushed, naked bottom smiled up at me. No need for those little blue pills now. Spat in my hand for lubricant.

"Hey, Cowboy, how about a fucking condom!" He reached into his pants pocket and tossed a foil packet back at me.

Those damn things are not easy to open when you're tense. A few seconds of fumbling rewarded me with latex, and it went on without too much complication.

I descended upon his nubile backside, penetrating him almost effortlessly. He wriggled and cried out, but I just took it as part of the game. Thrusting and thrusting, I vented my anger and frustrations, each slam conveyed the pent-up anger and frustrations from the people around me.

Top Dog—*Bam!*

Chrissy—*Wham!!*

Arnold Ziffle—*Jam!*

John Fuckgerald Kennedy—*Kablam!!*

Jeremy—*Gazang!!!*

Until I finally exploded in a finale of fireworks.

Collapsing on top of him in a sweaty mess, I looked down at his tightly-closed eyes and asked, "What the hell does 'gravitas' mean?"

He inhaled deeply, exhaled, then said, "My ass is so sore."

"Is that what it means?"

"Get off me. I need a shower."

"You sure do," I agreed.

Chapter Fourteen

Saturday

For once, I got a good night's sleep. Despite it not being my bed, my house, my town. Even with Jeremy's continuing, increasing anger. In fact, it was his shifting and moving that woke me. Not the sunrise.

Our motel did not provide morning amenities like coffee, and I tossed on the previous day's clothing and dashed across the way to get something from the Cozy Diner. Someone in their management must be a coffee snob, because not only did they offer different types of beans, they even had French Roast.

In an attempt to assuage his rage, I also brought back hot tea for Jeremy, who seemed to be sleeping fitfully when I left. I had hoped that he would have used the time to get himself ready to go, but when I returned, he was still in bed watching TV.

"This is tea for you," I informed him as I sat the cup on the table next to the bed.

He looked at me, blinked once slowly, and then resumed viewing whatever program he had been watching. I felt like taking the hot cup and spilling it all over him. A "thank you" would have been nice.

After taking a sip of hot coffee, I got out of the clothes I had worn and headed into the bathroom. The spigot squeaked as I turned on the hot water in the shower stall. When it warmed sufficiently, I adjusted the cold to make a comfortable temperature.

Under the stream, I considered various reasons for Jeremy's bad behavior this particular morning. Maybe I should send him back to San Francisco on a bus. If he's only going to be trouble, I've already got enough and don't really need more.

No, something else is going on. Probably some other new rule I don't know about yet. He already knew about the political leanings of this group before we sat down with Pig Man. He's upset about something, but I have no clue what it is this time. Maybe it's his unpredictability that keeps me intrigued.

With only the towel wrapped around me, I went to the television and switched it off. "Get ready. You're going with me."

He pressed a button on the remote control and the set came back on. "No, I'm not."

I pressed the power button again. "Yes, you are."

The TV sprang back to life. "No, I'm not."

This time I stood in front of the picture. "Do I have to order you to go?"

He moved around in the bed in an effort to see the screen. "You could," he challenged.

"What is going on here?" I shouted a bit louder than I had intended. "Give me a clue. Give me a sign."

"Give me a break," he mumbled to himself.

I really wanted to hit him. "Is it something I'm doing? Something I'm not doing? How am I not measuring up to your fantasy daddy today?"

He rolled over, face down. I stepped to the bed, grabbed the sheets and pulled them away.

"Answer me," I demanded.

"Just leave me alone," he muttered into the pillow.

It took mighty restraint not to grab him by the shoulders and shake him hard, the reaction I would have had previously. In this moment, I preferred to respond, rather than react. It was the desire not to repeat the previous cruelty of others that stopped me.

And maybe that's it. Maybe he wants me to play the role of his perpetrator. He thinks the only way to get attention is to work up the anger in his father figure. Geez, this is so horribly twisted.

Instead of giving in to my initial emotional reaction of smacking the heck out of him, I bent down and kissed him softly on the shoulder blade. "I'm going to get ready now." I walked back to the bathroom and finished up my morning routine.

When I came back out he had gotten dressed and sat on the edge of the bed looking down at his feet. Jeremy gazed up at me and narrowed his eyes. His nose moved a bit more off-center.

"Why didn't you hit me?" he asked.

"I didn't want to."

"But you did want to. I felt it," he accused.

"Just because I felt like it doesn't mean I have to do it." I stared at him, his emerald green eyes, his off-center nose.

"You still want me to go with you?" He picked up the tea and took a sip.

"Yes. Go shower."

"Hey, this is good!" Jeremy examined the cardboard container. "There isn't time. It's almost ten now."

Indeed, it was. I continued dressing, putting on my good suit. He just sat and stared at the television.

Before donning the jacket, I went to the suitcase and retrieved the gun and holster. After strapping it on and getting into the sport coat, I examined myself in the mirror to make sure I didn't bulge in the wrong places.

"You look nice," Jeremy complimented.

"Thank you. It's nice to have something, or someone, to get dressed up for once in a while." I kept checking and readjusting.

Three loud bangs on the door made us both jump. We looked at each other briefly. "Let's go," I said.

Jeremy switched off the set and leapt off of the bed. I opened the door to see one of Chrissy's boys standing there. Without saying a word, he cocked his head toward a rusty jeep, apparently telling us to get in.

Jeremy walked out in front of me and I pulled the door to the room closed. Then I felt in my pocket for the key to make sure I had it. Perhaps I should have reversed the order, but I didn't think about double-checking until after the door had clicked closed.

"Good morning, gentlemen," called an authoritative voice from the jeep. Arnold occupied the passenger seat. He hopped out to let us get into the back. "Ready?" he asked with just a hint of smarminess.

"As we'll ever be," I half said to myself.

"All right, then. Let's head out," he commanded.

The driver pulled out onto the main road without checking to see if it was clear. I heard screeching of tires, honking and, "Damn Nazis!" behind us. We turned right at the next intersection. Even though the light had been red, our ersatz chauffeur did not bother to stop first. We passed a speed limit sign, and I felt certain that our velocity was twice what was posted.

After a minute of breakneck driving, the driver turned right onto another main street, again without stopping against a red light. We passed other vehicles, despite it being a two-lane road.

By the time we pulled into the parking lot of the school, my heart had stopped and started at least a dozen times. This guy should be driving a roller coaster. Without realizing it, Jeremy and I had been holding hands, tightly.

Arnold looked back and said, rather nonchalantly for the ride we just had, "Well, here we are."

He hopped down and let us out of the back. I don't know how his long legs could be so steady. Mine felt rather rubbery.

As soon as we got out, the jeep wheeled around and sped off. I was quite sure I would prefer to walk back to the motel, no matter how far.

We followed the redhead, his limp still slightly evident, onto the grounds of Paradise Intermediate School. The eagle, their mascot, watched over us from almost every angle. Each school building seemed to have the emblem painted on it. We crossed the yard to an old auditorium.

The inside reminded me of Fort Dyck High School. Boxy and bright, the rays of sunlight fighting through dusty windows. Directly in front of me I saw a stage with steps leading to either side. Ghosts of my graduating class marched in solemn procession from right to left.

"Well, what do you think?" Arnold abruptly brought me back to the present.

I made a 360 and tried to catch all that I could. The main double door at the rear appeared to be the only way in and out. Two stairways at the back led to a small balcony, like a design afterthought. Folding chairs on racks lined the side walls. A side door drew my attention.

"Where does that lead?" I pointed at the door.

Arnold started toward it. "Let's look." He pushed the bar and swung the door into a side access hallway. To the left, a short stairway led to the backstage. To the right, a narrow passageway about 20 feet long ended at steps that led, presumably, up to the balcony.

"What do you think?"

Good question. This wasn't like the old days when ideas just came pouring out of my head. It took a few seconds to develop a plan.

"How many brownshirts do we have at our disposal?" I asked.

Dismissing my callous reference, he countered, "How many people do you need?"

I mentally added up two for the front door, one for each stairway to the balcony, one for each entrance to the stage and one for the side door. "At least seven."

"Not a problem. Where do you want me to tell them to stand?"

His last question caught my attention. "Won't I be instructing them?"

"That won't be necessary." He waved his hand in the air. "You just tell me what you want, and I'll communicate your orders."

This seemed unconventional and slipshod, but, again, it's not like we're protecting the President. I'm guessing the skinhead boys don't want to take orders from the old man with the young boyfriend.

"I want two at the main entrance," I pointed at the doors, feeling rather like a flight attendant indicating emergency exits. "One at each stairwell to the balcony–I don't want anyone going up there–one at each side of the stage, and one at this side door."

"Gotcha."

"Can the caterers set up in that accessway so that we can keep this area open? They can wheel their stuff in after the speeches."

"That sounds good. I'll let them know. Why don't you take a look around while I gather the troops." The word "stormtoopers" buzzed through my mind. "Chrissy should be here soon, and you can discuss any last-minute details with her."

"Sure."

Pig Man exited through the main doors, leaving Jeremy and me alone in the cavernous box. While Arnold and I had been discussing things, Jeremy had used the time to explore the big, rectangular, hollow room.

"Hey, look at this!" He held out an American flag with yellow fringe standing to the left of the stage. His finger pointed to the blue area.

"So?"

"It has only 48 stars. This is a real collector's item."

The whole town is a collector's item, as far as I can tell.

Jeremy and I walked up onto the stage together. I stood in various places and picked out one where I felt the line of sight would be best. It ended up being at the top of the staircase leading down to the access hallway. That would provide yet one more level of protection.

The front doors creaked open and I walked out onto the stage. Late morning sun blasted through the opening, and all I could make out were three silhouettes and their corresponding shadows.

The center figure stepped inside and pointed to the ground on either side of the doors. The backlit image appeared momentarily Christ-like.

"Stone!" boomed a gruff voice as Chrissy approached. "Good to see you, old man. Is the little pipsqueak with you?" She had on a respectable woman's business suit.

Jeremy stepped forward. "Present and accounted for, *mein Führer*."

"Very funny, asshole. Just keep out of my way." She strutted up the right-side stairs and stood in the middle of the stage. "Ask not what your country can do for you, rather, ask what you can do for your country."

The hoarse quality of her delivery added an unintended sinister tone. She might as well have said, "Today Germany, tomorrow the world."

"How was that?" she asked me.

A question I would rather not answer, being that there was no good response. "I'd stay away from quoting him like that. Be yourself."

She slapped me hard on the shoulder. "You're probably right. Arnold came up with some good shit."

As I rubbed my shoulder, I said, "Oh, yeah?"

Chrissy pulled some cards out of a pocket and turned back to face an imaginary audience. "Whatever it takes, we must protect this country's vital interests. If we have to deport every foreign-born person, if we have to imprison every wrong-doer, if we have to punish every unnatural act, we will eventually return this nation to its fundamental order, no matter the price!"

Jeremy squeezed my hand so hard it hurt. I turned to look at him wide-eyed and trembling.

"God, he writes good stuff!" Chrissy said to herself rather loudly. She put the cards back in her pocket and strode militarily around the stage.

Maybe Jeremy was right. I should not have been endorsing her candidacy. Oh well. It probably won't last very long anyway, and the two of us would go back to Indiana and figure out how to live happily ever after all.

— ♦ —

Around 10:30 the caterers began bringing in their tables and trays. Trying not to be obvious about it, I watched each one in turn, looking for any possible signs of sabotage or evil intent.

While this was going on, Arnold and a few helpers arranged the folding chairs in rows, leaving a large open space at the front. They placed a podium on the lip of the stage as well.

By the time everything got set up, it was quarter to eleven. One of the fellows at the front door nodded to me, and I walked up onto the stage and took my observer's vantage point. Jeremy followed and stood next to me. Arnold and Chrissy walked through the side door to wait in the hallway with the caterers.

First into the cavernous room were camera crews and other members of the press. Microphones got placed and wires laid.

People entered one or two at a time, presumably due to the frisking or whatever security measures the skinheads outside imposed. That gave me a chance to look everyone over as they came in.

When some of the folks tried to go up into the balcony, the assigned guards blocked their way silently. Good thing. I couldn't observe the balcony from my standpoint, and it looked like a bad place to have people anyway.

Two of the faces surprised me. The Walshes made the trip up from San Francisco. I wondered if Chrissy specifically invited them or if they heard about it through the media. There would be no chance for me to ask; besides it would be difficult to explain my presence without revealing the previous lies.

Some of the other white supremacy groups showed up as well, identifiable by shaved scalps and Nazi insignias. I guess this would be the time to set aside their differences and work together toward getting someone elected.

As I looked out at people's faces, the assortment of white faces, I could not help but wonder if the Kennedy clan had sent a representative, and who it might be. You would think they would have

Saturday

sent someone here to at least observe. Other than the Walshes, I did not recognize anyone.

Outside I could hear loud voices and chanting, most likely protesters. I couldn't imagine a situation like this without some sort of reaction. I'm sure Chrissy would attract a wave of opposition. Thank goodness I got assigned to inside work. The lieutenants outside would handle the demonstrators.

My attention must have drifted off for just a bit. While I focused on the noise outside, Top Dog and agent Hank had entered and stood at the rear of the room. Sheriffs and local police officers flanked them.

At 11:00 the front doors slammed closed. The voices from outside diminished to a distant hubbub. Arnold stepped up from the side hallway and moved to the podium.

"Good morning ladies and gentlemen. Thank you for being with us today. My name is Arnold Zemple. I am the campaign manager. We would like to start the proceedings with the Pledge of Allegiance. Let's all stand and face the flag."

Everyone in the room stood. I could see some eyes rolling, and beside me, Jeremy commented, "Oh, brother."

We all put our hands over our hearts, and Arnold started off, "I pledge allegiance." The rest of us droned along. I had a private snicker to myself as I recalled Jeremy's earlier discovery that this flag had only 48 stars. It now seemed more fitting to the occasion somehow.

As we concluded with "liberty and justice for all," Jeremy specifically emphasized the "all." I gave him a sidelong glance. I knew he hated being here, but if he chose to be part of my life, this was going to be one of the consequences.

"Thank you. Please be seated." The pink one paused and licked his chapped lips while the assembled mass returned to their chairs. At the rear, Top Dog vigilantly watched it all. I sensed his eyes scanning the room, looking for me, most likely. I could only assume that Jeremy and I were hidden in the shadows and not visible. However, Top Dog's gaze stopped suddenly when he reached my position. Maybe he could see me. Maybe he just sensed me. Whatever the case, he stared in my direction and patted his breast with his hand.

That did not make sense. Of course I knew he carried a gun. Was he trying to send a message to me that he was here to take care of Chrissy? If he were, why would he tip his hand? It felt like yet another gambit in his lifelong chess match. Nevertheless, I kept my focus more on him. And maybe that was part of his game too. Perhaps Hank would be the one to do the job. They had separated and I couldn't watch them both at the same time.

Top Dog's head rotated slightly and his eyes narrowed perceptibly. If he could actually see us, he was now looking directly at Jeremy.

When I turned, Jeremy seemed to be looking back and his head nodded slightly. I said, "Keep an eye on Hank for me. Tell me if he makes any sudden moves."

"Okay," came the whispered response.

Arnold started again, "Today is an important day. A very important day. Those of you with us will always remember it, and you'll be glad you were here."

Now I was thinking, "Oh, brother."

The tall redhead looked around and continued, "Only recently did we find out that one of our own had a family secret. A secret that would allow us the opportunity to make use of this infor-mation and initiate a write-in candidacy for the Congressional seat in the Second District of California."

One of the skinheads yelled, "Yeah!"

Arnold smiled in response. "Yeah, indeed. For years we have wanted representation in our government, a government that has become increasingly less responsive. A government that has become more worried about not offending people than protecting its own citizens. A government that has chosen to continue allowing foreigners to invade our shores despite the growing incidences of terrorism against its own people. The time has come, ladies and gentlemen, for a new voice in Congress. One that will stand up for what is right in this country. One that will not cave in to the special interests of the liberal causes. One that will take the floor of the Capitol and speak the words of eternal truth. A strong voice for the White people who built this nation, only to have it brought down by people of color and foreigners. Ladies and gentlemen, I give you the next Representative from the Second District of California, Chrissy Kennedy!"

People in the audience jumped to their feet, stomping, cheering, applauding. A chant rose through the crowd, "Chrissy, Chrissy, Chrissy."

With all the excitement, it became difficult to keep an eye on Top Dog. He didn't seem to be doing anything but observing.

"Can you still see Hank?" I asked Jeremy.

"Barely," he replied.

"How do you like you first day as a junior Secret Service agent?"

"Simply glamorous."

"I'll reward you later."

"Can't wait."

I felt a hand on my shoulder. Chrissy had appeared, presumably from the hallway. "Well, old man," she barked in my ear, "Here goes."

— ♦ —

Strutting out to the podium, Chrissy waved at the assemblage. She shook hands vigorously with Arnold, and then he hobbled off to the side near the flag. All the while, people cheered, whistled and hooted. I expect if guns had been allowed, shots would have been fired into the air.

One pair of hands went up to a mouth in the audience. It was Kat Walsh, presumably her reaction to seeing Chrissy's swastika tattoo.

The clamor continued for about a minute while she continued to wave and point at people she recognized. Eventually, she motioned for the crowd to sit down, and they followed her request reluctantly.

After taking a stance behind the podium, Chrissy reached into her pocket, pulled out the stack of note cards and placed them in front of her.

"Good morning," she started, "My name is Chrissy Kennedy and," but she was not able to continue because the crowd erupted again. After a few seconds she gave the sign to calm down.

"As I was saying, my name is Chrissy Kennedy, and I am running as a write-in candidate for the Congressional Representative from the Second District of California." Polite applause followed. "Thank you. As you might be aware, the

Second District is a large territory. Encompassing ten counties in Northern California, it stretches from Oroville in the south, to the Oregon border in the north. And speaking of Oroville, I would like to acknowledge my brothers present from the Aryan Nation." She waved her hand toward the crowd and a dozen or so thugs supplied whooping noises.

"You may be wondering about my last name, Kennedy. Some of you knew me as Chrissy Walsh. Well, let me tell you a little story." She cleared her throat.

"A long time ago, a certain First Lady of this great country was pregnant. Her husband got himself shot because he dismissed some rather good advice. Some government rat took it upon himself to take that baby," and Chrissy glared at Top Dog, who scratched at his chest in response, "and adopt it out, presumably for safekeeping. So, no one knew who this particular baby was, and a young couple from Boston adopted me and moved to San Francisco."

Interesting, I thought, how she skipped over the whole sex-change issue. Probably just as well.

"Just recently, a family friend explained the whole truth to me, and I had a startling revelation: I could take my original name again and use it to run for Congress."

Applause and cheers came up from the crowd. Top Dog appeared fidgety but attentive.

"I'm glad you agree." She laughed heartily, and the crowd began chanting her name again. A jarring thought slapped me upside the head: The two of us have something very significant in common. We both discovered our true natures late in life. Our approaches have been vastly different: While I cowered in fear about people finding out I'm really gay, Chrissy brandished her new-found identity like a battle flag. Whether I agreed with her or not, I did admire that she was taking advantage of the situation and using it to further herself.

As the roar quieted down, she went on, "Because this once fine country is in mighty sad shape, my friends. We used to be the supreme nation on this earth. We were unchallenged by our enemies. We were second to no one." She scanned the audience.

"Then we started giving our powers away. First it was the Black people, then it was the brown people, the yellow people, the red people, the lavender people, and now White people have no power left because we gave it all away."

Cheers went up and the "Chrissy" chant started again.

"Stone," Jeremy called out.

"Did pretty boy Hank do something?"

"No, I'm beginning to get worried about this. It's starting to sound pretty bad."

"We knew what we were getting into. Besides, it's just talk."

"That's how it always starts," he sounded despondent.

Chrissy started up again. "We need to rebuild this nation. We need to strengthen this nation. We need to purify this nation." Applause interrupted her. I glanced at some of the faces of the press, and I saw blank stares and aghast looks.

"This country was founded by White people for White people! We must protect ourselves from the evil of the ever-growing number of non-Whites among us. The evil of the invading foreigners who now disgrace our holy land. The evil of the Jews and Arabs. The evil of socialist liberals. The evil of sexual deviants. The evil of passive sympathizers."

"Stone!" Jeremy shouted.

"Shhh."

"I can't believe you're going to stand there and listen to that crap!"

"It's just talk," I replied, but started to think otherwise.

"These evils must be abolished. These evils must be removed. These evils must be destroyed!" Chrissy raised her hand in a way reminiscent of the Nazi salute.

The crowd started chanting again, "*Chris*-sy, *Chris*-sy, *Chris*-sy!" Then a new cadence blossomed out of the throng, "C-*K!* C-*K!* C-*K!*" in a rhythm reminiscent of "*Sig heil! Sig heil! Sig heil!*"

For the first time since this unnatural gathering began, I felt scared. That mob could erupt at any moment, incited by Chrissy's hateful rhetoric. I could see Top Dog starting to finger his lapel.

Jeremy shuddered and fidgeted. "Are you just going to stand there and let them spew their hatred?"

"What can I do? Now, shut up, you're distracting me."

"A new world order! My countrymen, a new world order. The time has come to reclaim our manifest destiny! Follow me, my friends. Follow me!"

The crowd erupted into the "C-*K!*" chant again. Chrissy held up her right hand just like Adolph Hitler did at Nuremburg while addressing the Party rally.

"Stone! I can't stand it! Do something!" Jeremy begged and stomped around.

"Like what?" I was afraid to move at all.

"Take her down! Don't let her win!" His hands waved about.

I looked down at him with suspicion and regret. "You know I can't."

"Shit!" Jeremy grabbed my right hand with his left and reached inside my jacket. "You pussy!" He grabbed the gun before I could react and ran down the back stairs.

"Jeremy!" I yelled after him.

"C-*K! C-K! C-K!*"

Chrissy screamed over the chanting, "We must do something, my friends."

I scrambled down into the accessway. Jeremy had already started up the stairs to the balcony. Trays of food lined the narrow hallway, and caterers blocked my path. I had to push people out of the way as I charged to the stairwell, hopefully in time.

As I started up to the balcony, I felt a pain, a tightening in my chest. Like an elephant sitting on me. Things started swirling around and it felt like I was about to pass out. I tried to take a deep breath, and the pain flashed white hot, then began to subside.

Chrissy's voice rang out from below, "We must cleanse these evils from our homes, from our streets, from our schools, from our government, from our nation! We must do whatever it takes!"

At the top of the stairs I could see Jeremy poised, aiming the gun at the stage. I wanted to scream out, but thought it might scare him into firing. Instead, I ran at Jeremy full speed in an attempt to knock him over before it was too late.

"C-*K! C-K! C-K! C-K!*"

"No matter the price!" Chrissy yelled, unaware of the balcony scene. "Whatever it takes, we must–"

A shot rang out as I leapt. The echo ricocheted around the stark, bright room. We fell together in a heap. I looked through the balustrade and saw Chrissy slumped down on the podium, the swastika emblazoned in red.

In attempting to wrestle the gun away from Jeremy, two more shots fired. He went limp. Loud footsteps rushed up the stairs.

I struggled to my feet, gun in hand. Jeremy lay on the floor, staring up at me with those bright green eyes. Blood dribbled down from under his chin, where a bullet had entered. The off-center nose pointed almost sideways as his face twisted into an uncontrollable sneer. People in uniforms approached us on both sides.

"Fuck!" the young man spat out, blood trickling down one side of his mouth. "You shot me, you assho—" and his breath stopped just as officers grabbed my arms and forced me back to the floor.

I struggled slightly, just so I could get to my young man, to hug him, to hold him. The frail carapace that was once my lover.

"Just stay still!" one of the men ordered.

The only thing I wanted, the only thing in the whole world, was to have Jeremy in my arms. One last time. The pain in my chest crescendoed. Breathing became labored, heaving. Voices of people screaming grew louder and louder. I started crying.

Through the tears, I saw Top Dog standing over Jeremy, shaking his head with a look of disgust. He aimed that look right at me. I wanted to slug the manipulative bastard for ruining our lives, all of our lives, and I fought to get free. If only to give the smug asshole the smacking he so rightly deserved.

When I started resisting again, the officers slammed my face to the floor. The pain in my head leapfrogged the pain in my chest, and I lost consciousness.

Epilogue

THAT is probably not how you wanted the story to end. Believe me, I did not want it to turn out that way either.

My version would have had Chrissy going down to a dismal defeat in the election and returning to the obscurity of her skinhead ranch in Paradise. Jeremy and I would have gone back to Fort Dyck and tried to pursue a somewhat normal existence. Including working out some acknowledgment of our relationship, whatever it would have turned into. We could have invited Henry over for Euchre on Thursdays, and watched the Dutch Days celebration proudly with the rest of the town. Darlene might get our food orders correct the first time. Top Dog could never bother us again. Oh yes, Jeremy, as Destiny, would launch his country music career and become the darling of the Gay Ole Opry.

But that is not how it worked out. Sorry.

By the time the case got to trial, I had already rationalized my acceptance of responsibility for two murders I did not commit. Sure, you know I didn't kill anyone that day, and any number of other people in the building had weapons plus a motive to kill Chrissy. Jeremy's death was just an accident.

All the evidence pointed to me. A renegade, closeted homosexual, former Secret Service agent, retired chief of police. The prosecutor wanted my head on a silver platter. Skinhead groups wanted to string my burning carcass up in a hanging tree. Top Dog probably wanted to see me fry as a scapegoat. I'm sure the Kennedys got whatever they wanted.

When I told my Public Defender the real story, he said no one would believe it, even though it was the truth. He suggested I throw myself on the mercy of the court, and maybe plead temporary insanity. That's not my style.

To my accusers I offered no resistance, and I willingly accepted the charges of first- and second-degree murder. In a strange way, a kind of delayed yet misguided justice has been served.

From the solitude of my penitentiary cell I have written this manuscript. No one bothers me here while I scrawl out the assembled stack of pages.

People should know what really happened, and that's why I've taken the time to write out these notes you are now reading. I hope it helps you understand the motivations and emotions behind this horrible incident that left me totally alone and friendless.

I will not be so remembered or revered as John Wilkes Booth or Lee Harvey Oswald, let alone Charles Giteau or Leon Czolgosz. Those who harbor anger about this crime will at least be able to put a name and a face on it.

When my death comes, I can take with me all the guilt for allowing the assassination of a father and son I had been assigned to protect. And the death of the only other person I ever loved who loved me back.

Now I can face my fate assured that at least one other person knows the truth. My truth.

WAYNE GOODMAN has lived in the San Francisco Bay Area most of his life (with too many cats). His published writing is primarily Historical Fiction, and eBook versions can be found online through Kindle Direct.